Mamma

Diana Tutton

Publisher's Note

This British Library Women Writers series brings back and contextualises works by female writers who were successful in their day. These authors have been selected, not just for the strength of their writing and the power of their storytelling, but for highlighting the realities of life for women and society's changing attitudes toward female behaviour through the decades.

The books in this series are historical texts and, on occasion, express views that are outdated today. In a few instances, the originals use dated racist terms and phrases which have been changed or deleted in this modern edition.

First published in 1956

This edition published in 2021 by
The British Library
96 Euston Road
London NW1 2DB

Copyright © 2021 Estate of Diana Tutton
Preface copyright © 2021 Tanya Kirk
Afterword copyright © 2021 Simon Thomas

Cataloguing in Publication Data
A catalogue record for this publication is available from the British Library

ISBN 978 0 7123 5388 5
e-ISBN 978 0 7123 6733 2

Text design and typesetting by JCS Publishing Services Ltd
Printed in England by CPI Group (UK), Croydon, CR0 4YY

Contents

છ

❧ ❧ ❧

The 1950s

❧

❧ Throughout the 1950s, a groom is (on average) approximately 2.5 years older than his wife, if both are marrying for the first time. The gap is about 3 years if the groom is remarrying.

❧ **1951:** According to the 1951 census, there are 789,803 people employed as indoor domestic servants (66,229 men and 723,574 women), down from 1.4 million in 1931.

❧ In the 1950s and 60s, it is estimated that half a million women became unmarried mothers. Many lived temporarily in mother-and-baby homes and chose – or were compelled – to put up their babies for adoption. In the 50s, a third of these children are adopted by a blood relative.

❧ **1952 (February):** Queen Elizabeth II ascends to the throne, after the sudden death of her father George VI. Her Coronation is June of the following year.

❧ Crosswords continue to grow in popularity in the UK, having first appeared in the *Times* in 1930. Initially consisting of simple 'straight' clues, crosswords gradually incorporated cryptic clues, and by the end of the 1950s most British newspapers are printing wholly cryptic crosswords.

❧ **1954 (June):** Food rationing lifts, with the final restrictions being on meat and bacon. Food rationing had been in place for 14 years.

❧ **1956:** There are 762,000 personnel serving in the UK armed forces, down from a peak of 4.9 million in 1945.

❧ ❧ ❧

❧ In the 1950s, approximately 80 per cent of men and 45 per cent of women aged 35–59 smoked cigarettes in the UK. The number of men smoking consistently fell in the decade, while the number of women consistently rose.

❧ 1956: *Mamma* is published.

❧ The pill is not marketed as a contraceptive in the UK until 1961 (though, from 1957 a pill marketed for menstrual disorders is available, which also functioned as a contraceptive). Once the contraceptive pill becomes available, it is only accessible to married women until 1967.

Diana Tutton (1915-1991)

Diana Tutton, also known as Dinah, was born Diana Godfrey-Faussett-Osborne in 1915. She was the youngest of four daughters, brought up at Pipe Hill House, a large eighteenth-century home in Lichfield, Staffordshire. Her family also had an estate in Kent.

Tutton lived at home until she married Captain John Tutton during the Second World War. As part of her war work, she drove a mobile canteen for the Women's Voluntary Services. After her marriage, Tutton moved with her husband to Kenya, where she joined the First Aid Nursing Yeomanry (FANYs). In 1945, they returned to England, and in 1948, the family, which by this time included two daughters, went to British Malaya for three years. When *Mamma* was published, she described herself as primarily 'wife and mother', adding that 'she occasionally finds time to act as a teacher and sick nurse, and of course, to write' with her only other activity 'a bit of backyard gardening'.

Mamma was the first novel Tutton wrote, but *Guard Your Daughters* was published first, in 1953. About an eccentric family of five sisters, it has many similarities to Dodie Smith's *I Capture the Castle*, published five years earlier. The novel was very popular, including being selected as Book of the Month for the Franco-British Selection Committee, and there is a currently unpublished sequel, *Unguarded Moments*. *Mamma* was published in 1956, followed by *The Young Ones* in 1959, with the unusual plot of brother-sister incest. Though Tutton lived for another three decades, dying in 1991, she didn't publish any further books.

꿔 꿔 꿔

Preface

꿔

Mamma, on the face of it, is a scandalously plotted novel about a mother who falls for her daughter's husband. However, this book is much more than that. It is a sensitive portrayal of 1950s middle-class family life, in which the contrasts and contradictions of the decade are strongly evident. It was Diana Tutton's second novel to be published, following on from the success of her debut, *Guard Your Daughters*, in 1953. *Mamma* is the story of Joanna Malling, widowed in her early twenties and now aged 41. Having come to terms with a life of quiet solitude, Joanna finds herself offering to share her house with her daughter Libby and Libby's new husband Steven. Soon Joanna is drawn to Steven, who at 15 years older than his wife is closer in age and outlook to his mother-in-law. Rather than write this as a melodrama, Tutton does something far more interesting.

The novel explores a series of contrasts inherent in 1950s society. In particular, the decade saw a rigid view of femininity and the role of women. Signifiers of soft, 'appropriate' femininity include Libby's enthusiastic adoption of the Women's Institute and her skill at cookery, as well as the more introverted Joanna's talent for gardening. Joanna's gentle, nurturing version of motherhood is contrasted with the outlook of Steven's mother, who shows no interest in her child's life and is 'an unbeautiful sight' in her outlandishly unfeminine folk-inspired clothing. Joanna's obvious unselfishness and her love and affection for her child makes her unwanted feelings towards her son-in-law even harder to bear.

❧ ❧ ❧

The demonstrations of snobbery within the novel provide fascinating commentary on mid-century middle-class suburban life. The central characters are entertained (and sometimes disgusted) by the supposed vulgarity perpetrated by their servants, neighbours, and even relatives. Class markers are everywhere and Tutton portrays a social hierarchy that subtly ranks people through what they eat and wear; whether they take in 'p.g.s' (paying guests); and even whether or not they sleep in a double bed.

The greatest and most important contrast in the novel is of the outlook of the different generations. *Mamma* was published 11 years after the end of the Second World War and portrays a tremendous void between those who were adults in wartime and those who were children. Joanna and Steven, who experienced at first hand the privations and trauma of the War are juxtaposed with those who, like Libby, emerged relatively unscathed. The novel deals delicately and poignantly with the societal view that it was more appropriate for a 35-year-old man to have a relationship with a much younger woman than it was for him to choose a widow of 41. While Joanna appears to the reader much more suited to Steven in both temperament and experience, society has written her off as a middle-aged mother whose best days are behind her.

Tutton's nuanced portrayal of her protagonists' characters is central to her novel's success. This fascinating study of family tensions is blended with sly humour into a book that has a timeless appeal.

Tanya Kirk
Lead Curator, Printed Heritage Collections 1601–1900
British Library

Mamma

I

🙰

The house was solidly built of yellow brick and was roofed with slates which, on this dripping day, gleamed back at the pale grey sky. But Joanna Malling, surveying her new possession from the squashy, weed-grown gravel, while the last few drops of rain fell about her, could see little else to please her, and even the roof wouldn't always shine like that. The paint was chocolate-coloured, and she couldn't afford to have it done this year, when there were so many things in worse condition. Really the whole effect was hideous. Joanna wondered whether she had been a fool.

She walked backwards, screwing up her eyes and looked again through a softening screen of lashes. That was much better. Whitewashed and with grey paint the house would look tranquil, for its shape was good and it sat well down among its dripping laurels and lilacs. "An old garden"—Joanna was so tired that she spoke aloud—"is worth everything, and just *look* at the Old Man's Beard climbing up that yew-tree!"

She plodded across to the little brown porch, hoping to find a bench. There was none, but she sat on the stone step, far too tired to worry about her health. "You won't know yourself," she told the porch, "when you have light paint and a wisteria, and new glass in that cracked, cobwebby window."

The drive curled away from the central plot of grass and a large snowball bush hid the gate. She listened. The first van-load should have been here by now. Perhaps it had broken down. What a fool to send away the taxi! Where was the caretaker who had promised to light fires, and where, oh where the front-door key?

"The furniture men will do something, I suppose, when they arrive. They'll break open a door, or climb in somewhere." After twenty years of widowhood, Joanna still occasionally, in moments of panic, looked round for a rescuing man. But she found the supply inadequate. She had quite expected to marry again, but in the five years after Jack's death she had had only one proposal, and that one so unsuitable as to be almost an insult. She had politely rejected a solicitor, twenty-four years older than herself, and had settled down to perpetual widowhood.

It is hard, when you've been told almost hourly that you are beautiful and desirable, to believe that you are suddenly no longer these things, but in the end Joanna had accepted the fact that no one wanted her except the elderly solicitor and her own small daughter. The solicitor had gone away, and Elizabeth remained. Darling Libby! If only she were here now the key would soon be found. But then it would never have been lost, for Libby would have taken charge of it in the first place. Unfortunately Elizabeth was in London, in the final stages of a course in Domestic Science.

For the twelfth time, and in the unreasonable hope of a miracle, Joanna searched through her disgraceful handbag. And now she at once saw the key, which leered at her from between the pages of a scribbled-over notebook. "Damn and blast you!" said Joanna ungratefully to the key, and with a trembling hand she fitted it into the lock. A moment later she was standing in her own hall, and even as she reflected that she need not now appear an idiot to anyone but herself, the first great van came gently up to the door.

The shock of finding the key and proving her own fatuity had bemused Joanna, and she would have liked a short rest; but here before her stood a square, sandy, white-aproned man, pencil behind ear, blinking his sparse eyelashes as he asked for her instructions. Two others were already depositing on the gravel a number of small objects—coal-scuttles, waste-paper baskets and saucepans—so that they might deliver from the van her dearly-loved walnut tallboy. Joanna put a hand to her head, pushing back a lock of almost black hair. She searched in her bag and was surprised to find the list that she wanted. The caretaker now came in, with a flourish and without apology for her tardiness, and she was asked to sweep the floors on which the larger carpets were to be laid. The sandy man produced a kitchen chair, wiped it with his apron, and invited Joanna to sit down, and with the help of her list she was able to direct the unloading, so that in an astonishingly short time the vans were empty and the house was furnished. The caretaker then volunteered to make tea; Joanna struggled from her state of lethargy to find a tea-pot, tea, sugar, half a cake and a few saucerless cups. The caretaker produced milk, and everyone sat at the kitchen table to eat and drink. Joanna began to feel better. Her legs and feet still ached, but the hot tea relieved the dreadful dryness of her throat and her head became clearer. She felt a great affection for the sandy remover and would have told him her life-history if he had not been so busy telling her his. She hated to see him go, half an hour later, and she over-tipped him and his fellows and waved to them regretfully as they drove away. What nice men! It was a pity she had planned never to move house again. Mrs. Tomkins the caretaker was hovering about her, making offers of help that seemed to Joanna intolerably officious. Should she open this? Should she transfer that? What would Mrs. Malling be requiring for supper? Joanna suppressed a snubbing rejoinder. She could not bear the woman for another moment; nor, under prying and probably hostile eyes, could she go upstairs and lie on her bed—and that she had to do immediately. So she thanked Mrs. Tomkins for her help and said she was not needed any more this evening. Would she be so kind as to come round in the morning? The caretaker demurred, bargaining for her due price of humility. At last Joanna managed to satisfy her, and she agreed to come, insisting that this was no precedent. She kept Joanna leaning against the doorpost for five minutes while she explained the sweeping of the flues, to be done six-monthly if Mrs. Malling desired any hot water. They had just been done now—the caretaker's son-in-law had cleaned them last week, and he thoroughly understood them—but what he had at the commencement found quite puzzling was this— And so on, until Joanna's replies became so lifeless and unintelligent that the caretaker was hurt, and drawing herself up said, "Good evening," and added as a final snub, "*Madam.*" She stalked down the drive, and Joanna, who had never noticed the snub but was faintly pleased to be called Madam, pulled herself upstairs by the bannisters and fell on to her bed.

It was six o'clock. She would sleep for an hour and then unpack a few essentials and find herself some supper.

Directly she lay down on the bare ticking she began to shiver. Although it was February she had been rather hot all day, but now suddenly she felt quite ill with cold. It took her ten minutes to make herself move off the bed, but once on her feet she wondered what she'd been fussing about; it wasn't really difficult to get some blankets and it was wonderful to lie down again with them wrapped tightly round her shoulders. Now she would go to sleep! Nonsense! she did *not* want a drink of water; she had just had tea. She shut her eyes and began to recite poetry, as was her habit when she found it hard to relax.

> So, we'll go no more a-roving
> So late into the night,
> Though the heart be still as loving
> And the moon be still as bright.
>
> For the sword outwears its sheath,
> And the soul wears out the breast,
> And the heart must pause to breathe,
> And love itself have rest.
>
> Though the night was made for loving,
> And the day returns too soon,
> Yet we'll go no more a-roving
> By the light of the moon.

("And it's no good pretending I'm not thirsty, because I am. I shall have to get that drink.")

Back once more on her bed, she lay unmoving, and thought of her life. It was not true in her case, alas, that the sword had outworn the sheath. She could not, after twenty years, think with any yearning of her husband, Jack. She must have loved him desperately once, and she tried to recapture her feelings when he died so suddenly at the age of thirty. She remembered her mother begging her not to go into the room after his death. "He never woke, darling; it would have been no use to fetch you, and now I do feel that you should stay away and remember him as he was at his best. Don't take any notice of the ghoulish servants who will want you to go in and look at him."

"But I must go in, Mummy," she had said. "If I don't look at him now I shall never be able to believe that he's really dead. I shall go on and on hoping that it's all a mistake, and that would be worse than anything."

And her mother had said, "Shall I come with you, darling, or would you like me to wait outside?"

"Please wait outside." And then, in sudden fear: "Oh, no, Mummy; do come with me!" And they had crept in, hand in hand, to the empty room, and Mummy had lifted the sheet that covered Jack's head. But there was nothing there, not even a question. The smooth, fair young face was of no significance at all; it was like a bad photograph. "He's not there," she had whispered, and had left the room again without touching him.

And had it really helped her to accept his death? Turning restlessly on her bed, Joanna thought that it had helped very little. At first she had made the sad mistake of wincing from every thought of Jack, of distracting her mind whenever he shadowed the borders of her consciousness. It was then that she started to recite poetry every night, occupying her mind until she could sleep with poems far too beautiful for such an abuse. This avoidance of her pain served only to keep it whole. She was for ever vulnerable, and constantly stabbed afresh. "I was only twenty-one," complained Joanna. "Not much older than Libby is now. I couldn't know, could I, that you must breathe in your pain until it loses all its power?" She beat her pillow and sank down again. Yes, in spite of that glimpse of Jack's body, she had half expected, stupidly, that he would come back to her. After the first year she had started to dream of him, and once in her dream he laughed at her and said, "Surely you didn't think I'd go without telling you?" Trying now to find feeling where none was left, Joanna remembered dispassionately her resentful bewilderment; that Jack, who never went as far as the pillar-box without calling out "Back in a minute!" should have disappeared so silently. But she couldn't bring back the emotion now. "I did it the wrong way round," thought Joanna; "I ought to have gobbled up the pain at first, till it was bearable, and then, when it began to be precious, have hoarded it away. As it is, I've nothing left now, and that's why I'm getting old."

She must get some sleep. She began to recite again:

> When I lie where shades of darkness
> Shall no more assail mine eyes—

But she couldn't concentrate. There was so much to be done before Libby should come down to help her at the weekend. Must have it looking a little nice for Libby.

Having Libby, she thought, ought to keep her young—one's children were supposed to do that. "But I'm not at all sure that it's true. After all, being a mother is a grown-up, rather unselfish sort of thing, especially if your husband is not there to help. I'm glad Jack saw her. He thought she was such a funny little thing. He said she'd never be beautiful like her Mamma."

Her little clock showed only ten minutes past six, although Joanna felt that she had been time-wasting for hours. She was longing to get up and start unpacking, yet she dreaded it unspeakably. "I can't lie here with the house in this state. Look at this room! In five more minutes I'll get up and start to sort it out; nothing else matters tonight."

It was Thursday, and on Saturday morning Libby would be arriving, tall, fair, calm and kind, to help Mummy get out of whatever muddle she might be in. It would be nice, thought Joanna, if Libby could find her not muddled at all. By a great imaginative effort she pictured the house furnished, its rooms shining with clean paint, its polished surfaces graciously reflecting bowls of flowers, curtains hanging in fresh folds, and herself, wearing her new red jumper, cutting for Libby's benefit a large piece of ethereal sponge cake. But after all darling Libby was not a guest, and it was very sweet to watch her taking care of her mother, or cooking for them both. Elizabeth's sponges were beautiful, while Joanna's—she had to admit it—were rather like biscuits. And she had never wanted to be a cook; all she had expected was to be left in peace to grow filthy and happy in her garden.

Joanna sat up with a jump. Good heavens! Libby's letter. The postman had handed it to her just as she was leaving that morning—it seemed weeks ago—and she had thrust it unopened into that hostile maw, her bag. Was it still there? She had noticed various envelopes when looking for the key; was Libby's one of them? For a moment she considered behaving reasonably, finishing her rest now and looking for the letter afterwards. But of course it was no good; she grumbled her way out of bed and round the room until she found the bag, and there indeed was the letter. Back in bed she doubled her pillow and tore the envelope.

Elizabeth's handwriting was large and childish and beautifully clear.

"Darling Mummy," she had written, "I hope you're not having a too frightful time and wearing yourself out completely. Do be sensible, darling, and leave some of the work for me to do. In any case you can't possibly get everything done, and you know I shall enjoy a strenuous week-end far more than a lazy one! At all events I can feed you properly for a day or two.

"Darling, I do hope you don't mind, but I've just got engaged to Steven Pryde!! I've mentioned him often, but I don't know if you guessed—I didn't myself really, till it happened. I know you'll love each other—all the Mortimers adore him—and as you were married at twenty yourself you can't mind about me being young! It happened last night, and I haven't seen him yet today, but I'm sure. ...

"*Later.* He rang up just then. I'm *so* happy, Mummy! I'll tell you all about it when I see you. Do be pleased, won't you? He's an angel, and so are you. I'm terribly lucky!!

"See you on Saturday morning, darling.

Libby.

"P.S. He's thirty-five. Quite a sober age, you must admit, but he doesn't seem old a *scrap*, and I don't think a fifteen years gap is too much, do you? L. xxxx."

Joanna's reactions to this letter came so quickly that they cannot be given in sequence. Whether her first feeling was selfish anguish or unselfish pleasure, or hope or despair, or the fierce resolve that Steven Pryde should be good to her unwary Libby, she could not have told. All these emotions seemed to well up from her toes and grip her at the throat and stomach. She did not know what to do with herself, and lay shaken and gasping for a moment before the pressure slackened, the tears rushed from her eyes, and she had time for gentler feelings.

Libby was a woman! It seemed impossible, and she read the letter again, wishing that she could ask someone else to tell her if it was really there or only imagined by her over-tired mind. She shut her eyes and saw a round-faced baby, dazzlingly fair, bowing to her from its pram with ineffable distinction; she saw it asleep, remote, cryptic, disdainful; she saw it staggering bandy-legged along a turf path. Then she saw a two-year-old waving good-bye, heard it cry, "Bah!" and saw a short arm straightened upwards, which barely brought the curling fingers above the blonde head. "How little their arms are at that age! Oh, Libby, you were sweet; you didn't really wave, you used to open and shut your fat little hand. I can see the smocking on your frock, and your knickers coming down as usual."

Libby had never been really ugly, although at one time her teeth had been too big for her mouth. She had been intensely happy at school, absorbed in work and friendships, a most conscientious prefect. She had run fearlessly into so many dangers, and Joanna had nursed her in so many illnesses. And now she would not any more be able to protect her, and this thought hurt Joanna, although she knew, with bitter honesty, that she had not protected Libby now for years. In any real difficulty Libby would turn to her friends, the Mortimers, for to them she gave unquestioning homage; their advice was always to be taken, their example followed, and to Joanna was to be brought the tale of their achievements. "And she's perfectly right," thought Joanna. "They are most excellent people, so well-informed and public-spirited; Mrs. Mortimer slaves for her blind people, and is an Alderman as well. And she would always know, if one asked her, which treaty happened where and who signed it, and what it was all about. And Janet would too, although she's so young." She sighed. "I could never be like that, but Libby may manage it; only I do hope she won't grow up without any imagination."

Who was this Steven Pryde? She had thrown away, before the removal, any of Libby's letters not already lost or used as spills, and she had to admit that the many friends her daughter had mentioned were utterly confused in her mind. Could he be the doctor? Or the young lawyer? (Poetic revenge, perhaps, for her own rejected solicitor.) Or the soldier—a captain, wasn't it?—whose company Libby had seemed to enjoy? Unfortunately it was her daughter's habit neatly to inventory her new friends, and then to assume that Joanna knew all about them; and short of a card index, she thought, it wouldn't be possible to keep them distinct. There was usually nothing very arresting in the description. "A tall, fair man of about thirty who works in Lloyd's." Or "A most attractive girl who's doing a secretarial course." How could one possibly form a picture from this? Sometimes they were "rather good-looking", usually "very friendly and nice", and occasionally "a bit com. but really quite pleasant".

Presumably Steven Pryde was "very nice". He was also thirty-five, and Joanna thought a difference of fifteen years excessive, but not fatally so. "He didn't seem a scrap old—well, I should hope not, poor thing! I only hope he is mature enough to be kind, and that he'll submit gracefully to being told things—rather a lot of things, if I know my little Libby. But, of course, you never know; she may adore him so much that she'll completely knuckle under, which would be dreadful. She doesn't say when she's bringing him down, but she does seem happy. Oh, how I wish it was Saturday now! I shall know if it's really all right the moment I see her."

She could lie still no longer. Absently she stood before the dressing-table and pulled a comb through her short, dark hair. The woman in the glass had a questioning look. It was an oval face, olive-skinned, with strong eyebrows that had never been groomed, quick dark eyes, sunken now with fatigue, and a mouth which closed in a sensitive, not quite straight line. "I might be a grandmother next year," thought Joanna feverishly. "How utterly ridiculous! I may not look young, but I certainly don't look like *that*." Indeed, her age would have been hard to guess. Her thin, upright body—boyish if you admire the type, lean if you do not—could have belonged to a girl of twenty, or to a woman of fifty. Her face was scarcely lined, and if she had smiled, her teeth would have been found perfect. The very dark and almost straight hair was not streaked with white. But her small brown gardening hands had lost their youthful contours, and her watchful expression was not that of an eager girl.

If she wrote to Libby now, and could make the dreadful effort to post her letter, Libby would have it tomorrow morning. Joanna looked hopelessly round the room; where on earth was her writing-case? She hunted vainly about the bedroom and then went downstairs. In the square hall her late Jacobean chest stood darkly gleaming across one corner. (Why couldn't they have put it straight? she wondered distractedly.) A roll of matting lay near the front door, but otherwise the room was empty. In the dining-room the Welsh dresser stood where she had pictured it, and on it was piled her china, unpacked without mishap. She longed to arrange it. They had put in all the leaves of the dining-table, and it looked too big, but that could be easily remedied. The room was rather dark, she thought; one might even call it dank. She must clear the laurels away from the windows and open up some sort of a view. She stood for a moment, looking out. What a blessing to have a house with proper shutters that fitted back into the walls by day and would keep the house warm on winter evenings! The windows were well-proportioned, too, with good sills for her bulbs. But the green leather writing-case was not on either sill, nor on any chair, nor on the little corner cupboard. She went into the drawing-room, and felt a shock of discouragement. She had thought so much of this room, and now she felt that it could never look nice; it was dreadfully overcrowded. The old green settee, without its loose cover, showed many worn places and careful patchings, and the two arm-chairs were equally shabby. Her writing-table had been pushed across a corner, where it could have no light, natural or artificial, and her tall bookcase stood unbeautifully half in and half out of an arched alcove. Joanna tried to think that the re-arrangement would be fun, but she could only feel hopeless; it was an enormous task and her courage was far from its flood. No writing-case was to be seen, and quite suddenly she had a vision of it lying abandoned on the built-in kitchen dresser of her last home. No good expecting to see *that* again, thought Joanna with dreadful calmness; it will be pinched while the house is empty. And my address book is in it! Oh, dear, what a *fool* I am!

After a long search she found a tangle of programme pencils, flung at the last moment into a drawer, and with these and a few pages from her note-book she sat down at last, dazed and aching, and tried to write to her darling daughter.

II

The letter, which was delivered to Miss Elizabeth Malling on Friday at the house of her friends, the Mortimers, seemed to her everything that a letter should be. To its tired, emotional writer it had been a failure, expressing little of her feelings and seeming both pale and wordy, glistening with false joviality in one sentence and withdrawing in the next into the formal expression of a platitude. Creeping out to the pillar-box she had hated it, and hated herself for its making.

She need not have worried. Libby, reading it again in the train on Saturday morning, basked in contentment. She leant her amber head against the cushion (first neatly interposing a silk scarf), put her gleaming brogues on the opposite seat, and smiled out of the window.

She was trying to picture Steven, and was so newly in love that her failure to crystallize his features, and have a good look at them, hurt and disappointed her. But nothing could annoy her for long this morning. She took his photograph from her cigarette case and smiled at that instead. It seemed to be mostly moustache—which was unfortunate, as she didn't like his moustache—but it was better than nothing. She kissed it, self-consciously, and tucked it away. It was beautiful to behave so ridiculously because one was in love, and she had never expected to feel like this. She would take Steven to be properly photographed soon, and doubtless he would want to have her done, too. She closed her eyes, and at once saw a large, highly polished drawing-room, herself seated before a bright fire, pouring out Steven's after-dinner coffee, and on various pieces of furniture huge leather frames, in which smiled, or meditated, her own slightly improved face. On her writing-table, beside her engagement book and blotter, one enormous photograph of Steven would stand. She opened her eyes. But first darling Steven had got to abbreviate his moustache. He didn't know it yet, but that was the first thing she was going to alter about him, bless his heart.

Steven was a soldier, and Elizabeth knew that her mother disliked soldiers, which was why she hadn't mentioned his profession in her letter. At first she had shared Joanna's prejudice, but her friend Janet Mortimer had pointed out, in her well-balanced way, that *some* regular army officers were quite intelligent, and possibly Mrs. Malling didn't know many? This was so clearly true that Elizabeth received Steven more tolerantly at their second meeting, and was soon in a state of soldier-worship the more engulfing because she had not been immunized in childhood. She had been too young to feel personally concerned in the war, and now war novels bored her, and she particularly disliked films in which crumpled, unshaven men did valorous deeds, occasionally pausing to make a valedictory speech to a dead friend. But this was different. Steven in uniform, courteously acknowledging salutes as they walked together, was impressive. She liked his M.C. ribbon and the crown on his shoulder, and she read up the campaigns in which he had served. She liked to be seen with him, and only wished he were a few inches taller; in fact, they were precisely the same height.

As her English teacher had been reared on Wilfred Owen rather than on Rupert Brooke, Elizabeth was a little disappointed that Steven did not turn pale or tight-lipped when the war was mentioned. She hoped that when he knew her better his heroic reserve might wear away and that she might console him for some of the horrors which must be burnt into his memory. It would be nice to comfort him, and he was obviously not the sort of man to cry. Elizabeth did not believe that men ever cried except in books. For that matter, she seldom cried herself, and needed to be alone to do it. And Mummy didn't cry now, though no doubt she had wept bitterly when Daddy died of pneumonia.

But though, as their acquaintance ripened, Steven sometimes laid his head on her breast, he was never seeking to forget with her the horrors of war, but only—she at last realized—to explore the delights of peace. Libby allowed him to explore them to a limited extent, and having been taught that the road to immorality was smooth and broad, it surprised her to find that a conscious effort was needed on her part to allow Steven any liberties at all. Now that they were going to be married, she supposed it would be fairly easy to lose her virginity, but it seemed that her will had to over-ride her instincts at every advance, which was the reverse of what she had expected.

Darling Steven! Every time she thought of him something swelled under her ribs like a bubble. Of course it would be all right; she would do anything for him, and all the books assured her that her pleasure—after a few preliminary setbacks, perhaps—would be as great as his.

It was Spring, too, or very nearly Spring, and after a week of wet weather the sun was shining today on the wet roads and soggy fields, punctuated, for her, by frequent tunnels. She wondered how her mother was getting on at the house. Why she liked the place, Libby couldn't think; it was Victorian, it was built of yellow brick, and it had long been neglected. Her own impression was of dripping trees, leaking gutters, and a brackish smell near the back door, where a slimy water-butt, half full of blackened leaves, stood overflowing gently on to the grass-grown cobble-stones. But Mummy said that the house had dignity and could be made perfectly charming, and there were times, as Libby knew, when her advice was not considered seriously.

"I hope it won't be too awful," said Libby, as she swung her suitcase down from the rack. The train wormed its way rallentando through the last hillside and stopped.

Tadwych Station, built between the gaping mouths of two tunnels, is practically underground, lit at night by too few lamps and in the day by a small amount of smoke-filtered daylight. Elizabeth glanced distastefully round as she followed the few passengers up a flight of dirty stairs and gave up her ticket. She blinked in the February sunlight, and saw her mother emerging in a hurry from a taxi. Joanna was wearing her green suede jacket and her oldest corduroy slacks, once rich brown but now faded almost to pink. They had long been condemned to the dustbin by Libby, and even their owner held them only suitable for gardening wear. However, Libby kissed her kindly, reserving her criticism, and the taxi drove off through miles of niggardly houses, redeemed from squalor only by the hills upon which they stood steeply terraced and by the felt presence of a river.

"Darling," said Joanna, holding her daughter's hand, "you look very well on it."

"I feel marvellous. Thank you for your letter Mummy. It was such a nice one."

"Not really. Not nice enough. Libby, when am I going to meet him?"

"The moment he can get away. He's had to go home this week-end to break the news."

"*Really* to break it? They'll be pleased, surely?"

"Only she. His father was killed in the war."

"Oh, dear! What an awful wedding it will be, Libby, with two lone lorn widow women as the only parents."

"It's going to be a lovely wedding. You wait!"

"What's she like?"

"I don't know. I think Steven's very fond of her, but they're not like you and me."

"Has he brothers and sisters?"

"No, he's the one and only."

"Oh, dear." Joanna's sympathy was not for Steven or his mother, but only for her daughter, doomed, it seemed, to marry the only son of a possessive mother. "Will she impinge much?"

"I don't think so. Steven finds her a bit of a bore."

"Poor Steven!" Joanna was delighted. "Thank heaven, darling, you won't have any of this 'wonderful mother of mine' business to contend with."

"Steven wouldn't be like that. He's really very level-headed." She blushed, and looked shyly triumphant. "Except about me," she added.

"Darling," said Joanna, too touched to find words. If only she were not so inarticulate, she mourned. It was true that articulate people embarrassed her acutely, but at moments like this she envied them. "I'm sure," she said, "that he's not a bit level-headed about you."

"He really thinks I'm wonderful," admitted Libby bashfully.

"Well, anyway, darling, he's very lucky, and I hope you are too. I wish you'd tell me what he's like. What about a photograph?"

"I've only this one."

It was handed over, examined, and praised. Joanna was disappointed. A boot-faced man, she thought; and what a moustache!

Libby said, "I'm going to make him cut off most of that moustache."

"Are you, darling? Doesn't he mind?"

"He doesn't know."

"Perhaps he'll refuse."

"Perhaps!" Her confident smile denied it.

"I was very nearly late for you. Thank goodness your train wasn't on time."

"I should have been furious with you."

"*I* should have been furious. But just as I was going in to change, I came face to face with a patch of *nettles*, just where my anemones are going."

"And they wouldn't wait, of course; so you donned your gloves—"

"And ripped them up. Great fun it was."

"Hence the trousers?"

"Yes. Sorry, darling. Anyway, no one knows me in Tadwych yet."

Libby thought that they would soon know her by her trousers at this rate. She glanced complacently at her own tweed skirt and at the well-gloved hands in her lap. Her mother glanced too. "'You can always tell a lady by her boots and her gloves,'" she said. "You pass on both tests, Libby. Mrs. March might have added, 'By her unexaggerated tweed shoulders', mightn't she?"

"Tiresome woman. Why couldn't poor Meg have had her fling, and a bit of flirting."

"The insufferable Laurie interfered."

"How dared he? He was only a schoolboy, anyway."

"All the same, there is something rather glamorous about the boy. I don't think one ever outgrows one's first feeling about a child's book. I still get awfully angry with Aunt March."

"Do you still weep over Beth?"

"In theory I laugh."

"But actually?"

"Yes, I'm afraid I still gulp, rather."

"Darling Mummy, you are sweet?"

"But don't you, Libby?"

"No, I skip."

"One does waste one's emotions, there's no doubt, but I suppose keeping them in a neat thermos flask would waste them just as much."

"*You're* not emotional, Mummy!"

"No, oh, no, I'm not." Joanna stared out of the window. But at this moment, my darling, she thought, I wish that we could have a good hearty cry together about this engagement of yours instead of talking about *Little Women*. I'm sure that would untie this knot in my middle, and I don't see how anything else can be expected to.

Libby, however, pink and smiling, showed no need of tears or even kisses. She seemed intensely happy, and it was natural that she should be more animated than usual—almost, Joanna thought, a shade nervous. Has she got something to break to me? she wondered for an instant. Then she ordered herself to relax. The news of the engagement had already been broken; there could be nothing else.

"Well, now," said Elizabeth, as they stood in the hall, while their taxi squelched over the weeds towards the road, "what's the programme? You seem to have done a lot."

"I've muddled along without a programme so far, except to get your room fairly human, and to eat at intervals. But now you're here I suppose I shall be forced to follow an exact time-table."

"It's 11.30. Is lunch organized?"

"If you don't mind bully beef."

"I like it. Anything to go with it?"

"Tomatoes and bread and butter. Will that be all right?"

"Lovely for me; but haven't you been eating that at every meal for about four days?"

"No, no," said Joanna, who had.

"Oh, darling, you *have* made it look nice!" Libby paused just inside her room to admire its white walls, blue cretonnes, white rugs and, on the walls, her own colour photographs of Swiss snow scenes. The little Davenport that had been her dressing-table since her tenth birthday stood below an old oak-framed wall-mirror, and she could see at a glance that the light would shine, not into the glass, but actually on to her face. "You *are* clever!" she exclaimed. "You've had the light moved for me. Did you have your own done too?"

"No, only yours and the spare room."

"Oh, Mummy, *why*?"

"I can see just as well as I shall ever want to. I'll promise to come in here to powder my nose on Steven's first evening."

Libby sat down on the bed and fingered the patchwork quilt which Joanna had made for her seventeenth birthday. "Darling Ma, you've made it so lovely; I feel awful to be leaving it so soon."

"But this is your room, my love. We can easily put in another bed—or a double one, whichever you like."

"Oh, a twin one, I should think."

"That'll be easy. The spare room one matches this."

"Thank you, darling." Elizabeth crossed to the window. "You shouldn't have bought those jonquils for me, Angel."

"But they look nice, don't they?"

"Lovely. Darling—"

Now it's coming, thought Joanna. I knew she had something to break to me. Oh, God, has he got a wife or something?

"What is it, Libby?"

"I'm afraid," said Libby, looking frightened, "that we'll be going abroad pretty soon."

"Abroad? Where?"

"I don't know."

"But why—"

"Steven's a soldier, darling. But truly an awfully nice one. He doesn't slap his boots at all. And he's a Major," she added proudly.

"How soon will you be going?"

"Steven thinks in June."

"Oh, dear!" said Joanna inadequately.

"Wherever we go, you'll come and stay with us, won't you?"

"Thank you, darling."

"Mummy, you won't *ever* think of yourself as a mother-in-law, will you? Promise! *You're* not like that and *we're* not like that. Steven isn't a bit. Directly we're settled you'll come out for a year or so, won't you?"

"It's very sweet of you, darling—"

"Oh, I know you're full of theories about leaving the young couple alone and so forth, but I tell you we're not *like* that!"

"I hope you are!" said Joanna briskly.

"No, truly! Janet's promised already to come as soon as she can for a long visit. So you can travel together."

Oh, can we! thought Joanna. I know what Libby and Janet are like together—I suppose I shall be expected to consort with Steven!

Elizabeth was still speaking. "Only, her boss relies on her so dreadfully, she says. Janet's marvellously efficient, you know, Mummy—"

"Yes, I do know, darling—"

"And she simply doesn't know how he'd get on if she took a really long holiday."

"And you don't know where you're going?"

"No idea. It might be Malaya, or Germany, or East Africa, or almost anywhere. I don't expect we shall know till the last minute."

"Will you be able to go with him?"

"Not if he flies. But I'm going to follow at once, anyway, even if I have to pay my own passage and go into a hotel when I get there. Steven says he won't be separated from me the moment we're married, no matter what it costs!"

"Steven's very wise. Has he *got* the money, darling?"

"Ah ha! Of course I must tell you all about his finances, mustn't I, as you're being a father to me, you poor pet. I think I understand the position, all right."

"Better than I should, I'm sure," hastened her mother. "But he's got something, besides his pay?"

"No, not really, but he's got a good life insurance. And there'll be a little something when his mother dies."

"Well, *your* prospects aren't terrific, I'm afraid. But there'll be the house, and the furniture's worth something—"

"Don't dare to start talking about your will!"

"All right, there's no hurry. Libby, tell me, when do you want to get married?"

"If you don't mind terribly, darling, we thought in May. Then we can have a honeymoon plus embarkation leave."

"Which end of May?"

"Early."

"H'm, about six weeks to get ready. Oh, dear, what a pity we've just moved—we're going to be busy."

"You're an angel to be so nice about it."

"Nothing else *to* be," said Joanna sincerely. "Well, we must really be very organized about this, darling. Oh, dear—your clothes too!"

"Janet will help me, and I'm not a slow shopper."

"No, you generally know your mind."

"As a matter of fact, if I give Janet my measurements she can buy quite a lot of things for me. Unimportant things, like stockings and cami-knickers and nighties—oh well, perhaps I'd better choose the nighties myself." And Libby blushed violently.

Joanna said, "I expect you'd rather choose all your own things, wouldn't you, Libby?"

"Ideally, yes, I would. But Janet's taste is so good, she could perfectly well get my underclothes, and things like table-mats and napkins."

Joanna found this attitude inexplicable. "But surely—" she protested, and then changed her mind. Probably she was a jealous mother, she thought, to feel such dismay. "Anyway," she said, "people will give you table-mats and napkins, with any luck."

"Perhaps they will," said Libby contentedly.

(And many of them, Joanna told herself crossly, will have far worse taste than Janet Mortimer.) Aloud she said, "A white wedding, darling?"

"Can we afford it?"

"We can afford that if it's the last penny we ever spend."

"It would be lovely—do you think white suits me?"

"Of course it does; you'll look perfectly beautiful." Joanna meant what she said. Elizabeth, with her height and carriage, her fair skin and amber hair, was made to be a bride. "Steven will worship you," said Joanna, and was ashamed that her voice sounded husky. She left her seat on the window-sill rather abruptly. "Do you feel strong enough to come and tackle the drawing-room now? I'd like to get it done today. We've no time to waste."

"No," said Libby happily. "We certainly mustn't let the grass—"

"Seed," cut in her mother concisely. And although they both felt that there was endless talking to be done, they spoke, for the rest of the morning, only of the work in hand.

III

On the morning of Steven's first visit, Joanna felt so nervous, when Elizabeth had gone to meet his train, that she found herself an almost unbearable burden. She walked quickly about the house, re-arranging her bowls of forsythia and early daffodils and her tall jar of cellar-white flowering currant. She took a duster and started to search in secret places for dirt; but with her new acquisition, Mrs. Holmes, to rush over the more obvious surfaces, and Libby—now at home—to follow conscientiously behind her, the house was remarkably clean. On the stairs, however, she triumphantly removed some cobwebs, and did not know that one of them had fallen in her hair.

To make a good impression on her son-in-law she had put on a dark-red, high-necked jersey and matching skirt, with fine lisle stockings which felt meagre to her trouser-accustomed legs. She stood in the drive, and her hands fretted to be among the weeds which encroached upon her polyanthuses. But she must *not* let Libby down by offering Steven a muddy hand to shake. Surreptitiously she tweaked up two healthy young plants of grass, using her left hand, and then childishly wiped her fingers on the backs of her stockings. Tomorrow, she thought, I shall get up in my slacks, and he can lump it. I will *not* have the garden looking a shambles for Libby's wedding. Damn it, it's his wedding too! He ought to be grateful.

Libby had gone off looking extremely well groomed, as was the habit of Janet Mortimer's apt pupil; very pink and happy and not visibly nervous at all. Trying to remember her engagement at the same age, Joanna decided that, compared to her daughter, she had been an hysterical little fool. Libby slept peacefully every night, and there was no place for fear in her happy excitement. She did not doubt her power to make Steven happy—why should she?—nor did she ever seem to feel herself sentenced to any kind of imprisonment.

Joanna walked across the drive, through an overgrown arch of roses, and on to the neglected tennis lawn. Useless for her to restore it, she told herself regretfully, as Libby was going abroad. She would get some wire netting, and keep lots and lots of runner ducks. But the lawn's great merit was that it was three-parts surrounded by lilacs. If only they will flower at the right moment, she thought, I can fill the house with them, and it will be good for the trees too—they can't have been touched for years. I must borrow a ladder; perhaps Mrs. Holmes will know who has one.

That sounded like a slowing car. Yes, it was turning in at the gate. With her heart bumping, and conquering a great wish to hide, Joanna walked slowly towards the house. "Oh, God," she prayed (not normally believing in prayer), "make us like each other. Make him nice!"

The young man who helped Elizabeth from the taxi was thick-set and well tailored. Being of Libby's height, he looked shorter, and Joanna at once noticed that he had not yet reduced his moustache. It was a lighter brown than his hair, and certainly very much too big.

"Mummy, here he is," said Libby, and stood proudly aside to witness their meeting.

They both spoke at once: "I'm so very glad to meet you, Steven—" said Joanna, and Steven said: "Mrs. Malling, I'm so delighted to be here at last—" and then they both stopped speaking, and Joanna said, "Really, how much simpler it would be to say 'Pleased to meet you' and have done with it." And was horrified that Steven did not even faintly, dutifully, laugh. She laughed herself, therefore, as she took Libby's arm and turned into the house, and she did not guess that the blank-faced Steven was wondering whether he ought to have kissed her, and wishing he had asked Libby's advice in the taxi. There were several small matters of etiquette that he had meant to lay before her, but when he had seen her—his beautiful, fresh-faced love, with her smile of radiant welcome— he had forgotten them all.

They went into the drawing-room, and Steven was awkwardly bringing his suitcase with him when Libby said: "Dump it in the hall, Steve."

Only ten-thirty, lamented Joanna. I can't even offer him a drink. She proffered cigarettes, which he refused, and hurriedly took one herself. His hand, as he lit it for her, was steady and he appeared unconcerned.

"What an economical couple you'll be," said Joanna feverishly, "neither of you smoking."

"But I do in the evenings," said Libby. "I've just started; isn't it silly? It must be the nervous strain of getting engaged. And as for Steven—"

"I do smoke a pipe," said Steven.

"Then won't you now?"

"If I may—when I've unpacked my tobacco."

"Oh, you didn't have it with you for the train?"

"Er—actually no." And Steven glanced at Libby, who beamed at him.

"Sore subject, Mummy. I objected to his bulging his pockets with a tobacco pouch. Don't you agree? It simply ruins that very nice suit."

"I'm sure it does," said Joanna. (Steven looked much nicer now that he was half-smiling.) "Would you like your tyrannical fiancée to take you straight up to your room?

"Thanks very much." Steven glanced towards the door.

"But first of all," said Libby, "there's a most important question to be decided."

"Oh, dear, is there?" said Joanna.

"What's Steven going to call you?"

"Good gracious! I've no idea."

"Well, he can't go on with Mrs. Malling."

Joanna was tempted to ask why not, and so, if she had known it, was Steven, but they both murmured politely, "No, no, of course not."

Elizabeth sat on the window-sill and smiled kindly at them. "Steven already has a mother," she announced.

"Yes, indeed," said Joanna, who would in fact have disliked being called mother by a perfectly strange young man.

"Of course there's Mater or Madré—" said Libby.

"I don't like them," said Joanna bravely.

"Nor do I. And as for Granny, which some people use straight away, long before there are any children, it would really be too ridiculous to call you that, darling."

Joanna bowed her head modestly, and Steven interjected: "Absurd, of course."

"So *I* think," summed up Libby, "that the nicest name is Mamma."

"Oh, yes," agreed Joanna. "That's very nice."

"Steven?"

"Yes, darling. Good idea."

Libby jumped down from her window-sill. "Then that's settled," she concluded. "Come on now, Steve; I'll take you upstairs."

Left alone, Joanna gazed at the shut door, and thought that she had quite lost her daughter. For years now Libby had shown her independence, but hitherto those friends to whom she had been drawn, while largely the cause of her mother's exclusion, had been known to them both, and Joanna had been able to understand their attraction. She was not herself fond of Janet Mortimer, but she could appreciate that she ought to be; Janet was, in fact, a sort of super Libby, lacking only, amongst all her excellencies, Libby's innocent charm.

But this young man whom Libby loved was, to her mother, *more* than a stranger. She felt his stolidity to be inimical, and knew that she would always feel it so. To think of Libby kissing him was an embarrassment from which her thought recoiled, and it was desolation to realize that henceforth whatever passed between herself and her daughter would, if of interest, be recounted to Steven. From Janet the loyal Libby would keep a secret if asked, but to Steven, now, all her loyalty must be given, and it would be cruel to strain it. Well, thought Joanna, I ought to be old enough to do without a confidante by now, and in fact I don't run to Libby with all my thoughts; I never have. Only it was nice to feel that I could.

She stood up. Remember, she told herself, that you are forty-one. And she was about to leave the house, turning for comfort to her garden, when Mrs. Holmes appeared in the doorway, her blue eyes lit with interest and sympathy. "Ow, isn't 'e handsome?" said Mrs. Holmes.

Joanna found this comment quite astonishing, but she managed to smile and to acquiesce. Mrs. Holmes, longing to talk, bundled down on her knees on the Persian hearth-rug and began to polish the little brass fender with all the strength of her shapely arm. Joanna inhaled smoke and looked on helplessly. How well she knew the type of charwoman who polishes and re-polishes the brass, while neglecting to wash the paint! She felt certain that she ought to protest, but by this time Mrs. Holmes had spread half a tin of Brasso over the immaculate surface of the fender, and it would have to be taken off again. "Mr. 'Olmes," she was saying, "used to 'ave a moustache somethink like your daughter's fellow's—what did you say 'is name was?"

"Major Pryde."

"Pride—eh?" Mrs. Holmes thought this exceedingly funny. The tight little auburn curls on her head quivered with mirth, and she sat back on her heels, turning her pretty, coarse face to beam at Joanna over her shoulder. "Well, I bet 'e's your daughter's pride all right, dear. Proper 'andsome! As I was saying, my 'ubby had a lovely moustache before 'e shaved it off. Wish 'e 'adn't now, but 'e done it to please *me* when Carol was on the way. (First one, she was, and we 'adn't been married long.) Just like Mr. Pride 'e looked when 'e had that moustache."

Joanna had seen Mr. Holmes, a strikingly beautiful young man of gypsy ancestry, with brilliant dark eyes and a rare flashing smile. He was infinitely better looking than Steven, and it would be vandalism to hide that well-cut mouth beneath a heavy moustache. "Really!" she said inadequately.

"Wish 'e'd kept it now," mused Mrs. Holmes. "I think Mr. Pride's a lovely gentleman. And you'll soon be having some grandchildren, Mrs. Malling!" She hugged her fine bosom with both arms, and rocked it from side to side. "I love to see the little kiddies," said Mrs. Holmes, squeezing herself ecstatically.

Grandchildren indeed! Joanna, outwardly unmoved, was searching herself for feelings of affection towards those potential babies. But they ought to be mine! she thought. You can't have *grandchildren* at my age! I could still have a baby myself, if I wanted to—which I certainly don't.

And my blessed little Libby is the most guileless baby herself. What a ridiculous idea!

"Makes you feel your age, don't it?" said Mrs. Holmes sympathetically. "Mum, *she* says to me when our Carol was born: 'Ow, Brenda,' she says, 'I feel ready for me tomb!'"

"Well, I hope I shan't feel as bad as that," said Joanna briskly. "When you've finished that fender, Mrs. Holmes—"

"What would you like me to do then, dear?" inquired Mrs. Holmes, quickly spreading polish over the gleaming surface of the copper coal-scuttle. "Course I'll have to do the scuttle," she added, deftly emptying the tin over the fire-irons, "and it'll be time for a cup of char then, won't it? We need some Brasso, Madam, next time you're shopping."

Joanna could hear Libby's voice on the stairs, and she surprised on her charwoman's face an expression of triumph. She decided, by way of spoiling sport, to take the young couple round the garden, but as she went to the door, Mrs. Holmes stood up, wiping her hands on her apron, with such a smile of happy anticipation that Joanna's heart was melted. After all, she would introduce Steven first, and then extricate him by proposing a walk in the fresh air.

The introduction was rather protracted by the ardour with which Mrs. Holmes shook Steven's hand; gazing up into his face with guileless admiration, while she told him that he would have a lovely bride. For to Mrs. Holmes this marriage, obviously not brought about by an expected birth, seemed entirely glamorous, and its hero and heroine shone almost as film stars shine. She sighed dotingly as she envied their handsome youth, and to Elizabeth she gave a wink, calling her "Duck".

In the garden Elizabeth took hold of Joanna's arm and Steven's, and the three walked about while they discussed the plans for the wedding. Joanna, conscious of every bud on every plant that they passed, wished that the children would show some interest in her recent work. The long bed against the wall had been cleaned of the weeds of years, and was planted now with daffodils and wallflowers, and later there would be hollyhocks. In the narrow beds under the front windows she had left the purple flags, which would be in full flower, if she were lucky, in time for the wedding.

And the stocks should be out too. But Libby was legitimately absorbed, today, in her own concerns, and she did not even comment on the cobweb in her mother's hair, although she did, as she talked, pluck it off with careful fingers.

"If we receive our guests in the drawing-room, Mummy," she said, flicking the cobweb into limbo, "where are we going to eat? Is the dining-room big enough?"

"It's much smaller than the drawing-room," said Joanna doubtfully, "but, after all, we shan't be a crowd. We hardly know anyone locally, and we can't expect all our friends to come from the ends of England."

"H'm, won't they walk in past the food?" objected Libby. "Oh, no, they can be shepherded *past* the dining-room door into the back passage—pity it's so dark—and get into the drawing-room that way. Then they walk past us—"

"Telling you you look lovely, and not knowing what to say to Steven—"

"And do they go out the same way?"

"No, no, you'd get a whirlpool. They'd better go into the dining-room."

"And across the hall to look at the presents in the study?"

"I suppose so. It seems rather untidy, doesn't it? Could you receive them in the dining-room instead?"

"Then we shouldn't have the alcove."

"Nor you would. The alcove full of flowers, and you two standing in front of it—quite right, Libby, we can't waste the alcove."

"Is the study *big* enough for the presents?"

"Quite big enough for all *you'll* get," said Joanna grimly. "It's as big as the dining-room, only longer and thinner."

"Then why not—"

"Yes, of course! Food in the study and presents in the dining-room. Then they can walk past you and go and waste a little time itching to re-arrange their presents, until you're ready to cut the cake."

"Will they be able to *see* us cut the cake in the study?"

"Yes—no—I'm not sure they will."

"Why not have the cake in the hall, Mummy, by itself?"

"Good idea. On—on what?"

"On a high stand on the chest—it'd look lovely."

"All right. Where do you suppose I'd better order it?"

"Oh, but Mummy, I want to make it myself!"

At this Steven, whose profound boredom had been plainly written on his face, turned upon Elizabeth a look of sentimental adoration. The darling! he thought. She actually wants to make the cake herself. How perfectly angelic of her!

"Oh, Libby, *can* you make a wedding cake?" asked her mother.

"Of course I can, darling idiot. What do you think I've been learning all these years?"

"All the decoration?"

"Lovely fun."

"But will you have time? You've so much to think of—"

"I *must* have time for that. Who's going to do the catering?"

"There's a firm in Tadwych who are supposed to be all right."

"Shall I go and talk to them for you?"

"Darling child, the bride shouldn't have any of these responsibilities, but of course it would be lovely if you would!"

"I'll go on Monday. Don't go into the Poor-House after this wedding, will you, Mummy? I wonder if we could do the food ourselves?"

"Of course we couldn't; it will be quite bad enough getting the house clean and tidy. Mrs. Holmes' mother has promised to come in as much as we want."

"What's Mrs. Holmes' mother like? Another barmaid?"

"Oh, *no*, darling! You've met her. She's Mrs. Tomkins, the caretaker. She's about the most refined female that ever set foot in a coarse and brutal world!"

"Oh, *that* woman. Give me Mrs. Holmes any day, even if she does waggle her ear-rings at Steven."

"She has lots of children, you know, but I suspect she's a disappointment to her mother."

"I bet she is. I think she's rather fun. Did you see her ogling Steven?"

"I certainly did. She thinks 'e's proper 'andsome." She stole a glance at Steven as she spoke, hoping for a smile, but he only looked disgusted.

Joanna sighed. I can't make *all* the running, she reflected; he really might try a little.

"Steven will wear his blues," said Elizabeth proudly, thinking of his M.C. ribbon, and hoping it would be recognized by all the guests.

"His *what*?" said Joanna blankly.

"His blues. Walking-out dress."

"Oh! Very nice, too."

"And we've decided all about me, haven't we, but the point is Janet."

"Haven't you got her fixed yet?"

"It's a bit difficult. I wanted pink, but she says it doesn't suit her. I thought pink always suited dark people."

"Not necessarily, I suppose, *I* never wear pink."

Elizabeth thought that at forty-one it was natural to leave pink for one's juniors, but she was too kind to say so. Steven unexpectedly said: "You'd look very nice in pink. Dusty pink, I think." And he added, with only a very slight stammer, "Mamma."

"How *clever* of you, Steven," said Elizabeth, changing her mind. "Of course she would. Mummy, will you get a dusty pink outfit for my wedding?"

"I'm too old," said Joanna.

"Rubbish!" Libby sounded almost too emphatic. "You'll look lovely, and Steven will give you some gorgeous flowers, won't you, Steve?"

"Of course!" said Steven, looking astonished.

"It's your job, you know, to provide the flowers. But don't worry, you don't have to choose them yourself. Promise, Mummy?"

"I'll promise to consider it," said Joanna. "In any case, I shall probably get precisely what you tell me to, as you very well know. The really catastrophic thing is that I shall have to have a hat."

"'The bride's mother started a new fashion by wearing, instead of a hat, a single, tellingly-placed cobweb!' Don't worry, Mummy, we'll get you a dream hat, and Steven will give you some carnations."

"Not carnations. Sweet peas, if you don't mind, Steven. I'm afraid they'll be rather expensive in May!"

"Of course he doesn't mind. Now then, what about Janet?"

"Blue?"

"I suppose it'll have to be. Would green be unheard of?"

"I'm afraid it would upset some superstitious people."

"Do they matter?"

"I think perhaps they do."

"I'm afraid mother's frightened of green," said Steven, "though of course she can't dictate—"

"Then of *course* green is out," said Joanna. "You'll be seeing Janet on Monday, won't you, Libby?"

"Yes, she's taking the day off to help me shop."

"Then you can thrash it out with her. It's no good our deciding on something she'll hate." And she thought that, as Janet was sure to have clear-cut, positive wants, it was waste of time to discuss the matter further with Libby. In any case Steven looked so bored that she did not know whether to feel pity or annoyance. "Let's go in now," she said. "Mrs Holmes will have some tea for us."

As they drank their tea Steven searched the face opposite to him for those qualities Elizabeth had described in her mother. "Sweet." Oh no, that mobile mouth, those ironic brows, were never sweet. "Kind." Yes, that might be true. But "helpless"? She did not seem helpless in the least, and as for "shy", the suggestion was laughable. There she sat, erect and wiry in her dark red clothes—he hated flat-chested women—and she seemed in no way disturbed by his presence. She and Liz chattered on, planning, objecting, planning again, agreeing, and he might as well have been in London for all the part he took in the discussion. Liz, it was true, gave him, now and then, her warm, confiding smile, and Mrs. Malling—Mamma— tried with an occasional lift of those winged eyebrows to include him; but he remained painfully aloof, conscious of his hands and knees, and of his dumbness. Couldn't they see, blast them, that he wanted to be alone with his darling? She had been loving but hurried, upstairs; her calm ruffled a little by her ardent wish to see affection spring up in a moment between these two whom she loved. She had hustled him down after a few kisses, and now here he sat, while the imagined figure of Mrs. Malling, built up during the past months, dwindled, a sweet-faced wraith, from his sight.

What on earth would Mother think of Mamma? he wondered, brushing aside the question of what Mamma would think of Mother. How restful were his mother's banalities when compared to Mrs. Malling's elliptical speech. Mother's bosom might be worn rather low, but at least she did *have* a bosom. To hear Liz call this stranger "Mummy" actually shocked him, for there was nothing motherly about her, nothing. She was just an attractive woman (attractive, that is, to others, he supposed) who was slightly past her first youth and consequently rather stringy. She spoke too fast and disagreed too often with Elizabeth, whose happy nature took no umbrage. Now they were discussing the invitations, arguing about people he'd never met. What could possibly be duller?

Joanna suddenly gave him her whole attention. "Steven, has your mother made a list of people to be invited?"

"No, I'm afraid she hasn't."

"Oh, Steve, darling, I did ask you."

"I know, Liz, but Mother probably forgot."

"Sure to have!" laughed Elizabeth sympathetically. She had seen for herself how Mrs. Pryde would forget the essentials while busying herself about the trimmings.

But now Steven seemed disinclined to laugh about it. He was frowning moodily. "I expect I can make a list."

"How many cards have you ordered, Mummy?"

"A thousand."

"A *thousand?*"

Joanna jumped. "Sorry, no, I mean a hundred!" She was still toppling, it seemed, after hearing Elizabeth called Liz. What a thing to say! How *could* he be so crass as to reduce a beautiful name to one odious syllable. But Lizzie would be worse still, she told herself.

"Will a hundred be enough?"

"Oh, yes, darling. Only one card to a family, you know."

"Yes, that's true. Would you hate to make the list now, Steve?"

"Not if you'll help me."

"But I don't know the people."

"I'll describe them, and then you can tell me if they ought to be asked."

"I've got five thousand things to do."

"Then you can't do them all today."

"Quite right," insisted Joanna. "Would you like to have the study to yourselves? There's paper and everything on the writing-table."

"And an arm-chair with plenty of room for two people!" said Libby lightheartedly, jumping to her feet and holding out her hand to Steven, who stood up, looking studiously boot-faced.

Joanna imagined that he was blushing. How odd of Libby to say that! But no, the child was merely being natural. Far odder that she herself should be embarrassed. She had thought of the chair already, for that matter, but had shooed her thoughts onwards to the writing-table.

"By all means," she said tamely. And added: "I'll try to ward off Mrs. Holmes."

Steven held Libby's arm and urged her towards the door. Then he seemed to remember his manners. "Thank you, Mamma," he said, and smiled beautifully. Yes, really beautifully! she thought as she went into the dining-room. His small grey eyes almost vanished, his excellent teeth appeared below the moustache, and he became suddenly charming.

"So *that's* what Libby first saw in him!" murmured Joanna, as she went to lay the table.

IV

❧

Surely that was the loveliest May in all memory. It came suddenly upon Joanna, who had been almost impervious to April, because the Spring had seemed to be merely one more preparation for the wedding. The lilacs had flowered in time for Libby, and the little crap-apple tree, which she had discovered near the rubbish-heap—covered with red blossom and half hidden by brambles—had simply been uprooted and made to stand before the drawing-room fireplace, where it had looked quite unreal and given the guests something to talk about. And all of the immoderate bud-bursting in her garden had remained unworshipped.

But now, a week after Major and Mrs. Pryde had driven away to a Cotswold village for their honeymoon, the Spring was violently upon her; she felt buffeted, washed over, soaked in it, and the minimum of housework became a frittering of moments that should all have been spent in the garden. Filled with delight, she ached with loneliness; but as this happened every year, it brought her no surprise.

In the vegetable garden, improbably enough, she had found a mass of iris plants, nettle-crowded, strangled with bindweed, and persistently managing to flower. Someone must have collected them with love, for there were many varieties, some of them strange to Joanna. Today, hovering over a clump of nettles like an arrested butterfly, she found one tall white one, delicately marked with gold. As she tugged with her gloved hands at the nettles, ripping up the roots and scattering small balls of earth like rain on the surrounding leaves, a part of her mind was with Elizabeth and a part, admiringly, with the white iris. She threw a handful of young nettles on to the rubbish-heap, and wondered whether Libby, were she here, would condemn her for wastefulness. She could imagine a reproachful voice: "But darling! They'd make *lovely* soup!" And she smiled as she stooped again to her task. In Libby's absence she would not cook anything that needed to be sieved.

Steven would eat like a king, and probably never realize the skilled processes through which his food went, on its way to his plate. Joanna hoped anxiously that he would insist on helping in the kitchen. He had been quite good, if a little distracted, in her house, but would he keep it up? Would Libby *make* him keep it up? She knew that Libby wouldn't lower her standards, and if Steven didn't follow her into the kitchen they would spend many needless hours apart. "I hope he's *sensible*" she whispered as she unwound the bindweed that was choking a Spanish iris.

Later, when they had finished flowering, she would prepare honourable beds for the long-neglected plants, making a formal design in the middle of the drive, where now an unsightly plot of grass with nibbled edges exasperated her on every walk. The plot was oval, and if she crossed it with a long X of paving-stones she would have four more or less triangular beds. Or she could think of another design. But taking away the turf would be heavy work, and the paving-stones which she had joyfully discovered piled up in the shrubbery could not be moved by her alone. Perhaps Mr. Holmes, when not lorry-driving, might be persuaded by his wife to put in a few hours in the garden. He was an expert gardener, she knew, and if once she could get him interested, he might be of enormous use to her. So far he had been rather unfriendly. He had greeted her woodenly and turned his greasy cap in his greasier hands, casting down lashes of childish beauty. Twice only he had smiled his unforgettable smile. What an ornament to the village! Joanna wondered whether Mrs. Holmes was much troubled by lapses in her husband's fidelity. He looked like a D. H. Lawrence figure, full of beautiful, dumb virility, and he must be younger than his wife. He was away so often at night, however, driving right across England, that his indiscretions might all be done at a distance. For Mrs. Holmes' sake, she hoped so.

Joanna straightened her back and shook the heavy gloves from her narrow hands. A nagging hollowness would no longer be denied, and she must go and eat something. She walked back to the house, and paused for a moment to enjoy her projected iris patch, flowering more lavishly than it ever would in fact. In her vision all the plants had together reached perfection, and were quite hidden under their elegant flowers; over whose transitory beauty hovered more transient butterflies. It really ought to be lovely, she sighed, as she went indoors.

She was hungry enough to enjoy a snatched lunch of two cold sausages, a lettuce and a tomato, with brown bread and butter. She read a book as she munched, and used her fingers, so that there would be no washing up. Afterwards, smoking a cigarette and too lazy to make coffee, she let her mystery story lie in her lap. The book was dull, she thought, and the vulgar and ill-mannered little detective was as dead as the over-plentiful corpses. She could not be bothered to read another word, and she thought wistfully of other more cultured detectives, whose well-bred investigations always entertained her. Libby would say she was a snob—dear Libby, who had herself been so relieved to find Steven's mother only queer, and not common!

What a woman to be called Aimée, poor thing! with her short, yellow-white hair, small grey eyes (like Steven's, but busier), her low-slung bosom, her pince-nez, her poked-forward head. At dinner, the night before the wedding, she had worn a long knitted jacket, rust-coloured, and pinned to it with a safety-pin a bunch of home-made woollen flowers. She had eaten outrageously, complaining of each dish that it was bad for her blood pressure and that she must only have a morsel, before piling her plate high. She had smiled all the time, following Libby and Steven with her short-sighted eyes, and had killed each burgeoning conversation with one inept remark. They had led her round the dining-room where the presents were arranged, and she had chosen to admire the most extraordinary things— hideous flower-vases, a horrible little coffee-table, and a green lamp with a pink-and-green shade. Her own presents were an old and exquisite ruby ring and a very ugly bedside rug. Libby was perfectly charming to her, and Joanna felt proud of her child, while Steven was affectionate in an absent-minded way, as one strokes a cat without knowing that it is there.

Watching Libby that evening, so fair, so unafraid, one would have thought her immune from all human ills. Her looks, which to her mother that evening and to Steven were pure beauty, seemed compassionate and enfolding, as though her companions were loved children. Remembering now, and trying to find words for her daughter's radiance, Joanna thought that she was like a mother who had no fears for her children—like an impossibility, in fact, or a goddess.

This blossoming before her eyes and its effect on the dazzled Steven had lit for Joanna what would otherwise have been a dark evening. She had been very tired, her legs had ached, her eyes had felt hot and dry, she had looked fifty, she knew; and despite Elizabeth's assurances she had been convinced of a thousand things left undone. Ashamedly, she had leaned on the reassuring bride.

Steven, pale and bright-eyed, bore little resemblance to the young man whose stolidity had offended her. She knew that he was awed too. And amongst all these intense and almost holy emotions Mrs. Pryde, impervious, had babbled on about—of all things—her "unmarried mothers"!

It seemed that she belonged to a society which found work for these unfortunates in homes where their babies would be welcomed. This was an excellent idea, thought Joanna, and she wondered whether it might solve her servant problem, but when she asked for details, she was disappointed. The girls took up their posts in early pregnancy, she learned, and worked as long as they comfortably could. They spent a fortnight in hospital and then returned with their babies, "And then it's our turn to look after them!" said Aimée beamingly, "and for the next few months we give them all the help and motherly advice we can. You know, Mrs. Malling, how a young mother worries over her first wee babe. That is why we like to send them to homes where children are understood, so that they will really be helped and cosseted."

Joanna wondered who paid whom. "And wages?" she asked.

"They have at least the usual cook-general's wage and their keep. And some of us manage to pay the littlest bit more."

"And can they cook?"

"My Celia can cook *beautifully*, but we're not all so lucky."

Joanna had already decided that she would stick to Mrs. Holmes.

Tucking Elizabeth up in bed for the last time (which happened also to be the first time for some years), Joanna said: "How *do* you suppose they get anyone to take on those wretched mothers?"

"I simply can't imagine. The whole thing wants reorganizing. I must talk to Mrs. Mortimer about it."

"Well, don't you take on any good works just now, will you, darling? Are you going to sleep all right, do you think?"

"Yes, of course. Why not? I'm blissfully happy, and I don't believe in brides who flap." And as Joanna went to the door she added: "I'm sorry Mrs. P. was a bit of a bind tonight, darling. But she's really very sweet, and not a bit pushing."

"She's certainly not that. In fact she seems to be living in another world."

"Yes, doesn't she, poor little thing? But Mummy," she whispered, "isn't it a blessing that she's Top Drawer? She may be a bit funny, but no one could possibly call her com., could they?"

"Oh no; she's unmistakably a lady."

"That sounds very snobbish," said her daughter reprovingly.

Joanna laughed and came back from the door to kiss her again.

"All right, pet! Put it any way you like, and now go to sleep."

And next morning, when Elizabeth came to breakfast looking pale and even suety, and showing a tendency to snap, Joanna rose to the occasion—or hoped she did—and at last played the mother's part of calm upholder. Libby suddenly changed her mind about the nightdress she would wear that night, and rootled through three neatly packed suitcases to find the one she now imperatively needed. Nothing in the world, thought Joanna, silently re-packing, can be of less importance than a bride's first nightdress. But it was done at last, and the morning dragged on until the welcome arrival of Janet Mortimer, immaculate and unexcited, who shook out the folds of her white bridesmaid's dress and asked for an iron. The electric iron fused, and while Joanna was looking wildly round for Steven (traditionally absent), Janet mended it herself and got to work. She then dressed herself and Elizabeth; and Joanna, duly wearing dusty pink, came in to camouflage something on Libby's neck that she could barely perceive, but which Libby desperately declared to be an enormous spot.

Waiting in church for her daughter to arrive on the arm of an elderly cousin—a man with a fine paunch but few words—Joanna felt stupefied and not even, as she had expected, sick. She was an inveterate weeper at weddings, but today she felt no emotion of any kind. Dispassionately she watched the arrival of the white-and-gold bride, followed by her slight, dark bridesmaid, whose crimson roses were precisely matched by her lipstick. (Most efficient of Janet, certainly, but shouldn't the bridesmaid look just the slightest bit virginal, or even shy? Janet, as usual, was visibly self-confident.) Libby's face was hidden by her veil, but her dress was perfectly cut and her carriage superb. The flowers on her head made her seem a shade taller than Steven, but he looked well enough in uniform; his shoulders were good, Joanna approved of his ears, and he stood admirably still. Libby had recovered her self-possession, and her responses were spoken more clearly than Steven's.

Even the singing of "Oh Perfect Love" wrung no tears from Joanna. She only hoped that the caterers were ready, that the fresh breeze had not knocked over her jugs and vases of flowers, and that the lady-like young woman with rimless spectacles would justify her boasts as a photographer. She was surprised that no exalted thoughts or tender emotions came to her, and she wondered whether the young couple were experiencing anything more than a sense of dreaming.

Astonishingly soon it was over, and she was kissing Elizabeth Pryde in the vestry. Never had her daughter looked so lovely as now, when with flung-back veil she offered her flushed and smiling face to be kissed by those crowding around her. If the child could see herself now she would never again complain about the unconventional shape of her nose! Joanna was herself kissed by Steven, both of them feeling for the first time a real impulse to come together; the red-haired best man embraced Janet (which showed that he had soldierly courage, for no one could have looked cooler than she), and to the traditional Mendelssohn they all paraded down the aisle. Steven and Elizabeth, reminded by Joanna to walk slowly, swung along despite her as though out for a country walk. Mrs. Pryde's hat, a sort of toque made entirely of life-like parma violets, slipped on to the back of her head, and as she bustled, smiling and apparently astonished, down the aisle, on the arm of the paunchy cousin, Joanna was seized by laughter, which—painfully repressed—brought tears to her eyes at last.

It had really been a very commonplace wedding, reflected Joanna as she lit another cigarette and slid further down in her chair. The bride and the mother of the bridegroom were, each in her own way, remarkable to look at, and the flowers in the house were lovelier than she could remember to have seen elsewhere; but there was nothing else unusual. Steven, in an expansive moment at parting, told her that she looked "incomparably distinguished" in her dusty pink outfit, but she did not for a moment believe him. Libby's choice of music for the service was disappointingly banal, and so was the health-proposing speech. Steven's reply was unusual only in its brevity: "Ladies and gentlemen," he had said; "we both thank you very much indeed. That's all." And the best man had then cut in with, "For they are jolly good fellows", a demonstration that unfailingly embarrassed Joanna, but which the young couple endured quite calmly.

Dear, good little Libby (Joanna lit a second cigarette). Even on her honeymoon she did not forget to send her mother a string of uninformative picture postcards. The hotel was nice, the food very adequate, the Cotswolds heavenly. Joanna tried to picture the young couple, and managed to perch them, munching sandwiches, on a stone wall at the edge of a beech-wood. Would there be bluebells in the wood? Libby would be wearing the old tweed skirt that she had insisted on taking with her. Steven, by now, would surely have got rid of most of that moustache. They would be sitting as closely as they could, and Libby would be holding forth, but not, her mother hoped, about the Mortimers. Or would Steven be talking, and Libby—forgetful of the picnic food—gazing into his face? Impossible to say. In any case, they would be beautifully united, insulated from all outside interference, and beamingly happy.

Oh, enviable state, when pressure from without instead of driving the spirit hither and thither, merely presses it more firmly into its place.

Joanna envisaged Steven and Libby as being sealed in a transparent ball, so that when the world outside pressed close, they were driven more closely into one another's arms. To have perfect confidence in the sympathy and understanding of one loved person was to be at peace, she thought. She could not now experience the emotion, but she could try to recollect it in tranquillity, and perhaps, if only she had been a poet, here was the germ of a sonnet. But was peace of heart—heart's ease—really an emotion, or a suspension of emotion? However that might be, she knew that she, the watcher with her memories, could not claim tranquillity; all of that belonged to the dear children.

Joanna must have been drowsy, for her thoughts, usually adequately disciplined, strayed into the bedroom of that unknown hotel, and she was suddenly confronted with a view of Libby and Steven naked upon the bed, legs entangled, cheeks pressed together, and a hand moving in the slow ritual of love. She felt an extraordinary wave of pleasurable envy, that flooded her limbs and brought a rare blush to her cheeks. Strange! She could even see the brass knobs on the old-fashioned bed, and the warm red curtains past which streamed the sun—for this was a daylight love scene. Ashamedly Joanna sprang up. It was quite natural, she told herself crossly, that a sex-starved woman should have her occasional dreams and desires, but to allow her own daughter and son-in-law to figure in them was an offence against rudimentary delicacy. And besides, she ought to be past this sort of thing by now. If she felt the need of a little eroticism before inexorable middle age should put a stop to her sex-life, let her go and buy some filthy postcards. This thought amused her, so that her assumed cynicism fell away, and she laughingly admitted that she felt no real need of a last fling, and would embark on the change of life with barely a pang. Only she hoped that it would not make her irritable, or mad.

She carried her two plates into the kitchen and guiltily wiped the crumbs off them. Honestly, she told the vision of a shocked Libby, they were perfectly clean, and in any case only herself would be using them. She had better get back to her gardening, and work these stupidities out of her system. "Dig till you gently perspire," was the advice of Kipling, but for herself she thought a good muck-sweat was needed. The house looked a little neglected, just clean enough but not highly polished. She would chase Mrs. Holmes about it tomorrow. She would *not* stay indoors herself on this perfect day. And she hurried off to find a spade.

V

Steven and Elizabeth Pryde, who had expected to embark for a foreign station within a few weeks of their wedding, were still in London at the end of May for Steven's relief had not appeared at the War Office, and he had received no sailing orders.

As they would only be in London for a few weeks, they made no attempt to find a house or flat. Libby, indeed, had thought that they might well stay with the Mortimers until Steven went overseas, but surprisingly he had objected. Unreasonable though she thought him (for the Mortimers were so tactful and kind that they would never seem intrusive), his masculine assertiveness rather pleased her, and she agreed without argument that they should go into furnished rooms.

The rooms that Steven, after many struggles, had engaged for them were both bleak and overcrowded; but, said Steven, at least we shall be alone, and it won't be for long. Elizabeth was content; she would be out all day, shopping, seeing friends, and meeting Steven daily for lunch, and it was certainly nice to be alone in the evenings, even if the arm-chairs in their little sitting-room *had* been designed to fit some creatures of inhuman shape. It was just as well, she wrote to her mother, that this state was not to last long. "All our money goes on food, although we go to the cheapest places we can find, and we never feel really well fed after lunch. Supper is better because we generally picnic at home—I make a salad or cut sandwiches, and we have fruit and coffee, and although the meal isn't very exciting, at least we can have as many helpings as we like. If only the damned woman would let us have a gas ring I could produce lovely food at a quarter the cost, but she won't co-operate at all—I think because she makes a hundred per cent profit on the very bad breakfasts she provides."

It was hard for Elizabeth not to be able to cook for her husband. She itched to show her skill, and to have watched her delicious mixtures disappearing down Steven's throat would have been an exquisite pleasure. But there were many compensations in her present way of life. She could amass her trousseau and her household linen without making any flurried mistakes, and her lunches with Steven—so different from their meetings in her student days—were always delightful adventures.

Arriving early (that none of Steven's time should be wasted), young Mrs. Pryde would select a table in sight of the door and sit there peacefully, remembering how Miss Malling had been carefully late, and how she had been used to worry over her appearance. She would glance complacently down at her smooth-knuckled hand, now carrying a narrow platinum wedding ring and a large and lovely sapphire. (Steven had wanted a gold wedding ring for her, but of course she had had her way.) She would light a cigarette (her case was from Steven, too) and go through her shopping list, marking off the things she had bought and noting what was still to be done, and she would look forward to the evening, when her parcels would be shown to her husband. The only snag was that those old pigs at the War Office still would not tell Steven where he was to be posted, and this made it rather difficult to buy clothes.

When Steven at last appeared in the doorway she would blush a little and give him her lovely welcoming smile, and he was always struck anew, as he passed among the tables to join her, by the freshness of her look, as though she were the only woman in the room whose skin and hair and teeth were utterly clean, and who slept well, and whose conscience was not troublesome.

For her part, Libby would feel a moment's shyness when he came, and a moment's pang at the sight of the moustache, which all her efforts had not, as yet, reduced. But as they talked, discussing the menu and reporting on their separate mornings, the slight tension which had been set up in her while waiting would gradually diminish, the little shyness cease and the man with the big moustache would merge into Steven—her Steven, near whom, a few hours earlier, she had lain asleep.

Steven's chief objection to their present lodging was that they must sleep in twin beds, and on this point Libby would not agree with him. How often had she and Janet, talking dispassionately of their distant married future, agreed that some privacies must be maintained, and that although one supposed one would welcome one's husband's visits to one's bed, one should be allowed in the end to sleep alone. Poor old Steve grumbled when he had to leave her, but much as she loved him, thought Elizabeth, she could not do without her sleep. "Good-night, my sweet," she would murmur, drowsy but determined, and Steven, grumbling obscenely or in a martyred silence, would creep across the dividing strip of carpet and into his own bed. He talked longingly of a double bed, in which they could really *properly* sleep together, and Libby, secretly glad of her hours of solitude, tried not to be snubbing about it. But he must have noticed her reserve, for when she bought two gaily patterned eiderdowns, saying that although they were expensive they were good value, as they would last for years, he made no comment, and after that he stopped talking about double beds.

Libby sometimes wondered if her husband were slightly over-sexed, for his passionate demands upon her came often and were far more intense than her responses. But it didn't worry her; she could give him what he wanted, and was content, if not exactly ardent. She would never, she promised herself, refuse him on grounds of sleepiness or anything less than real ill health. Even when he started a violent cold and racking cough she accepted his kisses, though she thought him a little inconsiderate.

He made a good deal of fuss about this cold. At first Libby was tender and solicitous, giving him numerous remedies in which secretly she had little faith, but which she thought might help him, if only he would believe in them. She was rather affronted when, taking them, he made it clear that he was the kindest of husbands so to oblige her, and that he was quite convinced of their uselessness. He *ought* to believe her, she thought indignantly, when she assured him that this or that would make him better! He sneezed, gasped, mopped, groaned, clutched his chest, and now and then, in a martyred tone, apologized for being such a nuisance, or hoped that she had managed to sleep a little despite his coughing. Libby began to feel bored. Steven didn't seem to listen to anything she had to say; all he did was to seize her in his arms now and then and cover her with germy kisses. Every morning she tried to make him stay in bed, and every morning he snubbingly got up and went to work. At lunch-times he sat huddled in his great-coat and ate hardly at all, and in the evenings he gasped, kissed her, groaned, and slept heavily in his chair, until it was time to go to bed and start coughing.

Libby caught the cold herself, and for three days she also sneezed, shivered, wiped her eyes, mopped her nose and pitied herself. But she did try to be cheerful during this trying time, while Steven, it seemed to her, made no attempt whatever to fight his depression. And on the fourth day, when the shivers left her and of all her symptoms only a blocked nose remained, there was Steven as ill and as consciously pathetic as ever. And it was June now (although wet and windy), and she had a new hat which blew off under the wheels of an oncoming bus, and Steven was too moribund to leap forward and save it.

If only, thought Elizabeth, they had already gone abroad, and had not had to come back to London at all! But she was a soldier's wife now, and must learn not to grumble at changes of plan, however frustrating, for they would be her yearly lot.

She woke one morning to see Steven, as usual, nearly dressed. She had given up the struggle to keep him in bed, and she watched him drowsily, without bothering to talk. Soon she would slip into her beautiful new dressing-gown, wash her face in cold water and have breakfast with him.

She had almost relapsed into sleep when she heard the springs of his bed squeak, and was astonished to see him, clothed in vest and pants, lying as though asleep, with a muddled twist of bedcovers half across him and his arm thrown up to cover his eyes.

"Darling!" she said stupidly. "You'll be fearfully late if you go to sleep again now!"

"I'm not going to work," said Steven, and began to cough.

She was accustomed to his coughing by this time, but he sounded dreadful this morning, and heaved himself up in bed as though he were in agony. In the next moment, as she jumped out of her bed and stood beside him, she saw how flushed he was, and that he looked at her without any love or interest, as though his cough were of sole importance in his life and she were only a stranger.

"*Steve*!" she said in terror, and then more gently: "Darling, did you have an awful night?"

"Yes, horrid. I kept forgetting who I was. Can I have some more pillows, Liz? Must keep sitting up."

Elizabeth silently propped him up with all the pillows and cushions she could find. Then she fetched her thermometer and a bottle of aspirin tablets. His temperature was 104.

"I've had lots of aspirins," said Steven hoarsely, "but they didn't help much."

"What time did you take them, darling?"

"No idea," said Steven.

"Oh, Steve! How many did you have?"

"Four, I think. Thought they might stop the blankets talking such a lot—they kept arguing, Liz; wasn't it stupid?" He groped for her hand and held it in a hot grip. "Oh, Liz, I *am* so uncomfortable!"

"Darling love," said Libby, her eyes full of tears. "Just keep still under the blankets for a minute, will you, while I ring up a doctor?"

"Don't be long," he said, giving back her hand with reluctance.

Libby struggled into her dressing-gown and rushed barefoot down the steep little staircase. It seemed hours before she got through to a doctor, and she had time to count and count again the blue swallows in the stained glass panel of the front door. Perhaps after all they were not swallows, but kingfishers, she thought dismally, as she leant against the chocolate-coloured wall and fidgeted her toes fastidiously on the oilcloth. At last she got the promise she wanted—Doctor Jackson would come round at once—and she rushed upstairs again; to find Steven apparently asleep. She hung over him, tearfully, feeling both frightened and ashamed. Her poor, darling Steve! Why hadn't he awakened her in the night when the blankets "kept arguing"? He must be really ill, and she had thought that he was only making a fuss! But how was she to know, if he wouldn't tell her?

She started to get dressed, with many pauses to look at her motionless husband, and with her dressing-gown at hand in case the doctor should arrive. All her convictions about sick-nursing had been destroyed. She had expected Steven, when ill, to do exactly as she told him, and to like it; and his obstinate independence had annoyed her, so that she had shrugged her shoulders and failed to realize that he was getting worse. Now she was feeling, in an intense degree, what one feels when one has dropped a valuable piece of china. To lose it is painful, and to lose it because of one's own stupidity doubles and re-doubles the pain.

But when the doctor came he was almost casual. Yes, a nasty neglected cold, certainly. A bad cough and a touch of pleurisy. "No, no, Mrs. Pryde, no pneumonia. We hope *that* won't develop. No need for it at all." Better get him into hospital, he added. She should have telephoned to an Army doctor in the first place, not to him, but he would hand the case over and recommend that they should send an ambulance along straight away.

He hurried off, and Libby started to pack a suitcase for Steven. Tears kept pouring down her cheeks, despite all efforts to stop them; she thought that she had never been so miserable in her life.

After the ambulance had driven away, Libby managed to swallow a little breakfast; and then, shivering and weak-legged, but not crying now, she went down to the telephone. She dialled a Park number, and could have wept again—with relief—when Mrs. Mortimer's deep, resounding voice answered her.

"Mrs. Mortimer speaking," said the voice, and Libby, making a great effort to be coherent, told her what had happened.

"Well, of course you must come here," said Mrs. Mortimer at once. "I'll be round to fetch you in a quarter of an hour, and you can tell me all the rest then. Go and pack your things now, Elizabeth, and bring a nice lot;—I expect they'll keep Steven in hospital for a week or so, and you won't want to keep going back for more clothes. ... Yes, I'll drive you round to see Steven directly you've unpacked; he'll like to know you're here with us. Now don't worry, my dear child; pleurisy is nothing nowadays. ... Oh, Elizabeth, I've got a dinner-party tonight, so bring a long frock. ... Yes, of course we want to have you; we can easily find another man. ... Yes, your green frock will be the very thing. I'll see you in half an hour. Good-bye for now."

As she went upstairs to pack her cases, Elizabeth felt cheered and quietened. The unruffled tone of authority to which she was so well used, and the knowledge that Mrs. Mortimer was in charge, calmed her strained nerves and illogically lightened her anxiety. When she had confessed to her hostess that she felt the fault to be hers, she would be still more relieved. As she folded the green dinner dress, which she had not yet worn, she wondered involuntarily who would be at the dinner-party. Dear Mrs. Mortimer, how like her, despite servant difficulties, to welcome two more people at her table; and of course the food would be excellent; it always was.

Libby exerted herself to be quick and efficient, but she was still parleying with her landlady when the car drew up. She hurried the conversation to a finish, and started to carry out her suitcases. The landlady, having secured what she thought too little money (but which Libby thought too much) for keeping the rooms until further notice, did not help her, but stayed sourly in her kitchen.

It happened, most fortunately, that Elizabeth had not seen the Mortimers for two days, so that there was small-talk to be exchanged when it seemed to Mrs. Mortimer that Steven had been sufficiently discussed. Her competent judgement was that Elizabeth had not been to blame. Steven had ignored her advice and neglected his cold, and there was an end of it. If yesterday he had felt worse, she could not be blamed for failing to see it. "You haven't been married long enough to recognize every little sign, as you will in a few years' time. That doesn't mean you're unobservant. It's just repetition—frequent repetition of behaviour—that makes a husband and wife understand each other pretty well, when they've been married for twenty years or so. No, my dear child, it's your Steven's fault for being so obstinate, but I don't expect you'll hold it against him."

"I knew just how to look after him," said Libby, much restored, "if only he would have let me."

"Of course you did, and it's a great pity he wouldn't. But I don't expect there's much harm done. He'll soon be out and about again, and then there'll be the sea voyage to put him right."

They were having lunch, and Janet, summoned by telephone at her office, had hurried home to join them. In her neat black suit and white blouse she was the epitome of a private secretary. She now began, without a perceptible break, to take the conversation over to her own affairs. Passing lightly over Elizabeth's chances of a pleasant foreign station, she alighted on the subject of clothes, and from this it was easy to start describing a dinner dress which she thought of buying. "Very dark red; d'you know how red ink looks, when it's in the bottle? The bulk of the liquid seems almost black, but on the surface, where it catches the light, the true red shows up. Well, it's like that."

"It sounds perfectly heavenly," said Elizabeth. "Do get it at once, Janet, and then you can wear it tonight."

"Oh, it's no good rushing it," said Janet sensibly. "If I do get it they'll have to alter it for me; it's just a shade too long."

"That wouldn't matter for a dinner-party."

"No, but I shall insist on having the alteration thrown in; at that price it's the least they can do."

"Quite right," approved Mrs. Mortimer. "I should be adamant on that if you buy the dress."

"I'll wear my old black tonight," said Janet with finality, and Elizabeth silently resolved to crush down a certain youthful enthusiasm, which, had she been in Janet's place, would have led her to buy the dress at once, wear it that night, and then be forced to do the alteration herself.

She was about to describe to Janet in detail her visit to the hospital, and her horror on finding that Steven was not alone in his ward, when Janet continued: "If you'll meet me for lunch tomorrow, Elizabeth, you can come and see it with me. Will you? They had one or two washing evening frocks which I think you ought to look at, in case you go to Malaya or somewhere hot like that."

"How exciting! But if I get one we shall be sure to go to Germany or Iceland or the North Pole."

"If you go somewhere cold I shan't come and stay," said Janet positively.

"If I feel like this in England in June, I hate to imagine how I'd keep alive in a cold climate. Go to Malaya, there's a good girl, and we'll have a wonderful time in Bikini bathing-suits and sun-frocks."

"All among the bandits," said Elizabeth, and she pictured Steven crashing heroically through virgin jungle with a tommy gun in his arms, mowing down bandits, and afterwards receiving a bar to his M.C. She would be frightened for his safety, but so proud that it would be worth it.

In this way the conversation was repeatedly turned back from the threshold of Steven's hospital, until, after they had drunk some admirable coffee, Janet stood up, said: "I must fly," and walked neatly and unhurriedly from the room.

Then Mrs. Mortimer said: "Would you like to telephone to your mother?"

"Good Lord! I must let her know; of course I must! But what on earth am I to say? You know how Mummy fusses."

"Has she got a telephone yet?"

"No, unfortunately she hasn't. I'd better write."

"I think a telegram would be wiser."

"Yes, I suppose it would. I'd better send one now. The thing is"—she hesitated—"she'll probably offer to come up, and I really don't want to—to drag her away from her garden."

"Certainly not. But if you tell her you're here, she will surely not worry about you."

Libby nodded, relieved. She picked up the telephone and sent this message: "Steven in hospital pleurisy don't worry am with Mortimers Libby".

To Joanna these words seemed to proclaim Steven's death sentence. She was taken immediately back to the most painful weeks of her life— the weeks when Jack, her husband, had neglected a cold, had started to complain of a pain under his ribs, had developed pneumonia, and had died. Libby, oh Libby! It would be too cruel if it should happen to her also. After she had telegraphed: "Terribly sorry darling may I come up Mummy", she walked about the house and garden in agony, twisting her hands, fighting for self-control, hurrying upstairs to pack a few clothes, hurrying down again to look for the telegraph boy, lighting countless cigarettes, and at last against all her convictions and in abasement of her pride, kneeling by her bed and praying, with painful tears, that Steven's life should be spared.

It seemed to her then that if Steven, whom she found it so hard to like, were to die, her pain would be too much to bear. To have lost one's husband was crippling, but for one's child to lose hers would be intolerable; she would not, she could not bear it.

When the telegram came: "No room darling thank you am really all right with Mortimers writing Libby", she made an enormous effort to control herself. Sitting before her looking-glass, worn out with emotion and hollow with fear, she told herself that she was the last person who ought to be with Libby now. If Steven died—well, then she would be able to sympathize as no one else could, but at present it was far better for her to stay away and bear it as best she could. Think of Libby, she told herself. The Mortimers will be kind but bracing, and will take her thoughts off it in lots of little ways. I will ring up from the call-box this evening, and now I will be sensible and try to stop flapping.

She did ring up—in the middle of the dinner-party—to be told by a calm daughter that Steven was said to be comfortably asleep and she was not to worry. "Thank you for telephoning, darling," said Libby; "it was sweet of you to go out in the dark. Forgive me if I rush now; we're in the middle of dinner." And picking up the skirt of her new green dress she ran back to the dining-room.

VI

❦

Steven Pryde did get pneumonia, but he was never in danger of death. After a few days Elizabeth could feel safe and cheerful, and it was then that he asked her to go and see his mother.

"Does she even know I'm ill, darling?" he said. "She hasn't written or anything."

Elizabeth was appalled. "Oh, Steven, how awful of me! I simply never thought about her. I *am* sorry!"

"I expect you did," said Steven kindly. "You very rightly didn't want to worry her."

"But I *didn't* think of her! I wish I had, but I honestly didn't. The only person I thought of letting know was Mummy."

"That was odd of you, I must say."

"Yes, it was. I'm terribly sorry. I was so worried that I didn't think straight."

Steve accepted this excuse without comment, but Libby felt ashamed, and willingly agreed to go out to Wimbledon and visit her mother-in-law.

She decided to go for tea. Mrs. Pryde had no telephone, and probably the 'Unmarried Mother' would loathe an unexpected visitor for lunch. Determined to be pleased and pleasant, she set off on the same day, a showery June afternoon, wearing her new violet-coloured mackintosh, which looked like a very smart coat, and which Steven said couldn't possibly be waterproof.

Walking to the Underground Station, she was able to prove the quality of her coat, and as she sat jolting in the red train she told Steven, in imagination, how wrong he had been. The rain had stopped when she came out, but the newly washed leaves still dripped on to the gravelled by-roads and on to her violet coat, and Wimbledon smelt of the country. All the bright gardens were a-shimmer as the sun came out and Libby, who had a prejudice against the suburbs, decided that they weren't so bad after all.

She tried to remember what her mother-in-law had said about the house, but unfortunately Mrs. Pryde had one of those voices to which it is almost impossible to listen. It was really rather odd, thought Elizabeth, that she'd never yet been invited there. When they had been engaged, Steven had spent a week-end with his mother, and had said afterwards that he'd never been so cold in his life and he didn't know how the old lady kept alive on that sort of food, not to mention folk-dancing on it, and doing good works. But this was before the appearance of the Unmarried Mother—what was her name now?—Phyllis?—Cicely? Her arrival had apparently brought the golden age to Mrs. Pryde. The baby was to be born in November or thereabouts, so Cicely?—Phyllis?—should have several cooking months ahead before she need temporarily retire. Elizabeth, who had moral views, hoped the baby wouldn't be mentioned, as she knew she should blush if it were.

She stopped at a gateway. 'Twyn Elms' it said, and, wrinkling up her face, she bent to open the gate. Why, she asked herself, have two gates, a narrow and a wide? It was like the story of the cat and the kitten.

Elizabeth walked up a path between nasturtiums and beat decisively on a small door studded with large nails. After a short wait she beat again, and this time the door was opened at once by a young woman in a smock, who said: "Good afternoon."

Elizabeth's thoughts, as she asked for Mrs. Pryde, were complicated and quick. Why the smock so soon? Surely she wasn't *proud* of her condition? Did one address her as Mrs. or Miss or treat her as a servant? This was going to be a perfectly awful afternoon. She smiled and followed the smock across the dark little hall.

She found her mother-in-law kneeling on the floor by a large old-fashioned trunk. Her short hair stood on end, her pince-nez were crooked, and she did not seem delighted to see her daughter-in-law. The little room was full of baby clothes.

"Elizabeth, dear child," said Aimée, and began to struggle to her feet. The smock at once took her arm, and Aimée stood massaging her knees for a moment. "Thank you, dear. Stiff! Stiff! I'm not very young," she complained; and then her automatic smile clicked on and she said: "Elizabeth, this is my great friend and ally, Celia Perkins. Celia, my dear little daughter-in-law Elizabeth."

Little forsooth! Elizabeth, towering above the other women, felt affronted. Christian names, too? She did not choose to be called Elizabeth by Mrs. Pryde's maid, and a fallen maid at that!

"Good afternoon," she said, and Celia bowed her head and said meekly: "How do you do, Mrs. Pryde, or should I say Mrs. Steven?"

Elizabeth became rather less stiff. "You do look busy," she said to her mother-in-law. "Can I help?" She wished that they could have been busy with something less embarrassing than baby clothes.

Aimée Pryde smiled rather nervously. "Yes, we were busy." She glanced sideways at the smock. "I was just going through this old ark"—here she patted the black trunk affectionately. "I wanted to see if the moth was getting into any of Steven's little things, and Celia was kindly helping me, weren't you, dear?"

"Shall I put them away now, Mrs. Pryde? Mrs. Steven won't want to be bothered with them."

"Yes, would you, dear? We can go through them tomorrow, or later this evening."

"But I'd love to see them!" protested Elizabeth; only to be taken by the arm and pushed firmly out of the room.

"They are very dull, dear. Come and see the garden. Celia!" she called over her shoulder, "don't attempt to move the trunk till I come! Now, Elizabeth, I'll show you my wee plot. It's looking so fresh after the rain. Kind Celia will soon be making some tea for us."

They walked up and down the little lawn, and Elizabeth broke the news of Steven's illness. She thought her mother-in-law would be resentful, but when she said: "There seemed no point in worrying you at the time," Mrs. Pryde answered:

"Very considerate, dear. Look at my aubrietia; isn't it rather sweet?

And is he really quite better now? Poor boy! what a horrid time he must have had."

"Lovely colours," said Elizabeth. "He's not *well* yet, you know, but he hopes to be out of hospital at the end of the week, and then of course he'll have sick leave. He's not awfully easy to look after, is he?"

"Men are always bad patients. Like big children, aren't they? Now can we—yes! We can tell the time by my sundial, do you see? He always was a difficult boy to nurse. Do you know, I've sometimes been quite cross when he wouldn't take his cough mixture? Do peep into the bushes there, Elizabeth. Can you see my little family of stone rabbits? They come out, you know, when we're all in bed at night!"

Mrs. Pryde's voice, lacking animation and almost without stresses, went on. Elizabeth thought about baby clothes. Surely Steven's first little frocks and boots were not to be given to the little illegit.? She wondered if Steven could be made to protest. Some day *she* would have babies, and it really would be too bad if all those dear little clothes had been given away. She would have to talk to Steven.

The tea was excellent. Anchovy toast and a chocolate cake. Perhaps after all there was something to be said for Phyllis—no, for Celia. Elizabeth took a good look at her.

No! *Not* attractive or in any way a *femme fatale*. Nor, she had to admit, was Celia tarty. She had a greasy skin with large pores, and her blonde hair, which was also greasy, hung diagonally across her forehead from parting to opposite ear, barely missing her eye. She sat hunched in her chair, elbows on table, smiling over her cup, which she held in both hands. Elizabeth felt sure that her legs were twined together under the table. Just like a schoolgirl! But all the same I wish she'd give me the receipt for this cake.

"Is Derek coming round to-night?" asked Aimée.

Celia put her head on one side. "I don't know if he'll be back in time. He's gone to Oxford today."

"Derek," explained Aimée, "is Celia's brother."

"Poor Derek! such long hours," said Celia wistfully. "But he comes in to see me whenever he can. He thinks it cheers me up. But *I* could tell him that I don't need cheering up, not with Mrs. Pryde so kind to me!"

Aimée was delighted. "Well, dear, if he does come round, be sure to give him a good big mug of cocoa and some bread and cheese. I shall be at the Women's Institute, so I hope he'll be back in good time. Otherwise you'll have a lonely evening. Derek," she explained to Elizabeth, "is a traveller."

"I see." Elizabeth wondered if he earned enough to help his sister. More likely that they both sponged on Mrs. Pryde, she thought. Really, it ought not to be allowed. But she had to admit that the house was exquisitely clean. The work was all right; it was Mrs. Pryde's manner that she didn't like. Celia was very discreet, but anyone could see that they were bosom friends, and not at all like servant and mistress. It was all very nice and Christian, no doubt, but she didn't like it at all.

When Celia helped her into the violet coat, she could hardly control a shiver of repulsion. She found the girl's face and hands, and her sturdy body bent in deference, actively unpleasant. But she only made herself tall, thanked Celia politely and brushed her mother-in-law's cheek with a parting kiss. Thank the Lord that was over! She strode back with a light heart to the station.

The Mortimers' house seemed more than ever civilized that evening, and Elizabeth valued the impeccable reserve of their parlour-maid. The rooms were big and expensively furnished, there were family portraits in the dining-room, water-colours in the drawing-room, sporting prints on the stairs. Everything was in its proper place, and if there was nothing very unusual to be seen, there was also nothing shabby or in bad taste. If only we were rich, thought Libby, eating, we could soon make Mummy's house look like this. Fitted carpets and proper pelmets would make all the difference. And a Hoover to save trouble. And we'd have maids, of course, and darling old Mummy could walk or garden all day if she liked, and come in to find a good hot meal ready for her.

"How did you find your mother-in-law, Elizabeth?" asked Mrs. Mortimer in her authoritative voice.

"She seemed all right," said Elizabeth rather doubtfully. "But I never quite know how well she is."

"That stroke," said Janet.

"Yes, if it really was one. But she must have been rather young for that sort of thing."

"How old is she now?"

"About sixty-two or three, I think."

"And she had the stroke—?"

"While Steven was abroad. It must have been—oh, ten years ago."

"Call it fifty-three," said Janet. "Surely that's too young for a stroke, isn't it, Mother?"

"Rather young, perhaps. But I've heard of people having them in their thirties or forties. Perhaps she worked too hard during the war and worried too much. Lots of people did."

"Perhaps," said Elizabeth with doubt.

"No one could have worked harder than you did, Mother, but you never had a stroke."

"My blood pressure," said Mrs. Mortimer with satisfaction, "is always about ten years younger than I am. James, will you have some more fish?"

"No, thank you."

Elizabeth waited until the maid had left the room. Then she said: "The dreadful thing is the Unmarried Mother."

"Oh, isn't she a success?"

"Oh, Mrs. Mortimer, she's ghastly! Kind of greasy and humble. I couldn't *bear* her!"

"But does she do the work?"

"Yes, she does that all right."

"And does Mrs. Pryde like her?"

"She thinks she's the uttermost summit!"

"Then, my dear Elizabeth, what are you worrying about?"

"They're such absolute bosoms! I'm quite sure that the moment I left the house they discussed everything I was wearing, what I'd said, and what they thought I'd thought, and had a good old giggle together."

"Oh *dear*!" Mrs. Mortimer was fastidiously distressed.

Janet said: "Did they seem—you know—very much attracted to each other."

"How do you mean?"

"Really, Janet," said her mother, "there's no need to jump to conclusions."

"Well, I think it all sounds very suspicious."

"Oh!" Elizabeth blushed, ashamed of her innocence. "Oh, do you mean that? Good gracious, Janet, I never thought of it! But surely not; I mean there's Steven; I mean she's a married woman; I mean—" She stammered into silence.

"There's no reason to suppose—" began Mrs. Mortimer soothingly.

"Janet!" said Mr. Mortimer, in a quiet, thin voice, and they all stared at him with their mouths open. He looked at his daughter over his glasses and under his eyebrows, which were white and bushy. "If," said Janet's father quietly, "you think this is a suitable conversation for the dining-table I am quite unable to agree with you."

"I'm sorry, Papa," murmured Janet.

And Mrs. Mortimer, looking less than her normal self, said: "Let's—er—talk about something else. Elizabeth, how did the new mackintosh look?"

VII

When Steven left hospital he joined his wife in the comfort of the Mortimers' house. Mrs. Mortimer would not let them go back to their lodgings, and so Elizabeth packed up, and paid off the landlady.

Joanna had suggested that Steven's sick leave should be spent in the country, but he was comfortable here and well-fed, and he showed so much daily improvement that Elizabeth didn't want to move. He would soon be having plenty of sea air, and for the present he chiefly needed rest. She was always very busy herself helping Mrs. Mortimer, and when the cook went out she enjoyed the run of a highly modern kitchen. The sun shone at last and Steven, in his shirt-sleeves, sat all day in the little paved garden; he grumbled because he had to put on a tie for lunch and a suit in the evening. The Mortimers always changed for dinner, although not usually into evening dress, and Steve loathed this practice, while Elizabeth enjoyed wearing her trousseau frocks. Steven was much liked by all the Mortimers, and after dinner he and Janet would have long friendly political arguments, neither of them giving way an inch. Usually Elizabeth listened proudly, but sometimes Mr. Mortimer would summon her to help with his crossword, and this made her even prouder, for it was the one thing she could do better than the Mortimer women.

She had decided generously that when Steven should apologize for his obstinacy, she would share the blame. She looked forward with pleasure to the little scene when he would say: "Darling, I know I was an idiot and gave you a horrible fright. I've learned my lesson now. Another time I'll listen to reason and stay in bed when you tell me to." And she would forgive him at once and tell him that she ought to have noticed he was worse and that she hadn't been as sympathetic as she ought. For Elizabeth was generous and had been brought up to forget an offence directly the offender apologized.

But the days went by, full of opportunities for little talks together, and still Steven didn't say his piece. After waiting confidently for some time, she so far sacrificed her self-approval as to arrange a few naturalistic openings for him. Oddly unobservant, he passed them by and would change the subject or fall silent, to her repeated disappointment. She began to think him rather grudging, and in the end she tried to make a joke of the affair, pulling his leg with rather ponderous good-humour. The Mortimers joined in until they realized that Steven was not amused.

Joanna came up to London one day and was relieved to find Libby so little changed by her recent ordeal. Watching the young couple, however, she thought that they were not yet quite adjusted to one another, and she had to tell herself that all marriages are notoriously troublesome at first. She in fact must have been unusually adaptable. They had been married for little more than year, and during that time she had borne a baby; it was odd that her memories of quarrels or hurt feelings should be so few, and should seem so negligible when she compared them with all those other memories. Somehow Steven and Libby did not seem so completely armoured against the world as she had hoped. They were not naturally tolerant. Dear Libby wanted to model Steven, and he was resistant. She and Jack had never been like that. Oh well, Libby and Steven would soon shake down when they went abroad together, and in their case there was surely no desperate hurry. She and Jack, thank goodness, had wasted none of their precious time.

As she travelled home in the evening light, by a train that stopped every few miles, she felt deeply thankful that the children would soon be off on their own. They would become really inter-dependent, complete when together and mutilated when forced apart. And this vulnerable state seemed to Joanna to be deeply desirable.

She would be bored and lonely while Libby was away, but she would not mind. She would look forward confidently to their return; a happy, properly married couple.

VIII

To Elizabeth, who had never been aboard, the prospect of a foreign posting was joyfully exciting. If they could travel together—and she had great faith in their united powers of persuasion—Steven would be able to steer her through the unknown conventions of shipboard life, so that the journey would be adventurous and not embarrassing. She thought that to stand by his side and see the English coast flatten away would be the most perfect happiness she had ever known.

As she dusted the Mortimers' drawing-room, on the first of July, she whistled a monotonous tune and let her thoughts fly. An ocean liner (it would be enormous, she imagined) and herself, in her new red travel coat, striding up and down the deck arm in arm with Steven. It would be a troopship, so she supposed he would be in uniform, which she loved; and they would be so happy, so absolutely absorbed in one another's conversation that they would never notice the other passengers, who would whisper: "What a distinguished looking young couple! Look, he's got the M.C.—I wonder who they are?" She was sure to have inherited good sea legs from her parents, neither of whom, as she knew, had ever been seasick, and so, when all the travellers retired below and the waves came "Whoosh" over the bows, she and Steve, flushed and laughing, would still pace the tilting decks. He would, of course, have to be well wrapped up, for it would be cold in the Bay; and here a gleam of reality pierced the dream; *would* he wrap up, as she bade him? With a change of her whistled refrain, she postponed the crossing of that bridge, and projected her ship into a halcyon Mediterranean, through which she and Steve would sun-bathe, and dance their long days and nights. Her skin, of which she was proud, must not be allowed to blister. She would be extremely scientific about her sun-bathing, and achieve an even tan. As for Steve, he was brown skinned and well protected by hair. Elizabeth smiled. Janet had often laughed at her for declaring that she could never marry a man with a hairy chest. How cocksure she had been a few months ago; how mistaken; how *young*!

She waltzed across the room with her duster and knelt down by the book-case. Time these books had a dusting, and as Steven had gone out without her this morning, she could do them properly. She hummed a few bars in a rather tuneless contralto, and then relapsed into the whistle. They would have a cool bungalow with a garden full of exotic flowers. She and Steven would sit on the veranda, watching an enormous moon come up behind the palm-trees, holding hands, and listening to—what? Frogs? Crickets? Some lines from Edward Lear came to her mind:—

> The little beasties' twittering cry
> Rose on the fragrant air.

All day the skies would be blue, and white-robed servants would bring round tall glasses, clinking with ice. They would entertain, and she would be famous for the excellence of her table. She would meet a snake in the bathroom; a flat head would rise swaying over the edge of the tub, but she would be very calm and brave, and Steven, revolver in hand, would arrive just in time. She would be photographed, in jodhpurs and an open-necked shirt, standing over the corpse of a lion (or a tiger), which she had just shot. Steven would be fit and brown and much more manageable than he was at present. She would send an endless stream of letters and photographs home to Mummy, and later on she and Janet could come out together to stay with her. (Janet would look after Mummy on the ship.)

Oh, life was lovely, lovely! No one had ever been so lucky before.

When Steven came in, she flew into his arms, and they exchanged a slow, luxurious kiss, of which Janet, standing in the doorway, was an approving witness.

Janet was not the girl to turn away in embarrassment. She prided herself on her detachment and understanding, and Steven and Elizabeth were an unfailing source of interest to her. She suspected that their sexual relationship still left much to be desired. Probably Elizabeth was not yet fully awakened; but she would be all right in a year or two, and would probably—when her troubles were over and done with—tell Janet all about them. It was, of course, a thousand pities that Elizabeth should have been so inexperienced. Janet, herself a virgin at twenty-one, intended to change her condition in a year or two, and to marry when she was twenty-five. She sincerely hoped that Steven was able to make up for poor Elizabeth's ignorance, but on this subject Liz was unexpectedly reticent, and her own study of Steven's character had so far told her nothing.

At lunch Elizabeth was in bubbling spirits, and Steven, as usual, watched her with a face like a boot, thought Janet. But after their coffee, when Elizabeth made her routine suggestion that he should go and rest, he astonished the three women by saying amiably: "All right, come along." And they left the room, arm in arm, while Mrs. Mortimer and Janet looked after them in pleased surprise.

"How very sensible of Steven," commented Mrs. Mortimer. "Perhaps he feels a little tired after being out all morning."

"Perhaps," said Janet, who preferred a more amorous interpretation of his behaviour.

In their bedroom Elizabeth turned round to kiss Steven, saying: "Darling, you are a good old thing to come and rest."

"I wanted to talk to you," said Steven, "and we may just as well talk in bed."

"You don't want *me* to rest too?"

"Of course I do."

"Oh, Steven, I've got lots to do."

"All right, then. Let's go down again," he said, turning towards the door.

"Blast you! All right, then; I'll rest!" And Elizabeth pulled off her frock, glanced with satisfaction at the reflection of her cami-knickers, and lay down with her hand under her cheek, and her attentive eyes on her husband's face.

Steven stretched a long, hairy arm across the dividing gulf, and Elizabeth put her hand obediently into his. "What do you want to talk about, my love?" she said cheerfully. "Us?"

"In a way. You're an awfully long way off, darling."

"Come along, then."

"Thank you. Oh, that's much better. There! Now you can't possibly fall off."

"Unless we both fall off together." Elizabeth had been secretly planning to creep away when Steven fell asleep, but now she was not sure if it would be possible, nor even certain if she would wish to do it.

"Liz, darling; I went along to the War Office this morning."

"Did you, darling? How are they all?"

"All right."

"Any news?"

"Well, yes."

"Oh, Steve! You're not going just yet, are you? Where is it to be? Can I travel with you?"

"Darling, I'm terribly sorry, but it's not abroad at all."

"*Not abroad?*" Elizabeth struggled up, propping herself on one elbow. "Oh, *Steve!*" Her tone was unfathomably reproachful.

"Not for about a year, they think. They want me to take over a job at home that'll be closing down next year; so then we're *sure* to go abroad, sweetheart."

"Next year!" Elizabeth's daydreams spiralled away and were gone. She stared after them, her eyes slowly filling with tears.

"Darling, I was afraid you'd be awfully disappointed."

"You must be too."

"In a way."

"What is this job?"

He went into details. The work sounded interesting, and it was a compliment to have been entrusted with it.

Elizabeth listened absently. All through lunch she had been so happy, and Steven had shown no sign of preoccupation; she hadn't dreamt that he had anything to tell her. This made her angry with herself and with him. "I can't understand you!" she burst out. "Do you mean that you knew all this before lunch? You didn't look different! You didn't seem—why on earth didn't you tell me at once?"

"I didn't think it was a suitable moment."

"*I* shouldn't have waited a *minute* to tell you!"

"You're so impetuous, beloved."

Elizabeth lay down again. She blinked, and two large tears slipped across her averted face. She felt inferior. A good wife would surely have noticed something odd in the behaviour of a husband who was suppressing vital news. And she was sure he despised her impetuosity. "I wish I'd known," she said listlessly.

"Darling," said Steven, hugging her tightly, "I'm terribly sorry you're disappointed. But you haven't asked where we *are* going."

"Does it matter?" Then she felt ashamed of herself, and turned to him with a smile. "Please tell me, Steve. Where? Any hope of a quarter?"

"None at all, I'm afraid. As a matter of fact, we're going to Tadwych."

"Good Lord! How incredibly handy! Mummy can find us a house."

"That's what I thought. Are there any, do you know?"

"Bound to be if one's on the spot to find them. Oh, Steve, that does make it better. It'll be lovely to be near Mummy, and we shall still be in easy reach of the Mortimers too."

Steven was delighted to find her more cheerful. He kissed her wet eyes and said: "Will you write to your mother straight away?"

"I'd better. Anyway, *she'll* be delighted. I'm glad someone will be pleased."

"Sweetheart, a year isn't so very long."

"I suppose not," said Libby, who thought it was endless. And she added plaintively: "Tadwych is a revolting town, you know, darling. I can't think why Mummy had to settle near it. She said the house had dignity!"

"I doubt if *our* house will have any. I shall be thankful if it has water and a spot of sanitation."

"And a gas cooker—"

"And no one else in it. That's the most important thing."

"Oh, darling, we couldn't possibly share! I'd rather do without the sanitation."

"Anyway, Liz, my darling, we'll be together."

Steven's arms tightened, and his mouth prevented her reply. He began to make love to her, and with a smiling side-glance at the clock, Libby submitted. As long, she thought, as she was in time to do her nails before tea.

As it turned out she did them after tea, and then wrote to her mother about a house at Tadwych.

"We're not at all fussy," she wrote, "as long as it's small and clean and we can have it to ourselves. Even a flat would do at a pinch; as if we've not got flowers of our own, we can come and steal yours!! Aren't we lucky to have an agent on the spot? I hope it won't be an awful bother to you, darling."

Knowing that her mother would be overjoyed to have them living nearby, it did not seem to Elizabeth that she would find it a bother at all. She did not know that the Americans had lately acquired an air base near Tadwych and that this had caused a desperate housing shortage. She guessed nothing of the exhausting days spent fruitlessly in Tadwych, of buses missed, taxis paid for, agents whose doors closed precisely as Joanna hurried up their steps, agents who promised and never performed, and agents who never even promised. "If I get something in the end," Joanna told herself, "all this will have been worthwhile." And she tried to forget her neglected garden, and to trust Mrs. Holmes to care for her house.

At first she relied on Mrs. Holmes also for news of small houses, empty or about to become empty. But she learnt to mistrust the daily discoveries of her charwoman, for they only led to rebuffs at front doors. Usually the firmly ensconced owners of these doors had once let their houses, ten years ago, or had toyed with the idea of taking p.g.s. Sometimes they even had names reminiscent of other people, whose houses were already let or sold.

Joanna told herself repeatedly to be more enterprising. She must push, she said, storm, waylay, invade and become immune to snubs. She went by bus to neighbouring villages and hurried shyly from door to door, asking if anyone knew of a house, or even of rooms, to let. Sometimes the householder would make a helpful suggestion: "Mrs. So-and-so in the white house by the church takes lodgers." And Joanna would hurry through a churchyard and up a little path under lime-trees, hoping as she knocked at the door, that poor Libby wouldn't be kept awake by the chimes.

Often though these plans fell away to nothing, with each fresh chance she planned afresh. Her pictured daughter unpacked her boxes in house after house, each of which had something to commend it. It was handy for the bus stop, or the curtains were pretty, or there was a tennis-court, or a weary pony was leaning over a gate, or sweet-smelling flowers grew under the windows.

But at last one day Joanna admitted that she had come to the end. She had one more address to try, and then she would give up. She caught her usual bus into Tadwych and set out to find the Grey House on Mervyn's Hill. It ought to be healthy, anyway, she thought, as she plodded up a long slope between substantial houses, each behind its garden wall. It depressed her that she was immediately passed by her own bus, which grated up to the top of the hill and there paused to take up an elderly lady. Having consumed her, it disappeared down the further side. "I might just as well have had a ride, and I expect that old girl was Mrs. Lane and I shall find the Grey House empty. However, Libby won't have to change buses when she comes to see me, which is something."

The road cut through the hill's brow, and the houses mounted high above. The Grey House was to be reached by climbing a steep path, laid in big concrete steps under a threatening wall. Joanna's calves ached as she hurried up, seeing nothing of the house. At the top the path turned back on itself between two old yew-trees, and she found that she was standing on a paved terrace with yellow roses running all over the floor. How lovely! Libby could do her sewing out here; the smell was heavenly, and there was a mumbling of bees. The house was hideous with stained glass and ochre paint, but those ugly great windows meant sunny rooms, and over the roses, the wall and the house opposite you looked down past smoke and dark chimneys on to pale grey water and long grey ships, and beyond the greys a clear green island, and beyond it again—across the river—the low, wooded slopes of another county.

All this kept Joanna staring until it struck her that it was rude to stand in other people's gardens helping oneself to their view and not even ringing their bell. She must find the front door. But oh, what a place for Libby!

A loud, triumphant laugh made her take her hand from the door-bell and look round. Astride the wall sat a small dirty child, arms stuck out for balance, watching her with bright dark eyes and wishing to be admired.

Joanna looked at it and thought of the path she'd just walked up. Concrete steps, and the wall *miles* high on that side! For goodness sake, child, if you're going to fall, fall this way!!

Never rush at a balancing child. Old stories of children on the ledges of fourth-floor windows rushed through her head, while the child said, "Ha ha *ha*!" for the second time. She said: "Hallo," rather huskily, and the child also said: "Hallo," and grinned right across its filthy face.

"Is it nice up there?" Joanna said.

"Yus."

"Can you get down?"

"Yus."

"Show me."

"All right, then."

The child swung a fat leg over the wall, teetered backwards for an endless instant, recovered its balance and slid down towards the yellow roses. With its feet a few inches from the terrace it stopped and began to yell.

Joanna advanced. The yells hurt her ears and paralysed thought, but she knelt and investigated.

The child was hanging by the seat of its red dungarees from a nail in the wall, and its sandalled feet hammered unavailingly against the stones and against Joanna as she tried to free it. Somewhat bruised, she picked it right up and turned, holding the little struggling body in her arms, towards the house. The child went on shrieking, and its mother appeared in the doorway. Joanna wondered if she'd be accused of brutality.

But Mrs. Lane accused no one. She soothed her son James and asked Joanna to hold him while she fetched the iodine bottle, for he has torn his plump little buttock as well as the dungarees. Joanna sat on a bench among the roses and crooned one of Libby's favourite nursery rhymes. James stopped crying to listen. When Mrs. Lane came back they were both saying: 'The House that Jack Built'.

Joanna looked doubtfully at the large blue bottle. This was not the moment, she supposed, to tell Mrs. Lane about modern and humane methods of first aid, but it did seem a shame to hurt poor James when he was being so good. He was standing between her knees with his dungarees round his ankles and staring into her face as he chanted.

Mrs. Lane, pale and agonized, advanced silently with the bottle. She poured iodine on to cotton wool, on to her fingers and on to the paving-stones. She stooped.

"This is the priest all shaven and shorn," declaimed her son, "That married the man all tattered and torn, That—ow! ow! ow! It burns! Ow! Blow, Mummy, blow!"

His mother blew. James danced with pain and sobbed. "Ow, Mummy, it's so hot! Blow! Blow some more. Mummy! That kissed the maiden all forlorn. Blow! Ow!"

Mrs. Lane kissed the back of his neck. "There's my good little boy," she said. Her eyes were full of tears, and she waved the iodine bottle dangerously to and fro. "Mummy's precious lamb. Better now. All better."

James stopped dancing. He looked at Joanna with enormous wet eyes and said gravely: "It was bitterly hot. I were brave, weren't I? Go on, That milked the cow—"

"I'm sorry," said Joanna to Mrs. Lane. "May we just finish this?—The cow with the crumpled horn."

"That tossed the dog."

"That worried the cat."

"That killed the rat."

"That ate the malt."

"That lay in the House That Jack Built." They finished together, and James, stepping out of his dungarees, strode in a manly way on to the lawn and there, standing with his back to them, bent down and looked at them between his legs. The two women laughed, and, suffering slightly as they were from shock, couldn't stop laughing. James, feeling clever, began to shout and prance.

Mrs. Lane wiped her eyes. "Let's have some tea," she said.

"Oh yes, let's," said Joanna, forgetting that she hadn't accounted for her presence. They went into a clean blue-and-white kitchen, and Mrs. Lane switched on the kettle. (Libby would like the kitchen!)

Joanna said: "You must think me very interfering. But that wall's so high and I was so frightened."

"How *am* I to stop him climbing on it? He doesn't take *any* notice of what I tell him, and I can't watch him *all* the time. Did you see him from the road?"

"Oh no, I—I was coming to see you. How awful, I haven't explained! Those nice women in the 'Work-basket' told me to come. I do hope you don't mind. They said—"

"Women in the work-basket? *What* work-basket?"

"The one in the High Street."

Mrs. Lane, who was a thin, faded blonde with mauve cheek-bones and too many teeth, looked at Joanna in alarm.

"The *work*-basket in the *High* Street?"

"Isn't it 'The Work-basket'? No, how silly of me, it's 'The Knitting Bag', of course. They advised me—"

"Oh, the Miss Laceys! Oh, what a relief! I was afraid you were getting delusions. Yes, 'The Knitting Bag'. So they sent you, did they?"

"They said you sometimes took lodgers—I beg your pardon, paying guests. Or knew of people who did."

"Quite right, my dear, I do. I sometimes think I'll set up as an agency. But I don't think I've anything at the moment. Is it for yourself?"

"My daughter and son-in-law." Joanna told Mrs. Lane all about Libby and made the most of Steven's illness.

Mrs. Lane was sympathetic. She made tea and carried out the tray. They sat among the roses and talked as much as James, who ate biscuits and interrupted, would allow. Joanna longed to tell him to shut up. He was a captivating child, but she wondered if Libby would be able to put up with him.

She need not have worried, for Mrs. Lane was not thinking of taking lodgers at present. If she did consider it later on she would let Mrs. Malling know. Anything she could do, at any time, would be a comfort to her, for she was irretrievably in Mrs. Malling's debt. Mrs. Malling had saved her son's life.

"But I didn't in the least!" protested Joanna, without affecting the glow of Mrs. Lane's gratitude. She tended to draw nearer as she spoke, so that the retreating Joanna found herself almost over the edge of the seat. But she liked her hostess and thought that Libby might have taught her some sense.

"Don't worry, Mrs. Malling," said Mrs. Lane at parting. "Something will turn up, it always does, and I shall be sure to let you know. Good-bye and thank you for saving my naughty little beloved." She and James waved from above as Joanna went down the path; James, indeed, still clad only in a little shirt, was standing on the wall, tightly encircled by his mother's arm.

So good for discipline, reflected Joanna. How *does* she expect to train him?

And now, she asked herself, as she walked down the long hill, what am I going to do about Libby?

IX

୨ଈ

Joanna really knew quite well what she was going to do. Only one thing remained, and that was to offer her own house. Very likely Libby was wondering, poor child, why it hadn't been offered long ago.

She brushed aside the tempting idea that they might all live together. Of course she must move away and leave them alone. They had had more than enough of other people's lives while staying with the Mortimers.

At present their days seemed to be occupied with their hostess's social and political work. Mrs. Mortimer was treasurer to various organizations, and Steven was apparently auditing all her accounts, while Libby made and sold sweets in aid of Conservative funds. It all sounded very busy and important, but Joanna sighed to see her daughter lapping up Conservatism from the Mortimers' cups and plates. She was indeed a Conservative herself, but she hadn't been at twenty or even at thirty. Libby's arguments were sensible and pat, and usually clinched by the telling phrase: "Mrs. Mortimer thinks," or: "Janet says." Mr. Mortimer was seldom quoted because he so seldom spoke.

She telephoned to Libby and said she was coming up to town for the day. "I'm sure," said Libby, "that Mrs. Mortimer would like you to come to lunch." "Thank you, darling, it's very kind of her, but I really think we'd better meet somewhere." This, Libby appreciated, was one of Mummy's rare 'definites', and she agreed, suggesting a restaurant that she and Steven liked.

Joanna was the first to arrive, and she plunged down the staircase from pavement level into a sort of baronial hall, heavy with carving and sprouting antlers. The food, she thought, would have to be awfully good. She sat at a table with a checkered cloth, and looked over a heavy balustrade to another full-size restaurant below, and beyond that she could see stairs down to a third. What an odd place! Fancy making huge terraces under the ground! And what happened *over* the lowest terrace, and under the one where she sat? Secret dens of unspeakable vice? She amused herself by looking for a waiter with a really depraved face; but they were all quite ordinary little near-Italians. She read the menu, which was good if true, and then watched the staircase for Libby and Steven, while she rehearsed her proposition. They would, of course, ask her to stay on with them, but she would know that they didn't—couldn't—mean it, and would be firm. She would take rooms for herself, somewhere where there was no housing shortage. She had to admit that it sounded unspeakably dreary. They should have the house, at a rent just high enough to cover her own lodging. She would find somewhere nice to go and something useful to do, she resolved bleakly.

She was still watching for the Prydes to come downstairs to join her, when Libby's voice in her ear said: "Hullo, darling. Are we late?" And there they stood, mysteriously arrived behind her.

"Darling! How did you get here?"

"By tube!" said Libby, amused.

"Yes, but—oh, you came up from below! Have I stopped at the wrong level? Were you waiting down there for me?"

"No, we've just come in at the lower entrance."

"Oh, I see. I didn't realize you could get out that end. There must be an awful lot of stairs, or have they a lift?"

"No, it's quite a short flight," said Libby, and she added kindly: "We're on a slope, you know, or rather *in* it. The street goes downhill, if you come to think of it."

"So it does. How disappointing! I was imagining—but never mind! Sit down, Steven, and tell me how you are. You look pretty well."

"Thank you, Mamma. I'm really perfectly fit now, though Liz won't admit it."

"He's awfully naughty, Mummy," said Elizabeth proudly. "I have a lot of trouble with him."

Steven asked what they would eat, and when they had ordered a delicious-sounding meal, he asked what news she had brought.

"Very little, I'm afraid."

"Oh, *Mummy*. No perfect cottage yet?"

"Not a whisker, darling. In fact I might say that I've no news at all, only a proposition."

"That sounds better. What is it?"

"It's really quite simple and obvious." Joanna's brown hands twisted together under the table, for she felt nervous. "You'll just have to take over my house."

"*Take* it *over*?" Libby sounded incredulous.

"Yes, darling. You can pay me some rent if you'd rather—in fact I think you'll have to so that I can—"

"Darling, what nonsense!" interrupted Elizabeth forcefully. "I've never heard of anything so ridiculous in my life. You don't really think we'd turn you out of your own house, do you? Steven, isn't your Mamma-in-law a complete idiot?"

Steven sat pulling his moustache and watching the two women alertly. There was no need for him to answer his wife's rhetorical question, for she went on speaking: "Mummy, dear, it's angelic of you to think of it, but couldn't we come and p.g. with you? That really *would* be fun."

"No," said Joanna, "you definitely couldn't."

"Would you hate it?"

"You and Steven would, dearest. Now don't be obstinate and awkward; you know it's no good arguing with me when my mind's made up."

"Ha ha!" Libby laughed derisively. "So *I'm* not to be obstinate and awkward! The blatancy of it!"

Joanna leant forward, her lips compressed and a little flush in her thin cheeks. Steven thought that he had never seen her look so attractive. He began to eat, glancing warily up from his plate to watch the battle.

"Mummy, now honestly, do be your age."

"That's exactly what I am being? You may feel, in your youthful exuberance, that it would be a success if we shared, but—"

"It's not at all fair to throw my youth in my teeth."

"Then don't throw my age in mine."

"Oh, don't pretend to be so worldly-wise, darling! I know you're right

– 81 –

in theory, 'Mother-in-law Destroys Happiness of Young Couple', and so on, but you know perfectly well that we're not a bit like other mothers and daughters, now *are* we?"

"Almost exactly like, I should think."

"Oh, Mummy! You know quite well that everyone says we're more like—"

"Rubbish, Libby! If there's one cliché that's more irritating and less true than all the others, it's the one about mother and daughter being more like sisters. In any case, you might just as well give in straight away, because *I* shan't, however long you may argue."

Elizabeth thumped on the table. Her face was red and she looked almost ready to cry. "But you can't just decide things for the three of us!" she protested. "*My* opinion's worth having too. And what about Steven's? He hasn't said anything yet."

"I agree with you, darling, of course," said Steven quickly.

He doesn't! thought Joanna. He'll really be thankful if I go. She glanced at her flushed and indignant daughter, and spoke gently. "There's some awfully attractive food steaming in front of us," she murmured, and took a mouthful. Oh, dear! she thought, I can't keep it up! Once I let myself cool down I'll never manage it. "This is a very good pie," she said flatly.

"Delicious," said Steven.

Elizabeth would not be deflected. "Steve will be out all day, Mummy, and if you insist we can retire to our own room when he comes in, and simply never *see* you! Oh, Mummy, we could have such fun! I could cook and you could garden, and after all we'll be going abroad in another year or so. You might as well see something of me while you can."

"That," said Joanna, "is a most unfair approach."

"Could we—" said Steven, and paused to choose his words. "Would it make you feel better, Mamma," he said carefully, "if it could be arranged for us to have a separate sitting-room?" He looked across the table with an air of polite enquiry, and was disconcerted by a gleam of amusement in his mother-in-law's dark eyes.

"Yes, indeed, Steven, it would make me feel much better—in fact I could not contemplate any other arrangement."

"Then you *will* contemplate it?" triumphed Elizabeth. "Oh good, Mummy, you *are* good! Now we can start planning, and it *will* be such fun."

"You can also do a bit of eating," said Joanna dryly. "Steven's ready for his pudding and you haven't even begun to eat, you talkative child."

Elizabeth beamed at her. "I shall enjoy my lunch now," she said, and she certainly appeared to.

Joanna asked a few polite questions about Steven's job, and irritated him by not listening to the answers. She was searching her conscience, for she had an uneasy feeling that she had always meant to be over-persuaded. Certainly to have left her house now, when she'd just finished unpacking, and bits of it were looking so attractive, and when there was so infinitely much to do, would have been hard. If I had gone, she thought, I should probably have felt martyred, and traded on it for the rest of my life. Perhaps this will be best, after all. But there mustn't be any nonsense about all being together in the evenings, and I must try to efface myself at the week-ends. Poor Steven! It was good of him to back Libby up, but he shall certainly have his sitting-room, and I only hope he'll stay in it!

Steven left them when lunch was finished, and the two women spent the afternoon in the shops. Elizabeth was happy, and cajoled her mother into various extravagances, after which she took her back to the Mortimers' for tea. Mrs. Mortimer gave her measured approval to the plan, and laid down one or two sensible rules for the sharing of houses. "And after all, Mrs. Malling," she concluded, "I have always felt that you and Elizabeth were more like sisters than mother and daughter."

Joanna could feel Libby silently resenting imagined criticism of her friend, and this made it hard for her to reply. "Thank you," she said quietly, with her eyes on her teacup, and hoped that Libby wasn't angry about something that was really not her fault. She was glad when Janet came in, to be told the news and to add her commendation.

"You and Liz are rather a special mother and daughter," ended Janet. "I've often thought that you—"

Joanna interrupted, rather rudely, Janet considered. "I'm awfully sorry," she said, "but I shall miss my train any moment now. Thank you so much, Mrs. Mortimer. Good-bye, Janet. You must both come down and see how we are all getting on." She kissed Libby and held her for moment. "Good-bye, darling obstinate child." And then she was outside and hurrying along the pavement towards her bus stop. She felt released, and the tap of her unwontedly high heels on the pavement sounded young and festive.

Darling Libby, what a loyal friend she was to the Mortimers! It was pleasant to see her fire up in their defence, but a little awkward at times. She wondered for a moment whether Libby would defend *her* as readily, but answered that she was disloyal herself to doubt it. If she had needed any proof of Libby's love for her, it had been abundantly granted today.

She imagined Steven protesting mildly against his wife's decision. Libby, she thought, would hardly listen; she would confidently sweep aside his doubts or march all over them. Poor Steven! Joanna smiled with careful sympathy. She was determined to go on liking her son-in-law, and she could well appreciate his point of view. No one wants a mother-in-law about during the first year of his marriage. On the other hand, no mother-in-law likes to feel unwanted. She cannot help resenting the feeling that she is only present on sufferance, particularly if she is in her own house.

I am not going to let this put me off Steven, thought Joanna. He has behaved most kindly and correctly, and it is not his fault if I happen to have guessed his private thoughts. I may even have guessed wrong! And she let herself play with the thought that she was really wanted—needed, in fact—to keep Libby company during Steven's absences. He would be glad, she asserted, that his wife need not be alone all day.

As if Libby need ever be alone! She would make more friends during her first week in the village than her mother had made in five months. Her gaiety, her refreshing looks, and her uncritical friendliness would always assure her all the company she wanted. But all the same she wants *me*! thought Joanna, and all the way home, in the jerky electric train and overcrowded bus, she applied this balm to the small itch, recurrently felt, of Steven's supposed antagonism. And she could not quell a secret pleasure in the Mortimers' despised cliché; perhaps, after all, she and Libby *were* a little closer than some mothers and daughters. After all, they had an advantage in their ages, not very many girls of twenty had mothers of forty-one. Twenty-one and forty would be even better, but she would have had to marry at eighteen, which would have been unreasonably young, and anyway she hadn't even *met* Jack then.

She got home late, and deliberately postponed the replanning of her house until the next morning, when she would not be tired, and should be able to face the upheaval calmly. Each time her thoughts strayed round the house she recalled them hurriedly after glimpsing some pleasant arrangement of furniture, now doomed to be disturbed. She read poetry while she sipped a brand of powdered coffee that she rather disliked and munched a large hunk of cheese and several digestive biscuits. With Libby here she would be able to enjoy neat little suppers, and she would still be alone in the evenings and have the privilege of reading as she ate. How she enjoyed it! It largely atoned for her moments of loneliness, and even for the monotony of her meals. Soon she would have the best of both worlds, which was almost unfairly lucky.

After she had put her cup and plate by the sink, for attention in the morning (her saucer, mercifully, was clean), she smoked a cigarette and nodded over the book. She read one poem several times before she realized that she was too tired to understand it, and decided to go to bed. To go round the house locking up was a cruel necessity, and she would willingly have reduced the doors and windows by half, but it was all done at last and she could go up, first exchanging her anthology for a detective story to which—having read the book last year—she knew the answers. She managed to go to sleep without either thinking over the day's talk or planning the work for tomorrow.

In the morning she read her way through a plate of cornflakes and two cups of coffee, washed up, and put a stew in the oven. Her steak, which she had ordered by telephone, looked rather tough and her only hope seemed to be to let it cook all day. She had a guilty feeling that Libby would have browned the unappetising lumps in a frying-pan before stewing them, but for herself she could not be bothered.

Luckily, it was one of Mrs. Holmes' mornings, so she could leave the routine housework, and start to plan and to sort. She turned Mrs. Holmes into the kitchen, shut the door against her friendly voice and went into the study. With that door closed also, she felt fortified against interference, and she sat on the window-sill and looked round the room.

As usual, her first feeling was exasperation. Why had the architect put the fireplace so close to the door, and why had the late owner decorated the room with jade-coloured paint? Apart from these marked disadvantages, the room was pleasant enough, having the well-shaped windows that were typical of the house, and a pleasant view down a sloping hayfield to the village roofs. Joanna's bedroom overhead was the only room to share this outlook, and she sometimes wondered what she would do if an enterprising builder were to buy the field. This was a chance she could not guard against, nor could she move the irritating fireplace, but the green paint might be eliminated if she could afford the cost, and if some small local building firm would do the work. Forgetting her earlier precautions, she went to the kitchen door and said inquiringly, "Mrs. Holmes?"

A smiling face and a pair of jingling ear-rings popped out from under the kitchen table. Joanna made a note to ask Mrs. Holmes why she didn't move the table and chairs, instead of scrubbing carefully round each leg, but this was no moment to be fussy. "Mrs. Holmes," she said beguilingly, "I need your advice. Can you spare me a moment?"

Mrs. Holmes was overjoyed. Every moment of her employer's time, she indicated, could willingly be spared from work. She trotted volubly into the study and looked hopefully round. "Well, now, Madam, what do you want doing?"

Joanna explained about the green paint. Mrs. Holmes was surprised, but willing to help. For herself, she told Joanna, green was her favourite. Mr. Holmes, indeed, had just painted her lounge in *navy* green with a frieze of wistaria top and bottom. But if Mrs. Malling fancied a light colour—well, it was her house, after all.

"But who can I get to do it for me?" asked Joanna hopefully.

"Well, dear, seeing as 'ow Mr. 'Olmes 'as got the week-end off—would you like him to do it?"

Joanna expressed gratification and surprise. "I suppose he'll be away tonight," she said, "or we could have talked it over."

"No, 'e's coming home today," beamed Mrs. Holmes. "I've made a apple-pie for his tea, special."

Joanna was mildly surprised, for she had seen a lorry parked at the cottage as she came back last night from the station, and had heard Mrs. Holmes's loud laughter at an hour when the little Holmeses must have been in bed. It was unusual, she knew, for Mr. Holmes to spend two consecutive nights at home.

"Well," she said, "if he wouldn't be too tired to come round this evening, I should be most grateful."

"Right-oh, dear, I'll see he does. Did you say *white* paint? Well, there! You know best. And 'ave you noticed my new ear-rings?" She jingled them beguilingly. Her pierced ears were small and pretty and her smile was coquettish below the dirty scarf which didn't hide her curlers. Joanna was touched rather than amused. "Aren't they *pretty*!" she said gently.

"Mr. Holmes likes me in ear-rings," boasted his wife. "And I've got a new blue dress to wear this afternoon—well, not new, exactly, but you'd never dream as it isn't—and he always says blue matches my eyes!"

And so it does, thought Joanna. Fortunate Mr. Holmes to have a pretty and loving wife awaiting him, in a new dress and new ear-rings, with tight auburn curls just released, and an apple-pie in the oven.

But navy green walls (what could they be like?) and all that wistaria, too! She felt irrationally that Mr. Holmes, that example of timeless beauty, ought to have better taste than his wife. He was himself so unaffected—could he really do with all this vulgarity?

What nonsense! Of course he could. She reminded herself that she had not yet suffered the disillusionment of seeing Mr. Holmes in his best clothes.

Feeling affable, and forgetting the kitchen floor, she invited Mrs. Holmes to come upstairs with her and look at the bedrooms. Libby's room looked delicious that morning, and she stifled a sigh as she spoke of moving in the bed from the spare room.

"'Aven't you got a *double* bed?" asked Mrs. Holmes, shocked. She tut-tutted and shook the ear-rings. "I've got *ever* such a big one. Pity I can't

– 87 –

lend it to you, Madam, but Mr. 'Olmes wouldn't hear of *that*!" She hugged her bosom. "Ah, well," she concluded, "there's times when two beds is useful."

"Major Pryde will use the spare room as his dressing-room," said Joanna repressively. "Shall we see if we can move that bed now? It will have to go here." She leant her shoulder against a wardrobe, which did not budge.

Mrs. Holmes came to lend her strength. The wardrobe grated a few inches over the boards, and then stuck.

"Do be careful, Mrs. Holmes!" pleaded Joanna. "Don't strain yourself, for goodness sake. Perhaps your husband will kindly give us a hand with it this evening."

But Mrs. Holmes would not hear of it. Men, she asserted, were not strong enough for that sort of work. Their poor insides were not built, as women's were, for heavy burdens. And she started to tell the sad tale of her father's end, he who had strained himself one day digging in the garden. "And when the Doctor came to look at him 'e said 'Well, I never!'" She broke off, momentarily coy. "Well, there," she continued. "I can tell *you*, dear, seeing as 'ow you've been married yourself."

Joanna turned away discreetly to flatten an upstanding corner of the shabby haircord carpet. She was extremely annoyed to hear a knock at the front door. Damn! Now she would never hear the rest of the story!

But Mrs. Holmes was not to be deterred. She bustled out of the room and then put her head in at the doorway, and said in a hoarse whisper: "Believe it or not, dear, one of 'is pelvises was as big as a coconut!" She nodded once, with pursed lips, and then vanished and could be heard scurrying downstairs.

Joanna docketed the story, to tell to the Prydes. She wondered if she really knew Steven well enough, and decided that if she didn't she ought to. One thing that she particularly detested was the doubtful story whispered into a wife's ear and immediately relayed by her—still in a whisper—to the husband. And then everyone sniggered together, and one might better have had the story aloud in the first place.

She followed Mrs. Holmes downstairs, and found her talking to her mother. "Well, there, Brenda," came the pinched tones of Joanna's ex-caretaker. "So you won't be alone tonight."

"No, Mum, he'll be home all right."

"I'm sure I'm pleased to hear it." And turning to Joanna she added, "It's lonely for my daughter in the evening, Mrs. Malling, when her 'better-half' is away. It's not as if she was one to go out and leave the little ones. No, no, Brenda was always a home girl. Never one for going with boys, my Brenda."

Joanna smiled sympathetically and went into the kitchen to look at her stew. The voices went on and on behind her. Mrs. Holmes sounded cheerful and her mother aggrieved. Joanna looked at the kitchen floor and then at her watch. It was time—she felt it—for Mrs. Holmes's cup of tea.

X

❧

Elizabeth, at breakfast, was reading a letter from her mother. The three Mortimers had already eaten their fruit and their toast, and had hurried away, Janet and her father to the City, Mrs. Mortimer to her hairdresser. It was nice, reflected Steven, as he ate his scrambled egg, that for once one of the Mortimers should be spending a really useless morning. He said as much to his wife, who pointed out, defensively, that with all the public functions Mrs. Mortimer had to attend, and the important people she must impress, a good expensive perm was neither useless nor extravagant. Steven let it pass; he was not in the mood for argument. "Eat your egg, my love, before it gets cold. You can read your letter afterwards," he said.

"I oughtn't to have an egg," said Elizabeth, still reading. "I'm getting fatter every day; I swear I am."

"Now listen!" said Steven emphatically. "If you go and starve yourself and get a figure like Janet's I shall leave you!"

"Darling!" she said absently.

"Liz, you didn't hear a word I was saying."

"Yes, I did. You said eat it up and be thankful." Elizabeth laid down her letter and contemplated the egg. "Oh, dear, it looks so good!" She took it, with a wicked little smile that delighted Steven. "If I had a figure like Janet's—or like Mummy's, for that matter—just think what lovely clothes I could wear!"

Steven cleared his throat. "This time I'll say it louder. If you get yourself a figure like Janet's (or like your mother's) I'll leave you!"

"You didn't marry me for my corpulence, did you, pet?"

"I married you for quite a lot of things. One of them was your nice bosom, one was your round face and one was your wholly angelic bottom."

"My face *isn't* round!"

"Well, it's not hollow-cheeked, thank God. Go on, eat it up!"

Elizabeth ate it, without reluctance. Then she picked up her letter. "Mummy says she'll expect us on Sunday night and everything will be ready except our sitting-room. She says, 'Tell Steven I'm very sorry, but I hope it will be done soon. In the meantime I've crammed two small armchairs into his dressing-room, but I'm afraid it's a squash.'"

"Oh, dear," said Steven blankly. "Did I make a *point* of the sitting-room?"

"Oh, no, she did herself. Such nonsense! As if we minded being with her, when I'm really simply longing for you to get to know each other properly!"

Steven smiled, but did not answer, and after a moment Elizabeth said: "Sunday evening! It does seem soon, doesn't it! I shall miss the Mortimers dreadfully, won't you?"

"They've been kindness itself, darling, but—"

"What?" Elizabeth began to smile.

"I want to be alone with you."

"I knew you were going to say that!" She beamed at him. "Funny! You want to take me off somewhere all alone, and I want to show you off!"

"Well, don't show me off in a big way to your mother, will you, darling? It'll make me extremely nervous."

"All right, I promise." She pushed back her chair. "What are you going to do this morning?"

"Take you out to explore London."

"Oh, no, you're not. I'm going to address envelopes."

"Don't. It's a lovely morning."

She hesitated, but stood firm, "I really ought to—in fact I simply must. Sorry, darling."

"Blast you, Liz," he said amiably. "I sometimes feel that I have no influence over you at all."

"Of course you have. What about that egg I've just eaten to please you?"

"That wasn't to please me. You always meant to eat it, and I obligingly gave you an excuse."

Elizabeth hit him, and went off to Mrs. Mortimer's desk.

Steven suddenly felt the restrained opulence of the Mortimers' house to be a little oppressive. He went out for a walk, and sat in the Park, smoking a pipe (which his wife would have disapproved of, as she thought it bad for his lungs) and looking peacefully around him at the dark trees and yellowing grass. July in London looked like September anywhere else, he thought.

There was a refreshing amount of bad taste about directly one went outside. A man in a deplorable mauve shirt was throwing orange-peel wantonly abroad and spitting pips, and a passing couple kissed, blatantly— at 9.30 in the morning! Darling Liz would have blushed and looked away, bless her. It was a pity she had refused to come out. It occurred to him that there had been truth in his laughing words as they left the breakfast table. He really did seem to have remarkably little influence over his wife. She basked in his admiration, she liked (as she had admitted) to show him off, and of course she loved him. But he had never yet made her change her mind. Perhaps, thought Steven, who had read some of the books appropriate to a bridegroom of his generation, his influence would grow with her growing powers of physical pleasure. At present she seemed disconcertingly placid about the whole thing, so that he felt he must curb his own emotions, which would be, heaven knew, deep and dark enough if he gave them their freedom. Of what passion he was capable he was not sure, but he did feel that their present embraces, while physically they relieved him, were emotionally little more than an introduction. He must not shock his young wife, and he was old enough to be patient. He thought that at present Liz regarded him as a cherished possession, one which added more lustre to her personality than any fur coat, bracelet or new car. Her kindness to him, as well as her happy sparkle when they were together, showed how much she loved him. But she expected him to be a precious adjunct to herself: in her mind he was far more her husband than she was his wife.

Steven knocked out his pipe. You could not expect, in a beautiful young wife, the selflessness of a devoted aunt. He was already unbelievably lucky, and he meant to be even luckier. How he longed to take his Liz far, far away from all these impinging women!

On their last evening in London, Steve and Elizabeth went to see Aimée Pryde. They had warned her that they were coming to supper, and, as Elizabeth remarked in the train, with any luck that oppressive Celia creature would take herself off for the evening.

They found Aimée in her garden. Three rustic chairs were posed round a wobbling table on which teetered a bottle of South African sherry. There were three glasses. "She *has* gone out!" breathed Elizabeth in triumph.

"Dear children, how good of you to come." Aimée vaguely kissed the air around their ears. "And are you really quite better, Steven! When do you take The Golden Road out into the country?"

"Quite recovered, thank you, Mother. We go to Tadwych tomorrow."

"I did tell you in my letter—" began Elizabeth, but her mother-in-law wasn't listening.

"Let me give you both a little sherry. Steven, dear boy, you pour it for me. Oh, we need a corkscrew. Now where does Celia keep the corkscrew? It must be found—it certainly must be found."

"I'll find it," said Elizabeth, and Steven said: "No, let me."

"If only Celia was here! But she's gone out for a ramble with her brother. It's so good for her, you know, to be refreshed. Everyone needs air and exercise, and especially at these times. Perhaps it's in the kitchen drawer."

They all went in together, and while Aimée and Elizabeth were ransacking the kitchen, Steven went into the little sitting-room. It looked vaguely different, and there were some framed photographs on the bookcase that he had never seen. Good of his mother to let Celia stick up her hideous relations. One young man, in a vast silver frame, he took to be the brother.

He was hunting methodically round the room when his wife joined him. "Any luck? We can't find it anywhere, but I must say Celia keeps the kitchen beautifully tidy. Your mother seems to think it may have been left out in the shed. She's gone to look."

"How typical!" said Steven absently. He was carefully turning over the contents of a drawer. "Old ping-pong set," he said, "spanner, corks, bits of—what are those bits of, Liz?"

- 94 -

"They're attachments for a sewing-machine."

"Thank you. And knitting-needles, and string, and three broken pairs of scissors." He shut the drawer. "No good."

"Steven," said Elizabeth, "it's all terribly cosy and—and *à deux*, isn't it? Two chairs"—she gave one of them a little push—"each with its work-bag beside it. The wireless in the middle. Over here, by this table, two more chairs and—oh look! It's a half-done jigsaw. Gosh! It's rather an interesting one!" She hovered, gripped by the conviction that she could finish the thing in no time if given the chance. Her analysis of the room's furnishings was forgotten. "That bit for his hat. A bit with a red feather, I think. It must be easy to find."

"Come on, Liz. What about the corkscrew?"

"You find that, darling. Is this it? No, bother, it's the wrong way round. This *is* a good jigsaw."

Steven pursued his search. "Two table-napkins in rings," he announced, delving in another drawer. "Salt, pepper, mustard. I suppose they have their supper in here. Patience cards. Spoil Five. Halma. Two lots of knitting wrapped in large handkerchiefs. How are you getting on?"

"Come and help. It's a lovely picture, Cavaliers and Roundheads and all sorts of delights. Do look!"

"*I* am working," said Steven. "Pen nibs, aspirins, buttons, a skewer, matches, used stamps—English ones. What *is* my mother expecting to do with these?"

"So am I working," said Elizabeth indignantly. "I've put in about twelve pieces! If I could just finish off this little boy's lace collar—"

"Wonder if it can have fallen down behind the books? No, lots of old bills—I'm sure Mother's been looking everywhere for these." He stared at a receipt in his hand. It was for a perambulator. "I say, Liz—"

"What, darling?"

"There's no corkscrew here. I'm getting fed up with this room. Let's go and look for Mother."

"You go. I must just put in one more piece."

Steve had another look at the receipt. Yes, his mother had certainly spent twenty-five guineas on a perambulator. But perhaps, he told himself, putting the papers back where he had found them, she had only advanced the money to Celia for a few weeks. He came over to the table where his wife was entrapped. "You feckless female. Come away from that."

He dragged her into the garden, where Aimée was discovered, corkscrew in hand, emerging from the tool-shed. "It's all right," she said, waving it gaily. "I remember now. I had it for the fertilizer." She gave it to Steven.

"But do let me *wash* it first!" said Elizabeth, horrified.

"Fertilizer, Liz, not weed-killer." And Steven opened the bottle.

They drank their sherry and stared at the roses, while from Mrs. Pryde the endless words came trickling. Elizabeth listened carefully, while Steven grunted and thought about the perambulator. He didn't reckon that his mother could afford to give presents on that scale. Liz had said something about Celia having an awful lot of influence, but he'd taken no notice. Liz had annoyed him by wanting his old baby clothes to be hoarded. He'd thought her entirely wrong. If Celia was having her baby *now,* for heaven's sake let her have the clothes. *They* might not have a baby for years (though he was doing his best to save up a little money for the possible creature's education). They couldn't grudge Celia any things that were lying there doing nothing. Liz had grumbled at him, but he'd told her not to be a fusspot, and she had shut up, hurt. Now he began to wonder if she was right.

They went indoors and had an excellent cold supper. They all washed up and they went into the drawing-room. They sat down. Mrs. Pryde continued to talk. Elizabeth was seized by a yawning fit which she struggled to control. It was painful. She tried to listen to her mother-in-law's little dripping words; her jaw quivered; she clenched her teeth. And it was a relief when Celia came in, followed by Derek. "May I introduce my brother to you?"

Derek was blond like his sister, but the resemblance went no further. He had short legs and wide shoulders, a low forehead and a wide smile. There was a portrait of the Royal Children on his tie. Steven instantly despised him. Elizabeth disapproved of him, but found him rather attractive, and therefore disapproved of herself as well. He sat on the arm of Celia's chair and kept referring to her fondly as "little Sis".

Elizabeth caught Steven's eye. "We really must be going," she said in a very grown-up-married-woman voice. "We haven't finished our packing yet, and I want Steven to have a good long night before the journey."

This was an excuse, because they were not in fact travelling down until the following evening. But Liz need not have bothered, thought Steven, kissing his mother; no one pressed them to stay. As they walked to the station he felt that the little room they had just left was drawn comfortably together. Now—he imagined his mother saying to Derek and Celia—now, my dears, we can talk.

XI

On Sunday evening, when the Prydes left London, only Elizabeth genuinely felt regret, and only she looked forward without apprehension to the months ahead. Steven, glad to be leaving the Mortimers and sorry to be going to his mother-in-law, reflected that it would take a train accident (non-fatal) to satisfy him. He must be difficult to please, he told himself. His Liz was in happy spirits, and so no doubt was Mamma. He must say she had been extremely tactful and kind about everything, and of course they couldn't possibly have accepted her kind offer to go away, but, heavens, how nice it would have been if she'd insisted!

In the taxi, absently answering Liz as she chattered and looking out at the sunlit summer evening, he toyed with the unworthy pretence that at the last minute Mamma had changed her mind, and that the house, when they reached it would prove empty. But no, when they rounded the bushes at the entrance, there she stood, tying up over the porch a long trail of honeysuckle, whose delicious smell of childhood was all about them as they kissed her. She looked very sunburnt and well; the whites of her brown eyes, as she smiled up at him, were blue, like those of a child; perhaps it was because she wore a faded blue cotton dress that he had not seen before. Oh, this would not be so bad, after all. Her welcome was charming, the house was full of flowers and looked its best as the late sunlight sloped in through its big windows, and supper was ready on the dining-room table.

Elizabeth was intensely happy, and her sentences cascaded after one another as she looked about her. "Darling, isn't it all lovely! Oh, *look* at your delphiniums! You should have waited for me to help with the—Oh, *Mummy*, what a lovely supper! You are naughty. Cold ham and a heavenly salad; isn't that delectable! And a glass of milk for Steve like I told you. Look, darling, *aren't* you spoilt? How are you, Mummy? Terribly tired getting ready for—Oh, and look! Raspberries for pudding and real cream!"

Steven, knowing that they had eaten raspberries and cream daily at the Mortimers, could hardly believe that all this gush was genuine, and he also obscurely resented the glass of milk. He mumbled something which was submerged in female clamour and sat down, rather glumly.

Poor young man! thought Joanna. If he is to be fattened up after his illness it must not be done so tactlessly in future. She wished that Libby would not, with rather over-weight humour, keep reverting to the subject of nourishing food, and speaking of a conspiracy "between you and me, Mummy" to control Steven. "I need your support, you know, Mummy, because he's most obstinate and naughty."

"How are the Mortimers?" said Joanna briskly, and the talk swung away from Steven, to his relief. As it happened, he was extremely hungry, but he made it a point of honour to take less than his share of the raspberries and cream.

Joanna insisted that she should be left to do the washing up while her daughter and son-in-law unpacked one or two of their boxes. She was aghast at the quantity of their luggage, which was thickly strewn about the house, making her pleasant, rather bare rooms look like customs sheds. Tomorrow when Steven had gone off to work, she and Libby must have a good sorting out, and perhaps the emptied boxes could go into the cellar, which was not, she thought, unduly damp.

She finished the washing up, with a swallowed sigh for her lost evenings of peace, for now, she supposed, there would always be plates to wash. She took the coffee-tray into the drawing-room and put it on a low table, and she stood looking around the room. Really, she could not think of a nicer drawing-room anywhere. Mrs. Holmes had been positively inspired this week and had polished until the old furniture reflected the beaming copper. Her tall windows caught the very last rays of yellow sunlight, about to be quenched by the elm-trees whose heavy heads were momentarily gilt; her curtains, relics of Jack's old home and now for the first time used by her, were of pearl grey stripes alternating with dark red, and up each broad stripe wound a chain of little roses. They suited the room perfectly. Lighting a cigarette, Joanna thought that only she, in her ancient cotton frock, was out of place. The coffee-tray should have been brought by a neat, elderly parlour-maid, who would have plumped up one of the cushions and silently withdrawn. The room looked so beautifully civilized; she did hope that Libby wouldn't leave her sewing things about in here, and that Steven's hair was not greasy enough to mark her chair-covers.

The sun sank out of sight, and immediately Joanna began to feel cold. She glanced towards the fireplace. Should she have a little log fire, on the children's first night, just to celebrate? But they would want to go early to bed so probably it was not worthwhile. She picked up the coffee-pot, and then, without pouring, replaced it. Just for tonight she wanted to treat the children as guests, and so she would wait for her coffee until they came. She rubbed her arms, which felt cold. Better get a jersey, and call out to Libby to bring one with her when she came. She went upstairs, suddenly—after a day of excitement and preparation—deadly tired.

The Prydes joined her after a few minutes, Libby wearing a housecoat of a soft brown woollen material, which was part of her trousseau. Huddling her old red jersey over her old blue frock, Joanna feasted her eyes on her pretty and well-dressed daughter. Steven, who had taken off his jacket to open boxes, was still in his shirt sleeves, and although he politely apologized to his mother-in-law for this, he obstinately refused either to fetch the jacket or—when Elizabeth herself fetched it—to put it on. He was, in fact, rather cross, and Elizabeth's repeated reminders that he had been ill did nothing to sweeten his temper.

Joanna felt for each of them, but could willingly have smacked them both. Libby was obviously fussing Steven to the limit of his endurance, but instead of so visibly resenting it, he might have shown a little gratitude, and he should have remembered that he *had* been ill enough to give his wife a very bad fright. In the end, after she had three times changed the subject, and Libby had three times reverted to the room's probable low temperature, she lost her own temper. "Oh, for God's sake, Libby, leave him alone!" she snapped. At this Libby looked infinitely surprised and hurt, and Steven, with a protective glance at her flushed face, at once put on the jacket, so that Joanna felt thoroughly snubbed. She poured out second cups of coffee and began to talk wildly—from bottomless ignorance—of film stars. Were the measurements for a film star's figure—she wanted to know—laid down in some director's manual? Because, whatever their faces were like, all their bodies were the same, whereas if you looked round among your friends they were all—even those with good figures—completely different from one another.

"All the manual insists on," said Steven, "is that they should be too thin."

"I don't agree," said Libby. "Even when fashion said we were to have no bosoms they always kept theirs."

"For the sake of the male film-goers no doubt." Steven seemed to have mellowed. He puffed his pipe and grinned in a friendly way at Joanna.

"You men like them juicy, do you?" inquired Elizabeth.

"Yes of course. You know," said Steven, and happened to be gazing at his mother-in-law, "I can't stand flat-chested women."

If he hadn't, the moment he'd said it, looked aghast, and if Libby hadn't appeared anxious and upset, it wouldn't have mattered, thought Joanna. Until that moment she had never thought of herself as flat-chested, and indeed she knew that she was *not* flat—not quite. She felt astonishingly hurt, and had to control an impulse to put her arms across her maligned bosom. She sat rigidly still and chattered on at random, saying that more variation was allowed among the men than the girls. "They all have to have wide shoulders and little hips, but at least some of them can be taller than others, which is more than the poor girls can be."

"And that's where you're wrong, darling," said Libby, who looked relieved. "Some of them are much leggier than others." And she mentioned two names which Joanna had never heard.

"Well, I expect I *am* wrong," said Joanna. "I hardly ever go to the things, as you know."

What an uncomfortable evening! she thought. If Steven and I are both going to try so hard to like and be liked we shall have nervous breakdowns soon. She gathered the red jersey together over the bodice of her blue dress. Stupid of her to mind. She had always been rather proud of her slenderness, and really, she supposed, she just looked stringy. Damn it, at her age—the age of a potential grandmother—what did it matter what sort of a figure she had?

"I'm afraid," she said cheerfully, "that you'll find your temporary sitting-room a bit cramped. In fact you may find yourselves with one foot up the chimney and one arm out of the window. But I shall be deeply offended if you don't pretend to like it, and the study—which I am going to call your sitting-room, and then it need never be called the study again, thank heaven—will be finished next week-end."

"Oh, darling, are you turning us out?" said Elizabeth, and Steven, labouring under a feeling of guilt, said quickly: "Mayn't we sit with you just until the study is finished?"

Joanna was so surprised at an attack from this quarter that she could think of no reply. "*Not* the study," she said automatically. "Of course you can, Steven, if you really want to."

"Thank you, Mamma," said Steven, trying to look pleased.

Twice during the next week Joanna made an excuse to go early to bed, leaving the Prydes in possession of the drawing-room, and twice Steven insisted that Elizabeth should take him for an after-dinner walk, pointing out that he had been sitting in the office all day. Mr. Holmes finished scraping the study walls next Sunday, and put on the first coat of white paint. It would need three, he said, and he really would get the room finished next week-end, unless, he added, he had to drive up to the North of England. His wife was encouraging about this: if he did have to be out driving next week-end he'd get time off in the following week to make up. Her admiration for Mr. Pryde, as she called him, continued to wax, and had the effect of energizing her arms, so that the house reached a new high level of polish. Elizabeth happily cooked, singing in a monotonous way that from anyone else would have enraged her mother. Steven disappeared on a bicycle at 8.15 every morning and returned in time for a late tea, and Joanna found time at last to enjoy her house and garden without feeling that every moment ought to be stretched to cover three separate jobs.

It was during the second week that they acquired the crossword-puzzle habit. All of them had toyed with the things now and then, and Elizabeth had sometimes had the honour of helping Mr. Mortimer with his daily effort, which he liked to finish over his evening coffee. Now suddenly they all became enthusiasts. Joanna would pick up the newly arrived *Times*, glance at the headlines and then, shamefacedly, make a dash to skim the cream off the crossword before Libby got at it. Libby was completely shameless. She rushed for the paper if she could hear its arrival and, beating her mother perhaps by seconds, would go straight to work without the most perfunctory glance at the news. And Steven, in the evenings, joined in the real work of the thing, for Elizabeth and Joanna only made darts at it during the day, and had no time for sustained thought, or the consultation of dictionaries.

Probably if Joanna had taken in a different newspaper, the study, when it was finished, would have fulfilled its intended purpose. But when at last the pictures were up on the glossy white walls, the books were in the shelves, and at the windows the faded chintz curtains, newly washed, were stirring in the summer breeze, it would have seemed to Elizabeth grossly unnatural to have broken off their sociable evening habit. On the first evening she invited Joanna, with an air, to "come and have coffee in *our* room tonight". The next evening was so cold that a fire in the drawing-room was positively necessary, and after that the habit seemed impossible to break. Elizabeth was content—as long as Steven was there she did not mind who else was there too—and Joanna was enjoying her evenings, and felt that she had really done all that could be expected of her. If at times she wished that she could read as she ate her supper, she suppressed the unworthy thought. As for Steven, after one or two efforts to get his wife to himself, he accommodated himself to the situation. They would all eat a delicious meal, the most important of the day; the washing up would be dealt with in turns—the Prydes doing two evenings to Joanna's one—and then they would go into the drawing-room and get to work. Elizabeth maintained her supremacy, guessing about half of each puzzle, and her mother and Steven managed the rest between them.

The study, now vaguely termed "your" or "our" sitting-room, became a dumping ground for the Prydes' personal belongings, and sometimes when Steven had work to do in the evening he withdrew thither unaccompanied by Elizabeth, who pointed out that if she did go with him he wouldn't have time to notice her. If, as he worked, he sometimes wished that he could glance across to see her fair head bent over a book, he never told her so.

XII

Often on Fridays Steven would bring home with him a file or two, and would work in the house on Saturday morning, instead of bicycling into Tadwych. On Joanna's suggestion, Elizabeth would roast the joint on Saturday, so that she might be free to share Steven's Sunday holiday, when usually they would go out together for the whole day, leaving Joanna to taste the loneliness—or was it peace?—of her silent house.

On these Saturday mornings Steven was quite approachable, and the two women soon gave up their careful avoidance of the study. He would join them for a cup of tea in the kitchen or drawing-room, and would not object if asked to carry a heavy coal-scuttle or move a piece of furniture. Elizabeth, in fact, tended to use him as a handy man-servant, although Joanna was more punctilious.

One Saturday morning in August, when Elizabeth had gone out to the village shop, Joanna made the tea at eleven and carried the tray into Steven's sitting-room.

She put the tray on the window-sill and poured out a cup for him, remarking as she did so: "Libby's not back yet, but I couldn't bear to wait, so I thought perhaps you'd like yours in here."

"Thank you, Mamma." Steven, who had stood up, subsided again, adding, as she picked up the tray: "Won't you stay and drink yours with me? As you very well know, we have two comfortable arm-chairs."

"Thank you," said Joanna, and sat down, not in a chair, but on the window-sill, looking at him thoughtfully, as he sat and stirred his tea. She couldn't help wondering whether he really wanted her company, or was acting on a plan. She had grown to like and to respect her son-in-law more than she had hoped for, and if his considerate and friendly attitude towards herself *was* a plan, he was sticking to it with almost superhuman consistency; but somehow she still could not fully relax when they were together, and when she was alone with him she felt she had to entertain him.

Their common ground, of course, was their love of Libby, and they were both extremely proud of her. So Joanna said: "Poor old Libby's having a very hot walk, I'm afraid."

"She won't have much to carry, will she?" asked Steven.

"Oh, no, I don't think so. I was only thinking of the heat; and she wouldn't take a hat."

"Never mind," said Steven tranquilly. "Sunstroke is quite out of date, and I like Liz freckled, don't you?"

"Not very much—I mean not very many. A few are rather becoming."

"They arouse my protective instincts," said Steven. "And she doesn't do that nearly often enough to please me."

He spoke flippantly, but Joanna's dark eyes searched his face. It was true, Libby was dreadfully self-sufficient, and even when she asked for Steven's help it was with an indulgent air. Steven was laughing now, and she lifted her expressive eyebrows inquiringly. "You've no idea how worried you sometimes look, dear Mamma," he said.

"Do I? I'm so sorry." Joanna hadn't been thinking of her own looks, and it had never occurred to her that her thoughts were visible. "I was just wondering about you and Libby," she said frankly.

"What about us?"

"Whether—whether you're content to be here."

Steven wondered what she would have said if she had spoken straight from her thought. The transparency was clouded now, and an expression of polite concern was all that he could read in her face. For a moment, as he made a civil reply, they both felt how nearly they had broken through an intangible barrier, and it was with something like regret that they saw Elizabeth come striding up to the front door, looking, with her flat shoulders and proud fair head, rather like an advertisement for some out-of-door scent.

"Here she is," said Joanna, reaching for the tea-pot, and thinking that Steven would be relieved to hear it.

"Good," said Steven, and went to the door, rather wishing that his mother-in-law would not look so pleased at the finish of their *tête-à-tête*.

Elizabeth came in, patting Steven's arm as he held the door for her, and dropping into an arm-chair, which shuddered as it took her weight.

"Darling!" protested her mother.

"Sorry!" Libby pushed a cushion behind her shining head and fanned herself with the Parish Magazine. "I've brought this," she said, brandishing it.

"What a thrill!" said Joanna.

"Do you read it, Mummy?"

"Never, I'm afraid."

"Well, you've jolly well got to in future. I've just promised to contribute housewifery notes to it!"

"You haven't!"

"I certainly have! One page every month—it shouldn't be very difficult."

"Darling," said Steven, enormously amused. "It hasn't taken you long to acquire this village, has it?"

"What do you mean?"

"You own it heart and soul already, don't you? Tell me, is there a Women's Institute here?"

"Well, as a matter of fact—"

"I knew it! And you're going to teach it to make jam—"

"Bottle fruit!"

"Same thing. Well, my poppet," said Steven, taking the Parish Magazine from her hand and rolling it into a baton, "never say again that you've nothing in common with my mother. I shall now expect you to write to her *every* week." He cuffed her with the baton, and she put her hands over her ears, laughing and protesting.

"Don't you do it, Libby," said Joanna. "There are two things that no wife should do for her husband: one is to pack his clothes and the other is to write to his relatives."

"Thank you, darling. But didn't you?"

"Never."

"Good gracious! I thought in those days—"

Joanna laughed. "We did have the vote, you know!" she said flippantly.

"You show a distinct tendency, Liz," said Steven, "to class your mother with the Victorians."

"Thank you, Steven, for defending me. Another cup of tea for you?"

"Please, Mamma. Now, Liz, suppose you come clean. What else are you going to do to put this village on the map?"

"Nothing else, really. Only to help with the church bazaar. And I did half promise"—she looked guiltily at her mother—"darling, I know you're not churchy, but after all this *is* one of the bigger houses in the village, and I do think—"

"Don't be so persuasive, Libby." Joanna looked at her with dancing eyes, and tried to appear solemn. "You feel," she said, with an attempt at pomposity, "that there are certain responsibilities which go with certain privileges. How well I've brought you up! Come on: as Steven rightly says, come clean."

"I half promised that you'd sometimes do the church flowers," said Elizabeth apologetically.

"Oh, Lord, is that all? I don't a bit mind doing that—in fact I shall enjoy it. Anything else?"

"Of *course* not, darling! You can't say I'm a busybody!"

Steven and Joanna burst out laughing, and Elizabeth's face became a deeper pink.

"You are pigs!" she said. "It all needed doing, honestly it did."

"Of course it did, darling," said Joanna. "You're a very good child, and Steven and I are extremely proud of you." She glanced confidently across for his support.

"Extremely proud," said Steven, in measured tones. "But you haven't finished yet, have you, Liz?"

"What do you mean?" Elizabeth shrank back, laughing and blushing more than ever.

"What about me? What is *my* contribution to be, towards this ideal state of yours?"

"Nothing really. At least, only—"

"Tell me, blast you."

"Only I thought you might sometimes play cricket."

"Cricket! Great God, you say *only* cricket!" He advanced upon Libby, waving his baton. "You mean to say you want me to spend my few precious hours of week-end freedom playing cricket?" He beat her, and she shrieked and struggled. "What are we to do with her, Mamma? I can't honestly agree that you've brought her up well. I think she's vindictive."

Elizabeth straightened up, gasping and pushing back her hair. "But you rather like cricket!"

"Well, yes," said Steven equably. "As a matter of fact I do. Thank you, my love, for arranging it. When do they play?"

"On Saturdays chiefly."

"Oh, Liz! Our Saturday afternoon together!"

"Sorry, darling, but it *will* be so good for you, and Mummy and I will come and watch."

Steven's face, which had expressed reproach, was perfectly blank as he agreed to consider the matter, and Joanna thought that Libby really had been a bit high-handed. She's so *young*, sighed her mother, and so awfully sure that she knows best! Her sympathy for Steven—quite unforced this morning—brought her to her feet.

"Drink your tea slowly, you two," she said, turning towards the door. But she was stopped at once.

"Oh, don't go, Mummy! I've got lots more to tell you!"

"Tell me later, darling." But she hesitated, with the cold brass door-knob in her hand.

"Oh, come on. Steven doesn't want us to leave him yet, do you, Steve?"

Steven glanced at the papers on his table, and then at his watch. "Not just yet," he said obligingly. "Come on in, Mamma; you may just as well obey orders." His smile was so warmly welcoming that Joanna, returning to her place on the window-sill, felt a little glow of pleasure. She really believed he was beginning to like her!

"I had a great gossip with Mrs. Hodge," said Elizabeth. "At least, *I* didn't gossip, but she did. I just listened."

"Who's Mrs. Hodge?"

"Oh, Steve, I've often told you! She keeps the shop!"

"Sorry. Go on, what did she say?"

"She says Mrs. Holmes had been a sad trouble to her good mother."

"I don't blame her," said Steven. "Of all the sour-faced mothers to have—"

"Hush! Listen! It seems that all her mother's savings had to be spent on that cottage the Holmes' live in."

"Hadn't they any money?" asked Joanna.

Elizabeth lowered her voice, dramatically. "It was to *bribe* Mr. Holmes to marry her! He only did it just in time!"

"Well," said Steven, "that's nothing unusual in a village. You mustn't be so naïve, my girl."

"Wait, I haven't finished. You know Mr. Holmes is away three or four nights a week driving his lorry—"

"Yes?"

"*Well*, she still does a roaring trade!" said Elizabeth, wide-eyed. "And that's why she has all those new clothes and ear-rings."

"Good gracious!" said Joanna. "And I always thought *he* was probably the one who strayed."

"Can you *imagine* it, Mummy? To be married to someone as devastatingly attractive as that man, and then to practise your trade as well!"

"She must," said Steven, "have had her idle moments. Damn it, she's got five children, hasn't she? They should have cramped her style a bit."

"Yes, and they all look completely different! That just shows! And her poor wretched mother's always trying to cover up by saying what a good quiet girl she is, and never goes out with other men!"

"Doesn't seem to need to, does she?" said Steven.

"It may not be true," said Joanna half-heartedly, and clearly hoping that it was.

"Oh, yes, Mummy! You've only to look at her! And nobody knows if her husband guesses or not. Mrs. Hodge said, 'Mark my words, dear! Some day he'll find out, and then he'll turn nasty!'"

"Good gracious! I hope he won't," said Joanna.

"Well, there you are. Isn't it frightful?" said Elizabeth cheerfully. "Do you suppose we ought to sack her, Mummy?"

"Whatever for?"

Elizabeth looked embarrassed: "Well, aren't we, perhaps, rather encouraging—"

"Oh, Libby, I'd encourage anything to get this house cleaned. And honestly I can't see that it has anything to do with us."

"No, I suppose not." She wrinkled her forehead. "Of course economically it's all wrong. We ought to be employing someone who's not—"

Steven gave a shout of laughter. "Oh, bless you, Liz!" he said. "You mean we should employ someone who's not otherwise employable. Mrs. Holmes (to whom long life) seems to be employable in a variety of ways, doesn't she?"

"Don't laugh at me, Steven. I only meant that that one family seems to be drawing an awful lot of wages."

"Including," Joanna giggled, "those of sin!" Then, seeing Libby's reproachful look, she sobered. "Darling, if there was a charwoman available who wasn't also a tart I'd employ her like a shot. For one thing, she might be a better cleaner. But there isn't."

"And anyway," said Steven, "I like Mrs. H."

Elizabeth laughed rather loudly. "Well, we shall know where to look for you if you're out late at night!" she said.

Neither Steven nor Joanna thought this remark funny, and their reactions to it were oddly similar. After an instant's hesitation Joanna smiled politely and said: "You've no idea, Libby, what bliss it is to me to know that the joint is in the oven at this moment without any responsibility on my part."

And Steven, taking his wife's hand, said: "And it will come out done to a turn, if I know anything."

"Thank you for these tributes," said Elizabeth, looking from Joanna to Steven with a puzzled smile. "Are you tactfully reminding me to go and turn the potatoes, or what?"

"We're not reminding you of anything, my love," said Steven. "We certainly don't want to send you about your business."

Elizabeth glanced at her watch. "They can wait for another five minutes," she said. "Did the post come, while I was out?"

"Now you come to mention it," said Steven, "I believe it did. No, don't break into a canter towards the letterbox; I brought them in here."

"Anything exciting?"

"Two bills for Mamma."

"Oh, Steve, nothing else?"

"I believe there was something for you."

"Interesting?"

"I shouldn't think so."

"Damn! I thought we'd get the photographs today."

"You don't call those interesting, do you?"

"Of course I do. Thrilling!"

"Well, in that case I wonder where I put them?"

"*Steve*!" Elizabeth was indignant. "Isn't he *maddening*, Mummy? Come on, hand them over, quick!"

Steven started to look deliberately through his papers. "Are these the things you mean?" he said mildly. "I'll open them for you; you'll only tear the whole thing if you fall upon it in your present mood. Now where"— he looked round, blandly—"did I put my knife?"

"Steven, you're doing it on purpose," said Joanna reproachfully.

"Doing what? I don't understand you, Mamma. Just a minute. There, Liz, you can have it now," and he handed her the neatly opened package.

"Thank you!" gasped Elizabeth. "Oh, do look, Mummy! They're not at all bad."

Steven stood up, with every appearance of boredom, and slouched across to look over his wife's shoulder.

"Stop posing, Steven," said Joanna. "You know you're interested. There you are! You look as if you were facing a firing squad, I must admit, but it's a good view of—She broke off, thinking that she must not laugh at his disputed moustache.

"Of what, Mamma?"

"Of your medal ribbons."

"Doesn't he look brave?" said Elizabeth teasingly. "Noble, almost!"

Steven turned away with an expression of nausea on his face, which the two women ignored.

"Let's see yours, darling. Oh, Libby, that's a nice one!" And indeed the photograph had caught Elizabeth's slow smile and seemed to have caught with it something of her inner contentment. "I call that a really happy picture," said Joanna, delighted. "Look, Steven, doesn't your wife look nice?"

Steven came back with alacrity. "H'm, not at all bad. I'd like a copy of that one."

"We must see how much they cost," said Elizabeth. "Do you want the biggest size, or the next one to it?"

"I want a little tiny one to go in my note-case."

"Do you, darling?" said Elizabeth, touched. "Well, what size do you want on your dressing-table?"

"None, thank you. I'd rather keep the wife of my bosom neatly tucked away where she belongs."

"Oh! Oh, all right! Well, I'd like some big ones for the drawing-room. Of us both, of course." And with a last lingering glance at her own portrait she turned back to her husband's.

"This is the best one, I think."

"Darling," said Steven, "have you got a morbid craving to see your own face all over your own drawing-room?"

Elizabeth seemed thoroughly taken aback. "I—I thought you'd want it there!"

"But I don't. I detest big photographs."

"But—but everyone has their photographs in their drawing-rooms!"

"Do they?" said Steven thoughtlessly. "How extremely suburban!"

Elizabeth blushed violently, and Joanna hurried to give her some support, although as it happened she entirely agreed with Steven.

"It is normally done," she said. "I think the idea is that you look at Libby, and Libby looks at you, and your guests look at you both."

"Whereas in actual fact the guests would be the only people to do any looking, because after you've lived with a photograph for a week you never notice it again."

"I suppose that's true."

"But they help to furnish a drawing-room!" said Elizabeth mutinously. "They make it look lived in."

Steven shrugged his shoulders. "It's for you to decide, darling; it's your drawing-room—or at least it will be. But if you want to know *my* opinion, I think it's ostentatious and vulgar."

"Steven!"

"Don't you agree with me, Mamma?"

"I shall have to think about it."

Steven gave her a glance of triumphant amusement. Obviously her non-committal reply told him all that he wanted to know. Then he said gravely to his wife: "Don't look hurt, Liz. You're much nicer than any of your photographs, I assure you."

Elizabeth smiled reluctantly. "You do have peculiar ideas, darling," she said. "Do they come from your mother?"

"Dear me, no. You know quite well that Aimée has photographs of herself folk-dancing! You know, waving a bunch of ribbons."

"Ah," said Elizabeth contentedly. "I expect she's put you off."

"Perhaps she has." Steven didn't look at Joanna. "Do you know, without wishing to seem unfriendly to you two girls, I ought really to do a little work this morning."

"Poor pet, so you ought." Elizabeth picked up the photographs and the Parish Magazine. Joanna took the tea-tray. They were on their way to the door when it opened a few inches and a coy smile topped by auburn ringlets came round it.

"Oh! Mrs. Holmes!" said Joanna, arrested.

"Good morning, Mrs. Malling. I've just popped up with a few new-laid eggs for your breakfast."

Mrs. Holmes sidled in, looking, with good reason, extremely self-conscious. She was wearing a cyclamen-coloured jacket and tight skirt, obviously new. She held out a paper bag, and waited expectantly.

"Oh, how very kind—" began Joanna, but Elizabeth cut in: "Mrs. Holmes! Another new outfit!"

"Well," said Mrs. Holmes, bridling. "I just thought that you'd like to see me new two-piece. I don't mind telling you where I got it too, dear, though I wouldn't tell everyone. Do you like it?"

"It's lovely," said Elizabeth reverently.

Mrs. Holmes giggled. "Know what my 'ubby said when 'e sees it? 'Brenda,' 'e says, 'you couldn't be smarter, not if you was Queen Juliana 'erself.'"

"Very true. You couldn't," said Joanna. "And as for the eggs—"

"'But just you wait till tonight,' I says to 'im. 'Till I got me new earrings on with it, to go to the pictures.'" Mrs. Holmes' pretty, coarse face was alight with happiness. "'You won't know me *then*,' I tells 'im; 'I shall be a habsolute Lady Godiva!'"

"So you will," said Joanna, heartily and indistinctly. "But really Mrs. Holmes, you shouldn't give us eggs. When they're such a price in the shops. Four of them too."

"Two for Mr. Pryde and one each for you two ladies, for your Sunday breakfast." Mrs. Holmes looked dotingly towards Steven, who, at the mention of Lady Godiva, had suddenly erected a file before his face and was presumably reading its contents. She pranced sideways and her head came past the file cover. "Nice *fresh* eggs, sir," she said. "Do you good, those will. Not like those things they call new-laid in the shops."

"It's exceedingly good of you," said Steven, tugging at his moustache. "Are you sure you oughtn't to keep them for the children?"

"Who, them? No! They got plenty. Mum, she buys eggs for them," said their mother smugly. "Don't you go telling *'er* I give you any!"

She retreated to the door and then turned and adopted a statuesque pose, obviously copied from an inferior mannequin. "So you like my costume, do you? Well, tata for now!" and she closed the door and could be heard humming as she bustled on her high heels across the hall to the front door.

Steven and Elizabeth, acting on a common impulse, hid their faces upon one another's shoulders. Joanna's hands shook as she carefully put her tray on the table. She wiped her eyes. "Queen Juliana," said Steven's voice, muffled by his wife's shoulder, "and Lady Godiva, all in one breath. Her poor Majesty!"

Joanna was so touched to see the children thus clasped together that she was the first to become sober. "This time," she said, as for the third time she took up her tea-tray, "I really am leaving you, Steven, and if that hysterical woman your wife will pull herself together and leave you too, you may get some work done this morning."

Libby's head lifted. "I was temporarily unwomaned," she said. "Mummy, don't sack Mrs. Holmes, will you? She's a jewel. You simply must go on employing her."

"All right, darling, to oblige you I will," said Joanna, and got herself and her tray safely out of the room.

XIII

"Steven," said Joanna one evening, as they were waiting for Elizabeth to join them for a crossword session, "I don't know how the village will ever recover from the shock when you take Libby away."

Steven smiled. "Poor village! She certainly seems to be very important to its well-being."

"When she was about four," said Joanna, looking out vaguely at the twilit garden, "I heard a great splashing coming from the kitchen one wet day and called to ask what she was up to. She said, 'Something very busy and 'portant!'"

Steven grinned. "She hasn't altered very much, has she? What *was* she doing?"

"Standing on a chair and washing her muddy gumboots in the sink. The whole floor was awash."

"She's more efficient now, anyway."

"She's certainly efficient about the crossword. If she doesn't come soon I shall be tempted to steal a march on her, but perhaps it would be a pity to break our new pact so quickly."

"Your new pact?"

"To wait till we're together and start fair. It was becoming such an ugly rush to get first whack at the paper and do all the easy ones."

Elizabeth hurried in with her work-bag hanging over one arm and a bunched-up eiderdown hugged to her breast. "You haven't started?" she said accusingly.

"No, darling; we've resisted temptation. What are you doing with that eiderdown?"

"It's pouring feathers, Mummy, and we don't want poor Aimée to be nested in them next week-end, do we?"

"Like Jemima Puddle-Duck? No, indeed we don't." Joanna's heart sank as she thought of Mrs. Pryde's intended visit. "Are you sure it's not thin all over?"

"No, it's quite mendable. Look, there's a rent here, and one here, and one down that end."

"Let me do it."

"Couldn't we both? Steve can read out the crossword. Oh, and by the way, we didn't finish yesterday's. Don't you think we should really tidy it up first?"

"Oh, yes, I suppose we'd better," said Joanna regretfully. She had been looking forward to the first canter through the clues when quickness of wit counted for more than downright knowledge.

"Pass it over, then," said Steven, subsiding comfortably on to the small of his back and sticking a pencil behind his ear—a habit that his wife was combating in vain. He folded the newspaper into a thick oblong and glanced at the clues. "I want a poet to start with," he said. "Five letters with an N in the middle."

Joanna threaded her needle and smiled amiably at him. "Afraid I can only think of Manet," she said placidly.

Steven began to laugh. "Or, come to that, Monet," he said.

"Or even Lenin."

"Or Banks (Leslie)."

"I expect they mean Canto, and they've got a little mixed."

"Or Sonnet!"

"Too many letters."

Elizabeth said: "But Manet was an artist!"

There was an instant's pause before Joanna, her head bent over her sewing, said: "So he was, darling."

"There must *be* a poet!" said Elizabeth. Kind Steven wasn't laughing at Mummy's absurd mistake, so she wouldn't either. It was lovely to see them getting on so well together, both chattering so fast, in fact, that she could hardly follow what they were saying. "Shall I look in the Oxford Book?" she asked obligingly.

"Yes, please do, darling. It's probably one of those fearfully obscure ones."

Elizabeth found the familiar blue-and-gold book, and started to read through the contents, starting at the end. "Plenty with six letters," she commented.

"Sorry, must have five." Steven doodled frowningly in the margin.

"Is William Jones any good?"

"Who on earth was he?"

"I don't know yet. Number four hundred and seventy-eight." She turned the pages.

"He certainly sounds obscure enough," said Joanna. "What's the poem called?"

"'Epigram.' Shall I read it?"

"Please do."

> "On parent knees, a naked new born child,
> Weeping thou sat'st, while all around thee smiled.
> So live, that sinking to thy life's last sleep
> Calm thou may'st smile, whilst all around thee weep."

"*Well*!" said Joanna. "Is that the only one of his?"

"Yes."

"Why *do* you suppose they put it in? No, Steven, Jones won't do. Five letters! I wonder—oh good Lord, what fools we are!"

"Who, then?"

"John Donne, of course!"

"Well, blow me down," said Steven. "We ought to have guessed that straight away; though I must confess," he added, "that I don't go in for him very much."

"Oh, I do," said Joanna, and Elizabeth said absently:

"We did him at school. You ought to pronounce him Dunne, Mummy."

"Oh, ought I?" said Joanna, and Steven looked amused and said:

"What a very improper school you went to, darling."

"Rubbish," said Joanna briskly, "I expect they did the religious ones. What did they make you study, Libby? The Holy Sonnets?"

"I can't remember," said Elizabeth. "I know I thought them very dull, and of course he's madly hackneyed now, isn't he?"

Joanna pushed back her hair, looking distracted. "It *is* a shame," she lamented. "Now I suppose they've spoilt him for you for ever. He really isn't dull or hackneyed; he only hair-splits rather."

"And doesn't scan," said Steven. He puffed his pipe, and glanced sideways at his mother-in-law. "None of the modern poets seem able to scan, of course, but I did think in the seventeenth century they knew the trick of it."

"Oh, the modern ones are all frightful," said Elizabeth easily, but Joanna was looking searchingly at Steven, and didn't notice her. "Steven, be honest. You're not nearly as limited as you like to make out, are you? Why do you do it?"

Steven withdrew his pipe and grinned at her. "Blast you, Mamma, to infuriate you, of course."

"You nearly succeeded," said Joanna coolly. "I detest sweeping statements about the arts. I suppose really you can spout Donne by the page?"

"Oh no. Only—

> Whoever loves, if he do not propose
> The right true end of love, he's one that goes
> To sea for nothing but to make him sick

which is a convenient argument, at times, to be able to quote."

"H'm, I'm sure it must be. There's the Flea, too, for a good bit of specious reasoning."

Elizabeth, who had been listening in silent surprise, now said inquiringly: "*The Flea?*"

"I don't expect you learnt that at school, Libby. He tries to persuade his lady to go to bed with him, and says she may just as well, as the same flea has already bitten them both. Very plausible."

"I don't see it," said Elizabeth, frowningly.

"Oh, it's only a joke, really."

"I thought he was always fearfully intense? I had to learn one about 'Death be not proud', and I couldn't make head or tail of it."

"It seems to have been badly wasted on you, darling," said her husband. "It's probably one of the finest poems in the English language—don't you think so, Mamma? But never mind, Liz, we'll give you a course in the love-poems—

> But O alas, so long, so far
> Our bodies why do we forbear?"

"Don't say it, Steven," interrupted Joanna. "Let her read the whole thing for herself." She went to the bookcase. "There you are, Libby." The book opened readily at the poem she wanted.

"One of your favourites, is it?" said Steven to Joanna, while Elizabeth was reading.

"Yes, I'm very fond of it." And she added diffidently: "I couldn't bear to read it for ages after Jack died, but now it's all so long ago."

There was quiet acceptance in her voice which hurt Steven, and he was touched by the unexpected confidence. He said gently: "He was fond of it too, then?"

"Oh, no, I used to try to get him interested, but poetry wasn't really his sort of thing at all. I always imagined he'd learn to enjoy it, but of course people don't. And anyway, the whole idea of Donne revolted him."

"You mean the sensuality of his religion?"

"More his preoccupation with death. Jack thought it morbid."

"As it was."

"Yes, but I can understand it, can't you? Surely they must all feel it in different degrees. If one wasn't troubled by the shortness of life, one wouldn't want to write poetry."

"I wonder if that's true? 'Easeful death-' after all?"

"Oh, but that was an idea Keats had for what one *might* feel, and he worked it up. It doesn't prove anything about his own feelings. To me the fact that he wrote poetry proves his longing to—to salvage from death some of the things that he loved. And do you know de la Mare?

> May the rustling harvest hedgerow
> Still the Traveller's Joy entwine,
> And as happy children gather
> Posies once mine."

"As you've just pointed out, that proves nothing about his own feelings."

Joanna had been leaning forward, all her long-lived shyness forgotten. She was flushed, and Elizabeth, looking up, thought that she looked positively young and pretty. Now, with a little smile, she relaxed in her chair. "It's not quite the same—" she was beginning, when Elizabeth closed her book, and said:

"H'm. Yes, a good poem, I suppose, though I agree with Steve about the scansion. Didn't Donne have himself modelled in his shroud or something?"

"Yes."

"Horrible!"

"But what a challenge! Are *you* ever frightened of death, Libby?"

"Not really. I'm afraid I don't think about it."

Joanna gazed at her in wonder, and Steven said: "How very wise you are, my darling."

"And you, Steven? In the War? Weren't you frightened of being killed?"

"I was always terrified I'd be hurt."

Elizabeth nodded. "Much, much worse."

"So everyone says," reflected Joanna, "but I'd have to be terribly maimed before I stopped valuing my life."

"Oh, Mummy, if you were crippled!"

"Even then."

"Have you read Hemingway's 'Fiesta'?"

"Yes, Steven. That's different, I suppose, and yet even then—surely one *could* get along without sex?"

It occurred to Steven that she must have done almost that herself

– 124 –

during the past twenty years, and for the first time he became really conscious of her as a woman, and a young one. There was something incurably innocent about her glance, an eager inquiry totally opposite to his wife's serenity, which was innocent too. Elizabeth's strong young figure—a little solid—and her fair face reminded him of a Flemish Madonna. She seemed absorbed in her own happiness, and unconscious that the world could be unkind. But Joanna, who should at her age have found security if she were ever to find it, seemed defenceless; gently questioning how soon she would be hurt once more. The sensitive, closed line of her lips showed control, but Elizabeth's mouth was untouched. He felt protective towards his mother-in-law, and he looked at his wife for a moment with detachment: a pretty fair girl who had everything she wanted. Then Elizabeth turned her head to smile at him, and it was as if a child had laid its hand on his knee; his heart moved with love.

"I don't see," said Elizabeth, smiling, "how anyone at all young *can* live without sex and not get warped."

Steven's feelings changed abruptly. Of all the tactless remarks! But Joanna answered peacefully: "Quite a lot do."

"Well, they all get a bit peculiar."

"I don't think that's altogether true."

"Janet says it comes out in all sorts of funny little ways."

"Well, good Lord, we've all heard *that* one," said Steven impatiently. "But it's by no means universal."

"Even if it's not visible," calmly continued Elizabeth, "it's still there. In fact if you can't see it it's probably worse."

"Darling," said Joanna, looking, as Steven gratefully noticed, not hurt, but amused, "we've all heard that, too."

"Often," added Steven.

"Oh, all right!" said Elizabeth, not at all offended. "But all the same, Janet says—"

"A course in so-called psychology," said Steven nastily, "doesn't guarantee a profound knowledge of human nature."

Elizabeth was astonished. She stared at Steven with her mouth open, and then, remembering Janet's saying that husbands were often sub-consciously jealous of their wife's friends, she smiled. "No, darling," she said soothingly, "of course it doesn't."

Steven found himself hating her. He turned to see if Joanna felt the same, and found that she was trying not to laugh. Her daughter's blandness and Steven's rage were almost too much for her, and she was biting her lips with the effort to keep a calm face. Steven relaxed, grinning, and at once she turned her eyes away, stiffening in her chair, and then standing up, nervously, to get a cigarette. It had shocked her profoundly to find that she and Steven were in danger of combining against Libby. She hoped that she had checked in time the disloyal message of her eyes and lips. If anyone was to feel shut out in this household of three, it should be herself; never, by any chance, darling little Libby.

Puffing at the cigarette, she returned to her chair. This was turning into a difficult evening, and a moment ago she had been so happily absorbed in her talk with Steven! It had been a delightful surprise to find him alive to poetry, and clearly he cared for it more than he was willing to admit. It occurred to her that she had never before met a man who was interested in it; she had, of course, known very few men well.

Certainly Jack had tried, but either you could be excited by poetry or you couldn't; Libby, like her father, never would be, although she was educated to the pitch of recognizing quotations, and knowing, with uncompromising certainty, which poets were "great" and which were "considerably over-rated".

She thought that she would enjoy a long talk with Steven, who probably knew far more about it than she did, if he had added an education like Libby's to tastes like her own. For herself, she knew very little, and admitted that her pleasure was largely sensuous and her favourites probably the obvious favourites of the anthologies. But they must not have their talk with Libby listening and perhaps feeling left out. Nor, naturally, did she at all want to get Steven to herself one day when Libby was busy. No, of course not. What a nuisance, thought Joanna, moodily inhaling smoke, that even one's own son-in-law, six years younger than oneself, must be treated in obedience to the good old conventions. It would be unthinkable that she should ever seek Steven's company in preference to Libby's, or he hers, and yet they liked each other, and were mutually nearer in age than either was to Libby. Feeling at last a real impulse of friendship towards Steven, it seemed sad to have to check its growth.

They had better talk about some non-committal subject now, she supposed, and was disconcerted when Libby said: "Go on talking about poetry, you two. I like listening to my clever relatives." And in fact she was filled with pride at Steven's unexpected knowledge.

Dear, generous child, thought Joanna. But you don't realize how nearly we were both disloyal to you, not in words, but in a shared look. You would not like us to have secrets from you. She said: "I don't think I feel so poetic now, but of course if Steven would like to recite something—?"

"He wouldn't," said Steven, rather rudely. "Let's get back to the crossword."

Joanna was delighted with him, and in a short time they finished one puzzle and started on the next. Joanna's brain, over-stimulated perhaps by what had passed, unhesitatingly produced answers to the most obscure clues, and even the anagrams, which she normally eschewed, fell into words for her with miraculous ease. Delighted as she was by her own unwonted brilliance, her conscience, foolishly sensitive this evening, grumbled that it was not for her to take all the limelight, and with it the children's unstinted admiration, Libby was meant to be playing the lead, and ought somehow to be pushed into doing so. She began to stall, frowning in affected perplexity, over something she had already guessed, but there was no denying it, Elizabeth was in poor form, and most of the carefully-left gaps were filled by Steven. The only thing successfully accomplished, she told herself ruefully as she went upstairs to bed, had been the mending of the eiderdown. And for what a purpose! The comfort of that unaesthetic female Aimée Pryde!

XIV

❦

During the next few days, however, Joanna became almost glad that Mrs. Pryde was to come. Her attitude to Steven had drastically changed, and she had to guard her behaviour when they were all three together. It seemed that a single evening of unforced friendship towards him was to be all her allowance. Before it she had been constantly trying to uncover interests in common, and to show Libby that he was liked by her: now she must check her spontaneity, lest she allow Libby to feel left out. It was good to find him suddenly so likeable, and she was pleased out of all proportion when Libby told her how much Steven enjoyed her company and admired her looks. She was half annoyed to notice that her looks actually did improve from that moment, and that she could not help taking more than usual trouble with her face and hair. Alone with Steven, when Libby was busy elsewhere, she found his company both restful and stimulating. But she took care, when Libby joined them, to retire into herself, and she found this oddly exhausting.

She expected, therefore, that her welcome to Mrs. Pryde would be genuine and warm. It was all there inside her, as she and Libby waited for the taxi in which Steven was bringing his mother from the station. She had taken a great deal of trouble over the flowers in the spare room and all over the house, had carefully chosen the books to put by Aimée's bed and had encouraged Libby to be rather reckless about the week-end meals. They were, for instance, to have a chicken. Now she was ready to be a good hostess and determined to like the odd little woman who must really be nice since Steven was her son.

It was a hot afternoon, with flies buzzing in the ivy-flowers by the gate and all the birds silent. They were to have tea on the lawn, which was now properly mown, although Steven—pulling off his damp shirt—had remarked that you couldn't see the grass for the plantains. Joanna hadn't yet bought her runner ducks, and as a tea-place the lawn, shaded by dusty old lilacs, was cool and pleasant. The table, in pride of scones and chocolate-cake, looked welcoming (Libby kept moving the butter and a ray of sun kept finding it again), and mother and daughter, clean and tidy, hoped that they looked welcoming too.

Sad that so much goodwill should be so soon dispelled. Mrs. Pryde, wearing a green frock which buttoned from throat to uneven hem and was clasped around her middle by a belt of many-coloured beads, was an unbeautiful sight against the background of grass and trees. She peered too closely into their faces with her automatic smile and there seemed to be no warmth in her. She asked a few obvious questions, but did not listen to the answers, and directly she had tasted Elizabeth's scones she offered her a receipt of Celia's. At this the warmth faded also from her two hostesses' smiles, and Steven, who had looked forward to his mother's visit, felt uneasily that it was not going quite as he'd expected. He looked from one to another of the smiling, talking women, and wondered whether he was imagining that there was something wrong.

Knowing her mother-in-law's tastes, Elizabeth had planned one or two little amusements for her stay. There was Square Dancing at the village hall, for instance, and there was a Women's Institute lecture. But Aimée Pryde had no zest for these things away from home. Her rheumatism had forced her to give up her folk-dancing, she said, and she did not wish to watch this modern American variety, which seemed rather vulgar, even if the dear Queen had—with her exquisite politeness—pretended to enjoy it. And she could listen to plenty of lectures at Wimbledon. She sat all day under the lilacs, smocking a hideous little garment whose destiny Elizabeth would not inquire. She and her mother felt it their duty to join Mrs. Pryde at intervals, leaving whatever they were doing to sit beside her and make dull and repetitive conversation. Joanna complained that never had she drunk so many unwanted cups of tea. In the evening they felt great relief when Steven, fresh from the Barracks, took over the task of entertaining his mother. But even he seemed to find the evening hours long, when he took her for walks and could not interest her in what they spoke about or saw, or when he played two-handed patience with her in the drawing-room. She had announced on her first evening that she disliked crossword puzzles, and now Joanna and Libby kept *The Times* in the kitchen and sneaked a few moments with it now and then as guiltily as drug addicts.

The weather turned cold on Aimée's last evening and Joanna decided to have a fire. Steven said to his wife, who was helping him to carry logs: "I haven't seen very much of you while Mother's been here, have I, sweetheart?"

"No, Steve, you haven't. I've been good, haven't I, about not butting in?"

"Very good."

Steven kissed her and dropped most of the logs she had balanced on his arms. One fell on his toe. "Damnation!" He hopped round the woodshed in pain.

"Oh, darling, poor love!" Elizabeth couldn't help laughing. She felt her spirits lift at Steven's words. Surely he was really glad that his mother was going next day. "Does it hurt very much? Steve, it'll be *rather* nice to be just the three of us again, won't it?"

"Well, yes," said Steven honestly, "I'm afraid it really will. It's been lovely to have her, of course, but the poor old darling does rather go on about her blood pressure, doesn't she? That and the ghastly Celia, with her little Pledge to the Future, seem to be the only topics."

Elizabeth was emboldened. "Steven, you don't think—Janet said once and I've often wondered since but I haven't liked to ask you—" She broke off, regretting her rashness. You ought to be able to tell *all* your thoughts to your husband (she sincerely believed this), but somehow she wished she hadn't started on this one. She began to pick up the fallen logs.

"Well, ask me now. What did Janet say?"

"Nothing. It doesn't matter. I'd rather not."

"Oh, all right. Come on, load me up; our mothers are getting cold."

Extraordinary of him not to press her. "Steve, just a minute before we go in. Janet wondered if there was something a little odd in your mother's affection for Celia."

"Perfectly extraordinary, I should say. How anyone in their senses can be fond of that lump of a girl—"

"But I mean, could they be—" Elizabeth began to blush and stammer. "Well, they couldn't of course be—well, a little bit, you know, in *love* with each other?"

Steven stood for a moment with his mouth open and a look of disgust on his face. Then he said: "*My mother?* Liz, for heaven's sake think what you're saying."

"I'm sorry. Janet only thought—"

"Janet at least had the decency not to make such a suggestion to me."

"Oh, Steve, I'm so sorry! I didn't really mean it."

"I should hope not. Give me those logs, for the love of Pete, and let's go in."

He left the woodshed without looking to see if she were following, and Elizabeth, thoroughly mortified, went into the kitchen and skimmed the stock-pot. How could she have been so crass? Of course Steven was furious; anyone would be. She felt ashamed yet rebellious, like a child who, encouraged by indulgent grown-ups, has gone too far and been suddenly snubbed.

The evening dragged. Steven was very polite to his wife and very attentive to his mother. Joanna's knitting became hopelessly involved. Elizabeth kindly pulled down all she'd done that day, knitted it up again correctly and handed it back. There was a feeling of strain which affected everyone except Aimée. She, pleased to be going home, hoped that Celia was well and had been taking her vitamin pills, and wondered aloud whether Derek had been able to pop in often and keep the dear child from brooding.

It was a relief to go to bed. But Elizabeth lay long awake, hurt because Steven had kissed her good-night so coldly, and angry because he had at once fallen asleep.

XV

Their next guest was Janet Mortimer, who came down for a week-end, and this visit was unexpectedly pleasant. Joanna's natural diffidence had become, where the Mortimers were concerned, a blend of exasperation with fear. Libby talked incessantly about Janet's coming, and planned meals that would display her choicest dishes, and she even bothered Joanna about the kitchen curtains, which she thought looked dirty and would be noticed by Janet. "I'm certain they weren't washed when you moved, Mummy, and everything of the Mortimers is always so clean."

"No, they weren't. They got forgotten somehow. I'm certainly not going to have them washed for the sake of Janet Mortimer. But if they really are grubby they'd better go to the laundry, I suppose. I shouldn't think they'd be back, though, by next week-end."

And they arrived back, in fact, about half an hour after Janet had come into the house.

Joanna's sense of inferiority was at once illogically allayed by the fact that Janet had a smut on her cheek. This was not Janet's fault, and in no way proved her less than competent, but it soothed Joanna all the same. She felt able to relax and to be kind to her young daughter's pleasant young friend, and Janet seemed happy and not at all intimidating. Perhaps part of her coolly efficient manner had been caused by shyness or by the effort to live up to her mother. ("At all events Libby will never be worn out with trying to live up to *me*!") It was delightful to hear the two girls giggling like a pair of ten-year-olds.

Janet didn't hide her envy of Elizabeth's married state. "Lucky brute, with such a nice husband as Steve and no worries about the future."

"But, Janet, you're always telling me that you don't believe in young marriages and want to get married when you're twenty-five."

"That's quite true. But suppose when I'm twenty-five all the people I like have disappeared and the new ones just don't turn up?" The two girls were sewing on curtain hooks, and at this point Janet interrupted herself to ask kindly: "Have you ever thought of Rufflette Tape for your curtains? We have nothing else in our house, and it would save you all this trouble when the curtains are washed. You simply slip—"

"Thank you, Janet," said Joanna firmly; "yes, we do have it in all the other rooms, but these curtains were given to me, and I really couldn't be bothered to make them all over again."

"I see." Janet broke off a length of cotton. "Well, as I was saying, Elizabeth, it's difficult to be sure that the right man will turn up at the right time, isn't it? I *ought* to be more attractive at twenty-five than I am now"—she glanced dispassionately at her reflection in a glass-fronted book-case—"but you never know, I might get fat or something."

"Well, *I* think if you're not ready to be married at twenty you never will be." Elizabeth sewed smoothly, never knotting her cotton or catching it on a hook. She added: "Look at me! I was ready."

"You couldn't help yourself. You didn't mean to get married young, but when Steve turned up you just couldn't resist him, could you?"

"But the point is that it's not going to stop me doing other things too. Of course, I'm having a holiday at the moment, but when we go abroad I'm sure to find a chance of teaching or something. Marriage doesn't mean stopping everything else."

"It does for a time. I mean to have my children straight away and get them over."

"*Over?*" said Joanna.

"Yes, Mrs. Malling. Then with a good Nanny one can turn back to one's career without fear of further interruptions."

"Well, some people say one should wait a few years," said Elizabeth. "Bung over another hook, Janet. Thanks."

"What do you think, Mrs. Malling?" Janet's inquiry was probably a polite gesture, but Joanna answered it seriously.

"I don't think your wonderful Nanny will quite protect you from interruptions. She'll probably leave you just when the children have measles."

"Oh, no, I don't think so. Not if she gets a good salary and is treated with consideration. People respond, you know, Mrs. Malling, if you treat them as human beings."

"Do they, Janet? Well, I'll tell you what else I think. If someone you really found attractive came along now, you'd forget all about this twenty-five business just as easily as Libby did. Now wouldn't you?"

To her surprise, Janet looked confused. "Well, perhaps I should," she said, and Elizabeth said, laughing:

"Just listen to old Ma! Practically talking about Mr. Right, weren't you, darling? Come on, Janet, tell us if there are any possibilities. What about Paul?"

"Too young," said Janet.

"Ian, then?"

"Well, he's the only possible, but he's only my age, you know, and can't afford to marry for a long time."

"Who's Ian?" asked Joanna.

"He's learning to be a solicitor. His father's firm does a good deal of Father's business and they all come to dinner sometimes. I like them all, but somehow—"

"Oh no, Janet! *Don't* marry a solicitor." Joanna was half amused at her own vehemence. Fancy poor old Tom raising his head after all these years! She had refused him, and that ought to satisfy her, but no! Up came her prejudice as fresh as ever. "They're such a *niggling* lot," she said, rather apologetically.

"I'm afraid," said Janet, "that I'm going to be very difficult to please. You see, Father's so marvellous."

"And so's your mother," said Elizabeth.

"Yes. A perfect relationship in its way. They each respect the other's judgment so much, and that's the most important thing of all."

"Yes," said Elizabeth solemnly.

"Rubbish!" said Joanna, and the girls looked astonished.

"Rubbish?"

"Of course it's rubbish. Do you mean to sit there, Libby, and tell me the thing you like best about Steven is his respect for your judgment?" She stood up, a little ashamed of her vehemence. "But I agree that it's *one* of the important things," she said more quietly. "And I've wasted quite enough time this morning. I'm going to make some coffee now."

Pausing in the passage to straighten a rug, she heard Libby say: "Darling Mummy, how she fired up! She's so romantic, bless her."

That afternoon Mrs. Lane was to come to tea and Steven was to bring a friend over from the Barracks. Joanna felt sure that he would be a dull, honest soldier, but perhaps he would amuse Janet. Almost anything would be better than a solicitor. Steven had announced that he was a nice chap and very good-looking, the sort of chap women liked, and Joanna was instantly certain that she would detest him. Whenever Jack had pronounced someone attractive, she had found him intolerable, and no doubt this would be the same story.

Although it was a Saturday, Mrs. Holmes had obligingly come in that morning, and when the late lunch things were washed and put away, Janet and Elizabeth began to lay tea in the dining-room and Joanna found that she had nothing to do but make herself tidy. It was rather fun to take a bit of trouble over one's appearance for once. Her dark hair, which had for years been unfashionably short, was now, Libby told her, quite up to date. It shone like old oak as she brushed it. She used her lipstick carefully and smiled at her reflection. An olive-skinned girl smiled tentatively back at her. Oh, nonsense! For heaven's sake, Joanna, don't start flattering yourself! She went downstairs, enjoying her white sandals as she planted them on the steps. She seldom wore them, and had meant to give them to Libby, but now she thought she should keep them.

She glanced into the dining-room. The table reflected her transparent old rose-patterned tea-set. Everything looked very nice. She altered the position of a rose in the shallow black bowl. Perfect now. She went into the drawing-room.

Libby and Janet could be heard running upstairs, shrieking with laughter as they went. Joanna, moving ashtrays a few inches and picking up some fallen petals, thought that Libby was at heart a schoolgirl. It was absurd for such a child to try to understand a man like Steven, who had fought in a war. Crossly she threw the petals towards the waste-paper-basket, and then knelt to pick them off the floor. Age didn't come into it. Steven adored Libby. Of *course* he did, and quite right too. She heard a car on the gravel and stood up. How dreadful! she thought, as she went towards the door. How I do detest having people to tea! It's quite the wrong moment to try and be sociable.

The door was opened before she reached it and Steven was bringing in his friend. Joanna wanted to laugh. The friend was well-built and had wavy fair hair, large blue eyes, a small fair moustache and, unfortunately, a small smiling mouth. He greeted her with, she thought unfairly, rather self-conscious grace. She was thankful when Janet and Libby, quite grown-up now and dignified, came down the stairs. They all went out into the garden, and Joanna willed Mrs. Lane to hurry up and arrive so that they could have tea.

Steven went up to change, and the others walked uneasily about the garden until Mrs. Lane's car drove up. Joanna was startled to find that James had also come to tea. He looked enchanting in a little blue sun-suit, but she feared for her cups and saucers. A glance at Libby, however, was enough, and when they went into the dining-room, a mug and thick plate were ready for him and Libby whisked him on to a chair piled high with garden cushions. His mother sat happily beside him and told Joanna how he had *insisted* on coming with her. "I tried to slip away quietly, but his eyes were too sharp for his poor old Ma!" she said.

Tea was not a comfortable meal for Joanna. James grabbed everything within reach, including his mother's cup, on which he burnt his fingers. He ate a few mouthfuls of this and that, and would leave half a sandwich on his plate and reach towards the chocolate biscuits. His mother, who never stopped talking for an instant, would say: "Oh James!" and offer him whichever plate his gleeful dark eyes had lighted upon. She appeared perfectly happy to eat up his cast-offs herself. She had made-up her face very nicely today, so that her prominent cheek-bones were rose-pink instead of mauve. Despite the teeth, she was now seen to be a pretty woman, and Joanna found her innocent pride in her son as endearing as it was exasperating.

The strange young man talked gallantly to Janet, and as that was what he'd been invited for, Joanna supposed she ought to be grateful. Half-extinguished by Mrs. Lane's effortless flow of words, she couldn't hear what the others were saying, but they looked quite happy. She poured out cup after cup of tea until her arm ached, laughed at Mrs. Lane's stories (most of which were told disarmingly against Mr. Lane), and felt a little hurt because no one passed her anything to eat. Elizabeth had made two heavenly cakes and Joanna was hungry. But Mrs. Lane and James on her left were entirely self-absorbed, and on her right Janet's head was turned towards the young man. Only Steven, at the foot of the table, seemed rather silent, and after a time he came round to see what she would like. Joanna felt disproportionately touched.

Amply fed in the end by her son-in-law's efforts, Joanna took her guests out of doors. Steven and the two girls had been making a putting-course in the garden, to be played with walking-sticks and ping-pong balls, and they now started to teach the other young man his way round it. Mrs. Lane preferred to sit in the shade, talking to her hostess and watching her son, who swaggered about, stomach well in advance, and picked, when he felt inclined, Joanna's flowers. He *was* perfectly sweet; Joanna admitted that she had never seen a more captivating child, but she couldn't imagine what would happen to him when he grew older.

The putting sounded hilarious, and Joanna would have liked to play too. Mrs. Lane apparently took it for granted that her hostess was a staid old woman and would rather not. Joanna realized with amused chagrin that she and Mrs. Lane were each deferring to the other. No doubt the mother of a married daughter seemed very elderly to Mrs. Lane. For her part Joanna, forgetting that she was herself forty-one, had written off her guest as well over forty, and wondered how she came to have so young a son. No wonder that the child was spoilt.

Steven came over, very dark and solid against the sunlight. "Mamma, won't you and Mrs. Lane come and play too?"

"What do you think?" asked Joanna of her guest, who answered:

"Oh, we old things rather like to sit in the shade and rest our bones, don't we, Mrs. Malling?"

Joanna smiled politely, and Steven promptly dropped on the grass and said: "Well, *I* should like a rest now. It's hot in the sun. Mamma, won't you take my place?"

"No, Steven, really—"

"Please, Mamma."

"Well—"

"Oh," said Mrs. Lane, "if you're not too tired, my dear, nor am I. Let's all play, shall we? And show the young things what the old ones can do."

As they crossed the grass, Joanna controlled her annoyance. Mrs. Lane clearly thought that in classing them together as 'old things' she was being magnanimous. My God, thought Joanna, eyeing her with hostility; look at her neck! Mine isn't like that, I swear!

Somehow the ridiculous game of golf failed to amuse Joanna. Everyone was very funny, she supposed, from Mrs. Lane, who swung at the ping-pong ball in professional style and flattened it against the front door, to the strange young man who lay down facetiously on the grass and played billiard shots with the end of his stick. But she couldn't laugh until, approaching the last hole, they rounded a big laurustinus and found James at the hole before them. He had hitched up the leg of his sun-suit and, with beautiful concentration—head bent, feet planted—he was making water into the hole.

Joanna gazed with incredulous delight at the rapt child and at the faces about her. Libby and Janet appeared shocked, the two young men had hurriedly assumed boot-expressions and Mrs. Lane was trying not to look proud. Joanna sank on to a seat, quite unable to speak and the tears began to pour down her cheeks. Then the others laughed too, but without her complete abandonment; indeed, they seemed rather concerned at her helpless state. Steven offered her a beautiful clean handkerchief, and she accepted it gratefully. Really, she must pull herself together; she must look ghastly. Odd that the tears should be so reluctant to stop even when she'd finished laughing. It was luxurious to sit there, in full view of them, crying without shame or disguise. They all thought she was crying from too much laughter, and of course they were all quite right. Were they right? She must not be hysterical. It was time to stop. But oh, what a relief it had been! She gave her eyes a final mop and stood up. The others were eyeing her with some embarrassment.

"I'm sorry," she said. "It was so t-terribly funny. What are we going to do now?"

"Well, I don't think we can finish our game today," said Steven, and Mrs. Lane said:

"I'm going to take this *bad* old thing home now. It's nearly his bed-time."

"And I"—said Steven's friend—"must be getting back, too."

So the guests departed and Joanna was left with the three young things, for so she tried to class them. She felt utterly exhausted.

XVI

∞

Janet went back to London and Joanna's household appeared to settle down. But although she often told herself during the next few weeks that her sudden sympathy with Steven was both pleasant and unimportant, she did feel the strain of being, in her own house and in the leisured evening hours, constantly on her guard. The little household was unquiet, and she soon noticed that Elizabeth was not altogether her tranquil self, appearing heavy-eyed in the mornings, and rather more dictatorial than usual. Joanna hoped that this impression was due to her own runaway imagination, rather than to any real change in her daughter. As for Steven, in this one particular she had no idea of his feelings. He was perhaps more resistant to Libby's rule, allowing his moustache to grow wider than ever, and flatly refusing the tonic she prescribed for him, but his manner was impassive, and he looked very well. Tiresomely enough, Joanna now very often knew what he was going to say before he began to speak, and he seemed easily to fill in the gaps in her own elliptical speech. Despite all her care, there were many times when Libby appeared to follow behind, anxiously trying to catch the thought which she and Steven tossed carelessly from one to the other.

She soon mastered the unworthy impulse which, for a few days, had driven her indoors to comb and to powder when Steven was due home in the evenings. Now she would retreat to a far corner of the garden, and involve herself in some active and dirty bit of work; but he usually sauntered out to find her when he had changed, mentioning casually that Liz was busy in the kitchen.

She tentatively suggested to her daughter that the cooking should all be done during the morning, so that when Steven came home he might find a tidy and leisured wife awaiting him. But Elizabeth said that she was perfectly tidy in the kitchen, and added that she thought it very important for Steven to have a good meal in the evening. "We must remember, Mummy," she said, "that he has been ill."

Joanna thought peevishly that no one—least of all Steven—ever had a chance to forget it, but she said nothing.

She was quite dazzled, a few days later, by the sudden idea of Elizabeth's being pregnant. She had noticed regretfully at breakfast that the poor child had two obvious pimples on her chin, a most unusual thing to happen to her, and one which she must feel humiliating. It *would* happen just now, Joanna had thought in exasperation, just when I particularly want her to keep her radiant look for Steven. Libby's whole personality seemed to her mother to be as dimmed as her complexion. With her self-confidence shadowed, her prettiness was shadowed too. But why should she be less than confident? Steven was as affectionate as ever, and never, now, did he try to give his mother-in-law a look of private understanding.

She was washing clothes when the idea came to her, and she stood still, with her wrists submerged in bubbles, gazing at it. Well, of course! If Libby were pregnant, that would perfectly account for the pimples, the irritability, the bruised look below her eyes—for everything, indeed, which troubled her mother. If only, thought Joanna rapturously, it could be *that*, making her look ill, and not my fault at all! From the thought of herself as a grandmother she turned away, shrugging; and she did not for long contemplate Steven as a proud and delighted father. He would, of course, love and cherish Libby *utterly*, once he knew about it. If it were true, she felt certain that Libby had not told him yet.

But the child must tell someone, thought Joanna compassionately. It would be very unlike her to keep it for long from Steven, in fact I should have expected him to have known of the very first indications. Perhaps she is not sure herself. I wish she would speak to me about it, the poor darling.

Squeezing out her own pants and Libby's nylons, she resolved to give her daughter an opening when she could. She left a row of limp garments on the line (for it was a close morning), made the mid-morning tea, and summoned Libby to the kitchen. "Always rather a relief, isn't it?" she said, "when Mrs. Holmes isn't here to entertain us."

Elizabeth sipped her tea frowningly. "To think," she said, "that I might have been riding on a camel at this moment, or scaling a mountain, or—well, anyway, doing something much more exciting than sitting here thinking of puddings." Then the frown relaxed and her sincere and lovely smile appeared. "Not that I don't love being with you, darling! You know I don't mean it like that! But it would be a thrill."

"It will still be a thrill next year, Libby."

"If they don't put it off again. I don't trust them an inch now."

"But surely they need lots of people abroad?"

"Oh yes. And the silly thing is that there are people living in *terror* of a foreign posting who would sell their souls to be in our shoes for a whole year."

"People," hazarded Joanna, squeezing her hands together under the table edge, "with children, no doubt."

"Probably."

"Better to get one's travelling over early," hesitated Joanna. And she added: "Although I believe a young baby travels remarkably easily and well."

Libby looked straight at her. "Does it? Anyway, that sort of thing won't affect us for several years. I wouldn't dream of starting a baby straight away; I don't think it gives one's marriage a fair chance."

"I see," said Joanna slowly. The disappointment was intense. She had been confident that all her problems would be naturally solved, but she had been wrong. So that was that; and now what?

Libby said: "Anyway, I'm going to London tomorrow. That'll be something."

"Yes, it's time you had an outing, but I do hope there'll be some air about tomorrow. It must be death to be in London today."

"I don't feel the heat very much, you know, and I expect Janet and I will pig ourselves with ice-cream at intervals all day." The prospect seemed to cheer Elizabeth. She pressed a silk frock, cleaned her white shoes and bag and looked much happier.

She went off next morning, telling Joanna that she would be back at 5.30. "But of course if I miss that train you won't worry. Good-bye, darling; have a happy day and don't forget to put your lunch in the oven at half-past twelve. Top shelf." She went gaily down the drive, and Joanna looked forward with pleasure to a solitary day.

But it proved disappointing: too hot to garden, much too hot to sort through clothes for the jumble sale, far and away too hot to wash blankets. She had particularly wanted to get the blankets done while Libby was away, but now she supposed she would give in and let Libby and Mrs. Holmes do it. She faced the fact—from which she had been wincing—that today was the day for letter-writing.

When Steven came in at tea-time he found her proud but exhausted. Twelve letters were stacked in the hall, and she told him that she never wanted to write another. He looked at her over his cup and said that she needed some fresh air.

"Yes, Steven, I do indeed; but where is there any?"

"I don't think it's quite so hot out now. Walk down to the bus stop with me to meet Liz."

Joanna looked at him. An ordinary, solid, pleasant young soldier, about whom, owing to the limitations of her daily life, she had been building a ridiculous structure of doubts and questionings. Why not go out with him? It couldn't be duller than sitting here. "Yes, I'll do that. Good idea," she said without interest, and went up to pull a comb through her hair. She didn't trouble about her face, which looked a sort of pale brown, but turned away contemptuously from her reflection. He *hates* flat-chested women, she reminded herself as she went downstairs.

He didn't look as though he hated her. When she joined him in the drive he lavished upon her a smile of such warmth and sweetness that she was awakened from her lethargy. They walked in silence, and Joanna became intensely conscious of herself, of the friction of bare arm against cotton skirt, of the beat of the road under her light shoes and of the sunlight on her cheek. She tightened her lips. She shouldn't have come, but thank goodness Libby would be with them soon, and then she could retire again into the background. I know my place, reflected Joanna, but sometimes it's hard to stay in it.

They walked the half-mile to the village without speaking a word. Joanna was profoundly depressed, and glad that Steven seemed depressed too. Cheerful and edifying talk, she felt, would be beyond her. They waited at the bus stop, forced now into making a few desultory remarks by the presence of various villagers. The bus arrived and Mrs. Holmes sprang forth, followed by two of her children. No one else. Mrs. Holmes seemed disposed to linger, but Steven said: "Come on, Mamma. Let's walk up the hill and come back to meet the next bus." And, Joanna silently matching her step to his, they turned away with such serious faces that Mrs. Holmes told her mother over tea that there was something up, and she didn't like the look of it.

They left the highroad at once, going across fields where cattle grazed. The yellowing grass was strewn with dung, and twice Steven touched her elbow to steer her past an unsavoury deposit. They climbed a stile, and Joanna hurried competently over it to show that she needed no help. The rhythm of the walk eased her and she dreaded any hesitation. The thin grass brushed her bare ankles with the feathery caress that she had loved as a child.

The silence which she had welcomed began to oppress her, but she could think of nothing to say. She quickened her pace up the hill, darting a glance at Steven's uncommunicative profile. She was breathless and her heart bumped. Steven began to laugh.

"My dear Mamma, is this the Derby or something?"

"Oh, Steven, I'm so sorry. I don't know why I was in such a hurry."

"Trying to get away from me, I should think."

"From myself. I'm fed up today."

"Oh, Mamma, I'm so sorry."

His sympathy filled her eyes with tears. She looked away and spoke in a high voice: "Oh, only the weather."

"There's an oak over there that's quite yellow already. The summer's nearly over."

His words sounded unbearably sad, and Joanna's voice shook as she answered him. "Nearly over. I wonder where you'll be next summer?" And she added: "You and Libby."

"I wonder," said Steven mournfully.

"We're in for a storm. Look over there."

"Hectic, isn't it?"

"The sky's literally violet-coloured, and just look at the green—the gold—of those trees!"

"A last hanging out of flags. A sort of defiance."

"Steven, we'd better go back."

"No, no, we must get to the top of the hill first." He caught her hand and began to pull her along. "I'd like to be out in a storm today," he said, and added (*did* she hear him add?) "with you."

They climbed on, while Joanna told herself that Steven had been ill and was in her care and that she ought to take him down to shelter before the rain started. Very true, she answered herself, and went on up the hill, held by Steven's large, warm hand. They stopped at last to watch the rain sweeping towards them. The trees nearby appeared searchlit, every leaf and twig brilliant against the indigo.

"Come on, Steven, I can hear the rain in the valley already. Let's run down."

"I don't want to," said Steven sulkily. He was still holding her hand.

"Well, *I* don't want to get wet, even if you do."

He looked at her with surprised concern. "Oh, gosh! I'm sorry. Let's go. We'll never get to the village"—the first drops plopped around them—"what about that white cottage?"

Joanna didn't want to shelter in any cottage, but she said: "Good idea." They began to run along a cart-track, stumbling in the baked ruts as the rain thickened and made dark discs at their feet. They rushed through a green gate between yew hedges, and up a turf path. Then Steven was knocking at a green door, and Joanna panted: "Oh dear, I believe they're gentry!" and put up a hand to her draggled hair. Steven released her at last as a grating voice called: "Come in!"

It was a very neat little sitting-room, highly polished and exquisitely clean. Whoever looked after it took great pride in the brass, the silver, the copper and the pewter which were everywhere grouped in—to Joanna—excruciating juxtaposition. Flowers cringed in brass shell-cases, lolled in wide silver bowls, peered over the rims of pewter mugs and copper jugs. Joanna found this upsetting.

But far more upsetting was the old man who scrutinized them from a wheel chair, by the window. He sat rigid and hunched, a mauve knitted shawl over his shoulders and a plaid rug on his knees. He had a high, pointed head, almost bald, and little blue eyes. He smiled, displaying two even rows of National Health teeth.

"Oh! Good afternoon," said Joanna. "Thank you so much for letting us come in."

"Er—good evening," said Steven; "very kind of you."

"Come in, come in," said the old man testily. "Don't stand in the doorway like a couple of keepers in a bloody lion-house. What have ye come for, eh?"

"To shelter," said Joanna advancing. "It's absolutely pouring outside."

"Want to see m' daughter, eh? Well, ye'll have to put up with me. She's gone down to the village and left me swaddled like a bloody baby." He made an irritable movement, and Joanna realized that he was crippled.

"Can I help you?" she said timidly.

"Don't know why she's not back by now, leaving me like this," he grumbled. "Always going out shopping and never coming back." His face puckered with self-pity, but he grimaced and began to smile again. "Well, who are ye? Eh?"

"We live at the house in Potter's Lane," said Joanna, speaking very clearly. "We're newcomers to the place."

"Potter's Lane," said the old man. "I know it. Damned ugly house. Been married long?"

Joanna laughed and felt her neck flushing. "No, no, we're not married at all. We—"

The old man found this diverting. "Not married, eh? Wait till m' daughter tells that to all the other old pussy-cats! Not married! Ha! That's good, that is." He shook with silent laughter.

"No," said Joanna. "Steven is—he's—you see, I'm Mrs. Malling, and this is Major Pryde, my son-in-law."

"Ha! Just you wait! What will the parson have to say to you, hey?" The old man struggled impotently in his chair and Joanna hovered, hot and unhappy, not knowing how to help. "Can't you get this blasted shawl off me?" he grumbled, and she took it from his shoulders and laid it aside. He was a shrunken little figure, and in his hand he held a ruler with a handkerchief draped over one end. As she watched, he dabbed with it, ineffectively, at his nose.

Steven advanced towards them, looking, Joanna thought, rather white. "I"—he said with a gesture—"am *son-in-law* to Mrs. Malling. I'm married to her *daughter*."

"Well," said the old man reasonably, "if you've got a daughter you ought to be married! 'Tisn't fair on the child." He chuckled and was seized with a fit of coughing. His face became dark red and the hand holding the ruler wavered so that he seemed to be doing a sort of semaphore. He was obviously in great pain. "Give me a drink!" he wheezed, and Steven was the first to find a jug and tumbler. The old man sucked noisily at the water and spilt some of it down his neck. "Mop me up, can't ye! No, not there, NOT there. Higher up. Can't ye see where I'm wet?" He was in a frenzy of frustration, the terrible rage of having to watch someone else bungling. He seemed satisfied in the end, however, and Steven, tight-lipped, put his handkerchief back in his pocket and the glass on the table.

"I'm sure it's stopped raining," said Joanna. She did not feel she could bear much more.

Steven went to the window. "Well, at least it's not so heavy now. Shall we go?"

"Do let's." Joanna went up to the wheel-chair. "Thank you so much," she said conventionally. "We must go now."

"Go, must ye? Do something for me first." The old man darted a lizard-look at the door. "M' daughter's not back yet. See those jugs on the chimney-piece? Turn 'em round, will ye? M' daughter will put them facing in; I've told her and *told* her I don't like 'em that way! No, no, *no*; those ones are all right. Move the other three. *That's* better!" He sighed with relief and so did Joanna as she stood back from the little jugs, now in orderly single file towards the left.

"Can we do anything else for you, sir?" asked Steven.

"Good-bye, good-bye. M' daughter won't know what to make of those jugs. She'll think I flew!" He laughed and coughed. As they went out he called: "Better think about getting married. This sort of thing won't do in a village, ye know, won't do at all!" They could still hear him wheezing as they squelched down to the gate.

"That—" said Steven in a clenched voice, "—was terrible."

"Ghastly." Joanna shivered. "Is the rain really any less heavy?"

"Shouldn't think so. We couldn't stay there much longer, could we?"

"We could not." Her cotton frock was soaked already and her toes were coldly wet in her shoes. She wondered what to say about the old man's mistake. No doubt it had been funny. They ought to laugh about it now, and when Libby got off the bus they could tell her and *all* have a good laugh. Libby would think it a great joke. The longer she kept silent, Joanna insisted, the more difficult it would be to start speaking. Why didn't Steven say something?

He said: "The poor old bastard," and Joanna began to laugh. It was a relief to be amused, even though she was amused at the wrong thing.

Steven looked surprised. He said: "What is it?"

"You never talk about bastards normally, Steven. That old man's infected you with all his bloodies."

"Sorry. Do you mind?"

"Don't be so touchy. Of course I don't. The person *I'm* sorry for is the daughter."

"She might have let him have his jugs the way he wanted them."

"Yes, she might. But think of looking after him all day." She waited for Steven to comment, but as he said nothing she continued tentatively: "It will make a good story for Libby, won't it?"

"Frightfully good," said Steven nastily, and Joanna said no more until they came to the bus stop.

After all, the rain was stopping as the bus came splashing through the puddles. No one got out, and Joanna began to feel anxious. "Of course there's some perfectly reasonable explanation," she said quickly, to comfort Steven, and he said: "Yes, of course," to comfort her.

"We'd better go home and change. Look, the sun's coming out."

"Come on, then. I wonder what the girl's up to?"

"Missed her train talking to Janet, I should think. I'd better do something about supper; she'll be hungry when she does arrive."

They splashed up the lane, and in a moment Joanna had ceased to worry about her daughter and was thinking only of Steven. He looked haggard.

They were walking side by side but leaving an exaggerated space between them. Joanna tried to see Libby striding along in the middle, in her rightful place between them. Steven was swinging his arms; that was the hand that had held hers. Remember! Libby is here too.

Some familiar lines came into her mind:—

> As 'twixt two equal Armies, Fate,
> Suspends uncertain victory,
> Our souls (which to advance their state
> Were gone out,) hung 'twixt her and me.
> And whilst our souls negotiate there
> We like sepulchral statues lay;
> All day the same our postures were
> And we said nothing all the day.

But that, Joanna cried out in silence, isn't what I want at all! I want Libby between us, not Steven's soul and mine. Oh, what *is* he thinking behind that tired face? He looks so much older suddenly. No wonder the old man—he looks quite old enough—oh, stop, stop!

She quickened her step, and this time Steven didn't try to delay her. They almost ran up the drive.

There was a telegraph boy just coming away from the door.

XVII

❦

The little yellow envelope was addressed to Pryde. Joanna gave it to Steven and said hastily: "I don't expect it's Libby at all. Something quite different, I expect." Her emotions had somersaulted again and she was all concentrated now upon her daughter. She felt sick.

Steven said, "Probably just to say she'll be late." But Joanna knew that Libby wouldn't have wired that message. The child believed that her mother was old-fashioned enough to be alarmed by telegrams, and this pleasant convention had had its effect; she really was alarmed now. Would Steven ever stop fumbling with that envelope?

He unfolded the paper, read it without a word, took one step forward and put his face down on Joanna's shoulder.

She stood still, not breathing. Then she cried out: "Steven, *tell* me!" And his muffled voice spoke against her collar-bone:

"It's Mother. She's dead."

Joanna's knees shook violently. She put her arms round Steven's shoulders and after a moment began to stroke his hair. "Steven. My dear. I'm so terribly sorry." Tears spilled suddenly down her cheeks. The relief of knowing Libby safe and at the same instant the exquisite pleasure of holding Steven in her arms had quite swept away her self-control. It's too much, she thought in delicious self-pity. Oh, it's too much, too much!

Steven lifted his head. "Joanna! You're not crying for me, are you?"

She nodded, dumbly. She really thought it was true.

He took her hand and held it for a moment to his face. Then reason and conscience began to take over and they moved a little apart. Joanna said: "How did she—what happened?"

"A stroke," said Steven. "My God, I never thought this would happen."

- 151 -

"Who wired?"

"The doctor. I suppose I ought to go straight up. There'll be things to do, and I can't let that Celia creature—"

"Tomorrow, Steven. There's no point in going tonight."

"No. No, there isn't, is there? Oh, Mamma, I never expected this."

He's calling me Mamma again now. But he turned to me for comfort; Libby wasn't here. And he called me Joanna because that's how he thinks of me. She said: "You couldn't have known, Steven. Don't for goodness sake start blaming yourself."

"Thank you. No, I suppose that would be stupid." He started to crumple the telegram, then smoothed it out and put it in his pocket. "She died this afternoon. It says, 'Suddenly and painlessly'."

"Thank goodness!"

"Yes. But the dreadful thing is that I never thought she was ill at all. I thought she made an awful fuss about her blood pressure. Didn't you?"

"Yes, I'm afraid I did. But Steven, even if you had realized, you couldn't have done anything."

"I might have stopped her eating all the wrong things. She did, you know. She liked her evening sherry, too. And at least I could have thought of her with more sympathy and—and respect."

"She never knew you lacked either."

"No, she never knew. But *I* know."

Joanna's mind was divided, and to her shame one part was calculating how much the children might benefit from Aimée's will. Surely it would make a difference to them. They could run a car. How extraordinary that she should stand here, with legs like cornflour shape, and a thudding heart—as much moved as she had ever been in her life—and think furtively about money! "You'd better change now and have a drink," she said.

"No, thank you, Mamma," he said formally. And then he looked at her and his face changed. "Yes, perhaps we'd both better. Go and get out of that wet frock. I won't be long, and we'll each have a whiskey."

Joanna went upstairs. He's thinking of me. Oh, Steven! She put on her old dressing-gown and came down. She sat in the drawing-room and closed her eyes. She could still feel his forehead on her shoulder and the strength of his springy hair under her hand. She had looked at that thick hair so often and thought that she would never touch it. She was actually sorry when Steven came in, as though he awakened her from a lyrical dream.

But she took her glass and drank, watching him over the rim.

"I must go and meet Liz now. Surely she'll be on this bus."

"She couldn't expect you to meet all the buses."

"But I must. Of course I must. Mamma, thank you for your sympathy. I'm sorry if I've behaved—stupidly."

"Oh, my dear!" Joanna wouldn't go to him, wouldn't even hold out her hand. Sit still, she admonished herself, or you'll be sorry all your life. "Yes, do go and meet her, Steven, and tell her about it. She'll be awfully upset."

"Right, then I'll go now," said Steven, without moving. "Are you feeling all right now? You looked a bit white."

"So did you. Yes, thank you; the drink has done me good. Do go, or you'll be late."

"All right." He paused, opened his mouth, thought again and quickly left the room.

Joanna considered quite coolly whether she durst go to her room and there, face down upon her bed, cry and cry. But she decided that there wasn't time. Libby would soon be back and would think it very odd if her mother were tear-stained on Aimée's account. Oh God, prayed Joanna, and now she was thinking only of Steven, let her be good to him. Give her kindness and tact.

Elizabeth was delighted to find Steven awaiting her. She had spent a refreshing day with Janet and had been to a film. How had Steven and Mummy got on? Had he met *several* buses, bless him? She chattered gaily, pleased with everything and overjoyed that Steven had awaited her return so impatiently.

They had come to the gate when she paused. "You're not saying much, old Glumboso. Tell me about your day."

Steven took out the telegram. "I'm afraid I've had bad news." He handed it to her.

"Oh *Steve*!" Elizabeth gazed at him with reproach. "Why did you let me go on talking? Why didn't you tell me?" She was frightened and ashamed. She ought to have noticed; she ought to have guessed. She had been childish again and a bad wife. "Darling, how *awful*! How could it possibly have happened so suddenly?"

"I don't know." Steven took her arm and they walked on. She didn't know what to say. What was he feeling? Was he really sad? How would one feel if one's mother were like that, and then she died. Not heartbroken, surely, as one would be if Mummy died. But sorry, perhaps. Yes, surely one would be sorry, and perhaps a little lonely and lost. She glanced at her husband's face. He looked dead tired and rather ill. "Steven, will you please go to bed directly after supper? You don't look well."

"I don't mind when I go to bed."

"Darling, it'll seem better in the morning."

"Why should it?" said Steven, and added, surprisingly: "A night's sleep won't give me back my mother."

"I didn't mean that. I only meant—oh, what can I do to help? Steven"— Libby turned at the door and put her hands on his shoulders—"darling, you mustn't feel alone. You've got me," and she added bravely, blushing, "and don't forget that you've still g-got a mother. You must try to think of Mummy as that now."

She was bitterly hurt when Steven broke into loud laughter.

XVIII

Joanna stayed late in bed next morning. To have watched Elizabeth fussing Steven at breakfast would have been unendurable, and she did not come down until from her window she had watched him leave the house for London.

She found her daughter heavy-eyed and unsmiling. They kissed, commented on the weather (which was still hot) and went in silence about their tasks.

Half-way through the morning Joanna realized that there were none of the broom-bangings and snatches of song with which Mrs. Holmes normally emphasized her labours. She went to find Elizabeth, who was cooking. "What's happened to Godiva this morning?"

"Heaven knows. She's never let us down before, and this is her day for the kitchen floor."

"How maddening of her!"

"It wouldn't be so bad if I'd known. I could have got it done in the time I've been hanging about waiting for her. And if I start now she's sure to turn up just when I'm beginning to *enjoy* it."

"*Enjoy* it, Libby."

"Oh yes, you do, when you've made up your mind to it and got started."

"Well, let's have some coffee now, and then think again. I don't see why the floor shouldn't be left for once. Shall I put the milk on?"

They took their cups into the garden and were relaxing together in sad, affectionate silence when across the lawn came hurrying Mrs. Holmes's mother. "Good Lord!" said Joanna, "something's wrong with Godiva! Mrs. Tomkins never comes here in the mornings." And she went forward to meet her.

Mrs. Tomkins was looking draggled. Her hair was wispy and two of her buttons were in the wrong button-holes. "Oh, Mrs. Malling!" she gasped.

"Good gracious, Mrs. Tomkins, what is it? Come and have a cup of coffee. Is there something wrong?"

"Oh, Mrs. Malling, I do hope you'll pardon me for intruding on your privacy just when you and Mrs. Pryde are having your lunch. But my daughter required me to say that she regrets it will not be convenient for her to oblige you this morning."

Miss Otis! thought Joanna. She said: "Oh dear, I hope she's not ill?"

"Not to say ill, Mrs. Malling. Only a little in—indisposed!" Mrs. Tomkins words went up with a squeak, her face slipped sideways, and drawing a small handkerchief from her sleeve, she held it to her nose in the manner of a weeping film-star. Tears washed unimpeded down her cheeks and plunged into the bosom of her dress.

"Is one of the children ill?" began Joanna. Then, aghast at what she saw, she exclaimed: "My dear Mrs. Tomkins! I'm so sorry. Do tell me what it is." And she laid an uncertain hand on Mrs. Tomkins' shoulder.

"No no! The children are all well, the darling little things. But he said such dreadful things about them!"

"*Who* did?" interposed Elizabeth, interested but baffled.

"Mr. 'Olmes—Holmes!"

"Look now, Mrs. Tomkins!" said Joanna with artificial brightness. "What you need is a nice cup of coffee, and then you will tell us all about it, and perhaps we shall be able to help!" She pushed the woman into a chair, and Elizabeth ran for a cup.

They gave her the coffee, well-sugared for shock, and made her take a cigarette. The first mouthful of smoke seemed to make her feel better. She began to mop up the tears from her face and neck, though Elizabeth was concerned to see that she was too polite to tackle those that had poured down inside her bodice, which must be very wet and tickly.

Her story, when at last they heard it, was melodramatic. Mr. Holmes, it seemed, had come home unexpectedly last night, to find his wife entertaining a friend. Although, Mrs. Tomkins assured them, it had been an evening of limpid innocence, Brenda being found in the kitchen helping her guest with his football coupons, he had immediately misinterpreted the scene and had turned nasty. The other man—a friend of theirs from a boy, and such a nice quiet young fellow—had been thrown from the house, and Mrs. Holmes had been struck and locked into her room. Mr. Holmes had put the key in his pocket, and had then taken a great deal to drink and gone to sleep on the kitchen floor. He was still there, sleeping heavily, and his wife had told the dreadful story to her mother through the bedroom window.

"Still asleep!" exclaimed Joanna. "What time did all this happen?"

"At about four o'clock in the morning," said Mrs. Tomkins unguardedly.

Some football coupons! thought Elizabeth, catching her mother's eye. Aloud she asked: "What about the children?"

"Oh, they're at my little abode. Brenda utilized a crack in the wall to whisper through, and sent them all round to me for breakfast. Only fancy him saying that they are not his, the cruel beast!" Mrs. Tomkins began to cry again. "And Brenda always such a quiet, refined girl from a baby! The times I've said to that girl, 'Brenda, you ought to get out more and make additional friends!' and she always answered: 'I prefer to be at home with my better half!'"

"Oh dear!" said Joanna faintly, and looked to her daughter for help.

"The police," said Elizabeth briskly, jumping up. "Mummy, you stay with Mrs. Tomkins, and I'll just go and—"

"No, no!" said Mrs. Tomkins in horror. "Oh no, Mrs. Malling! Never, *never* have the police had any call to interfere with us. I would prefer to be in my coffin!"

"Perhaps," said Joanna, "he will wake up in a more sensible state of mind. But I really don't think poor Mrs. Holmes ought to stay locked in her room all this time. She must be terribly hungry."

"I'll come back with you, Mrs. Tomkins," said Elizabeth. "Surely there must be another key to fit that door?"

"I couldn't trouble you, Mrs. Pryde." Clearly Mrs. Tomkins was bouncing about between fear of her son-in-law's violence and terror that he might shame her before the ladies.

"I'll come too," said Joanna.

"I really couldn't permit you to be troubled," faltered Mrs. Tomkins, and then with a fresh burst of tears she confessed: "He's—he's got his gun!"

"Oh Lord! In that case don't you think, Libby—"

"Yes, I do." Elizabeth looked very determined. "I'm going to the police *now*! If only the telephone had been put in! They said they'd do it today! Did he threaten her with the gun, Mrs. Tomkins?"

"Yes, Mrs. Pryde!" Mrs. Tomkins snuffled into her handkerchief and was difficult to hear. "He said the most shocking things to her, poor dear; I couldn't *tell* you what 'e said!"

"Right!" said Elizabeth efficiently.

"Oh no!" Mrs. Tomkins actually caught at her skirts. "No, no, don't go for the police!"

"Libby, let's just go down and have a look round first. He may be perfectly all right this morning!"

"But Mummy, while we're wasting time having a look round he might—"

"I don't for a moment think he will." Joanna was not able to fit Mrs. Holmes credibly into a picture of tragedy. Never that vulgar, jolly, joke of a woman! "Oh, come on, Libby. We'll just have a look through the window. It can't do any harm, and we don't want to panic."

They set off down the road, walking fast and taking little notice of Mrs. Tomkins, whimpering at their heels.

It was such a beautiful September day, thought Joanna! Surely nothing frightening could be happening this morning. They climbed a stile and hurried across an orchard, where the grass was parchment yellow and scattered with sheep droppings and fallen fruit. Joanna longed to eat a plum, but she felt that Mrs. Tomkins would think it heartless. Elizabeth, striding like a purposeful angel, showed no interest in plums; she seemed to be taking the absurd Holmes affair seriously. From the next stile they could look down a slope where wheels had flattened the orchard grass in two pale parallels, and could see, at the end of this ghostly track, the roof of the Holmes's cottage. They paused to gaze, and even Mrs. Tomkins stopped talking.

Joanna was suddenly reminded of the beautiful, dewy mornings during the Battle of Britain. Just so peaceful had they seemed. No smoke came from the red chimney ahead, and not a sound came up to ears alert for angry voices or even for the crack of a gun.

"I wish Steve was here," said Elizabeth softly.

Joanna was startled. She had actually not thought of Steven since Mrs. Tomkins' arrival in the garden. Well, she told herself as she climbed the stile, it had been a respite, and it was good to be acting in perfect sympathy with Libby. What fun to tell Steven about this adventure, making a dramatic story of it. Surely, surely the story would not end in tragedy! As they walked silently down the slope she felt suddenly terrified.

Mr. Holmes's dahlias were a gorgeous sight. They crowded the little front garden and brushed their heavy heads against the dresses of the three women who walked quietly up the path. The front door was shut; its brass knocker shone in typical Holmes manner. The windows were shut too, and it was not easy to look through the small panes against which pressed pink geraniums. "I wonder if Mr. Holmes would give me some cuttings," thought Joanna inappropriately. She peered into the room. Certainly he was not on the floor now; the room seemed only to be occupied by flies.

The bedroom window, above, was open, and towards it Mrs. Tomkins addressed a wavering cry. "Brenda! Coo-ee! Brenda, are you there, girlie?" Her compromise between a whisper and a shout would at any other time have been funny. But there was no answer, and the three women glanced at each other's paling faces, and turned to the front door. With unexpected valiance Mrs. Tomkins laid her hand on the latch; the door opened easily, and she started without hesitation to climb the steep stairs, Joanna and Elizabeth close behind her.

The cottage smelt of closed, low-ceilinged rooms, of sunlight through glass, of apples, of furniture polish and of very old clothes. But the window in the front bedroom was open; and here only a suggestion of sweetbriar was in the air. The bed was rumpled, and across it lay a pair of imitation Chinese pyjamas, with dragons on the legs. Mrs. Holmes had brought them proudly home from a second-hand shop, only last week.

All the drawers were open, and the room looked as though a burglar had ransacked it. But Mrs. Holmes, alive or dead, was not there.

After the first sighs of unacknowledged relief, the three women separated. Mrs. Tomkins, tut tutting in a whisper, began to fold the scattered clothes and put them into various parts of the yellow bedroom suite that was Mrs. Holmes' pride. Elizabeth went to look round the cottage, although she felt sure it was empty, and Joanna, suddenly exhausted, sat on the window-sill and picked a sprig of sweetbriar that was trying to climb into the room. She sat sniffing at it, and resting her trembling knees, until Elizabeth came up the stairs at speed and ran into the room. "Mrs. Tomkins!" she said. "There was a note on the kitchen table addressed to you."

Mrs. Tomkins, forgetting her manners, snatched the sheet of ruled paper and pored over it. Then she looked up, smiling beatifically. "'Dear Ma,'" she read aloud.

"'Please keep the kids today. Bert and I are off to Tadwych. He's going to buy me a present. Will drop in tonight.
                    Cheeribye,
                        Brenda.'"

After they had left the palpitating Mrs. Tomkins at her house, and to the care of her five grandchildren, Joanna and Elizabeth walked slowly home together. They both felt limp, angry with themselves and furious with Mrs. Holmes. Elizabeth began to plan how she would cheer Steven up with an account of her terrible adventure. Joanna also strung phrases together, although she ordered herself severely to leave the story to Libby. It might be fun to see Steven's reactions; she only hoped that he would not be too unhappy to show any interest. Doubtless Mrs. Holmes would come round in the morning with the full history. Praise heaven, she felt hungry for lunch.

Coming into the house, they met a smell of burning. "Oh, *Mummy!*" wailed Elizabeth. "My pudding's boiled dry! This has been the most damnable morning!"

XIX

Steven was not expected back until late. He suddenly appeared, however, when Joanna and Elizabeth were having tea on the lawn and discussing yet again what Libby called The Godiva Case. He strode across the garden and dropped on the grass, not seeming to notice his wife's upturned face expectant of a kiss.

Elizabeth jumped up. "I'll get a cup. Oh, Steven, I'd have made a cake, but I thought you wouldn't be back. There's only bread and jam, or would you rather have honey? Shall I make you some toast; it won't take a minute?"

"Sit down, Liz, and don't fuss. I'll share your cup. How are you, Mamma? I didn't see you this morning."

Joanna answered that she was very well. She had a good look at him and decided that he seemed less dejected than she had feared. He looked grim, but excited; he must have news to tell, and she wondered whether she ought to leave him with Libby. But she was so tired, and this was, after all, her garden. If they wanted to leave her, she wouldn't resent it.

She leant back with closed eyes and listened to the two voices. If she hadn't been in a state of humourless gloom she would have found them funny. Elizabeth was bursting with the Godiva story, but determined to be really grown-up and listen to Steven first. As for Steven, Joanna felt that he also had news to impart, but maddeningly he drank his tea, ate his bread and jam and said almost nothing. Joanna thought, from the sound of his monosyllables, that he was looking chiefly at the grass. She hoped vaguely that he wouldn't glance at her, for she knew that she looked antique and a mess. Her chair was comfortable, and it was restful to listen and to take no part. At this rate she would have time for a sleep before either of them came to the point!

"But tell me about your day, Steve." Libby sounded determined. "Did you see Celia?"

"No, I didn't. Can I have some more tea, please?"

"Of course, darling. But why not? Wasn't she there?"

"Thank you. What about you? Have you finished?"

"Yes, the cup's all yours now. Bread?"

"No, thanks. It's cooler today, isn't it?"

"It's cool enough for just sitting. But if you do anything in a hurry, or walk fast—"

"Have you been walking fast?"

"This morning. Well, we had to, didn't we, Mummy? But Steven, where *was* Celia?"

"Out." Joanna could hear Steven stretching himself.

"But she must have expected you?"

"She had gone," said Steven deliberately, "to buy black clothes."

"*Mourning*?" Libby sounded as though she thought it an impertinence.

"I suppose"—something in Steven's voice warned Joanna that he was coming to the point, and she opened her eyes—"I suppose she thought it was the least she could do." He was rather flushed, and was grubbing up moss with his finger-nails.

"From gratitude, you mean?"

"Exactly, Liz. From gratitude. You see, she's the principal legatee."

"The prince—oh *no*, Steve!"

"Oh yes." He took out his penknife and began to attack a daisy root. "She's been left pretty well everything that's of any value at all."

"But when did this happen?"

"Mother must have made a new will just after she'd stayed with us here." The daisy broke off, and he started to dig round another. "Odd, isn't it?"

"But, darling, why on earth? Did we do something that annoyed her?"

"I don't think so. She told old Turner that she'd been thinking while she was away about poor defenceless Celia and her unborn child, and she wanted to make them safe in case anything happened to her. She said she'd missed Celia so much and worried about her." Steven abandoned his digging and cleaned his nails with his knife, which was something Joanna could not bear to watch. She shut her eyes again.

"You saw Mr. Turner, then?"

"I saw Mr. Turner, and he told me the whole thing. If Mother had told me herself, I shouldn't have felt quite such a bloody fool. But as it was, it was—a surprise."

"We could dispute the will, couldn't we?"

"Oh no, Liz, for heaven's sake! She had every right to do it, and no doubt Celia's need is greater than ours. Only I think she might have told me."

"Steve!" Elizabeth was excited. "What did the doctor say?"

"He said he'd told her a thousand times not to eat so much, and not to garden in the hot sun. She wouldn't take any notice. She did it once too often, that's all. Well, you know it was hot yesterday." Opening her eyes, Joanna found him gazing at her, but he instantly looked away.

"And you're quite sure—"

"I'm quite sure, my dear, melodramatic wife, that it was a natural death which we ought to have been prepared for. She was stooping over the herbaceous border and—well, she never came to."

"Very merciful," said Joanna.

"Very," he said crisply. "Turner tried to dissuade her, of course, but she knew what she wanted."

"The house?" said Elizabeth.

"Oh, that's ours. Heavily mortgaged."

"Well, that's something."

"Indeed it is. When Mother bought that house I put down a thousand pounds, and a building society did the rest. What my mother has kindly done is to leave me in her will the thousand pounds she owed me. That's all."

"Oh, darling!"

Steven looked at his mother-in-law. "You haven't commented very much, Mamma," he said accusingly. "What do you think?"

"I'm very sorry," said Joanna.

"I'm not." Steven stood up. "I wish I was sorry. I'm bloody angry, and it's a very bad thing to be angry with one's mother when she's only just dead." He looked in surprise at his hands and put the penknife back in his pocket. "I think I'd better go and wash," he said, and walked away.

Elizabeth started to follow him, but came back again to her mother. Her face was bright pink and she was almost in tears. "Mummy, isn't it abominable? Poor, poor Steven!"

"Ghastly," said Joanna.

"And after all the help he's given her. She's had a monthly allowance from us, you know. Shall I—would you go to him if you were me?"

"I don't know, darling."

"He almost seemed angry with us, didn't he?"

"He's had such a shock, and he feels hurt and humiliated."

"What shall I do?"

"I can't advise you, Libby."

I can't, she thought, and I mustn't. Poor Steven! if only he wouldn't feel so bitter. There's nothing I can do, nothing at all. I expect he's forgotten all about yesterday.

"What a shame!" said Elizabeth thoughtfully. "Now I can't tell him about Godiva. It wouldn't amuse him a bit."

"Perhaps after supper it would. Why not take him for a walk now? And—perhaps not say much about anything at all." Damn! Now I've advised her, and I particularly didn't want to.

"I'll try; that's a good idea. But of course," said Libby, with a grown-up air, "he may *want* to talk to me about it. It may do him good. Just the two of us."

"Of course, darling. I do hope so."

Elizabeth went soberly indoors, feeling her responsibilities. She forgot the tea-things, and Joanna found enough energy to take them in herself. She thought that she would develop a headache and spend the evening in bed. She simply could not be with Steven in his present state and do nothing to help him. Libby, poor child, must cope.

Elizabeth had her walk with Steven and spoke very little and only on neutral topics. She was rewarded when Steven's rigid shoulders gradually relaxed and when at last he took her hand. They started the walk at a gallop and finished it, to her relief, sauntering arm in arm. But this had been achieved simply by listening to Mummy's advice. Elizabeth wished that wifely intuition would tell her what to do next.

She was glad to find that her mother had gone to bed, and she cooked Steven's supper and did not coax him to eat more than he wanted. She watched his face with loving anxiety, and as the evening passed, and she thought all the time of Steven, not of herself, something quite new came into their relationship. She no longer thought of managing Steven, but only of comforting him, and she did not watch with approval her own efforts.

He began to talk in the end, releasing his bitter feelings, and she listened almost in silence. When he had finished she told him of her day, not dramatizing the Godiva affair but letting him have the whole story. To her delight, he was really interested and asked a great many questions. They sat on the sofa together and she leant against his shoulder while he told her that she'd been very brave and he did wish he could have been there to look after her.

And then he said something perfectly astonishing. "Liz, about that house?"

"Your mother's, do you mean?"

"Ours now, provided we go on paying the Society."

"Yes, Steven? What about it?"

"How would it be if we tried living in it?"

"When we've been abroad, do you mean?"

"No, I mean straight away."

"But your work's here!"

"Lots of people travel to and fro."

"They travel *up* to London and then *down*. Not the other way."

"Nice to be different."

"But, darling, are you utterly loops? The trains would be all wrong, and you'd be dead tired, and what on earth would Mummy think?"

"She wouldn't mind, would she?"

"You haven't quarrelled with Mummy, have you, Steve?"

"No, of course not."

"Then why—"

"Liz, my darling. We're man and wife. Did you know?"

"Some of our activities would be awfully odd if we weren't."

"Then let's live alone and think about each other, and build our marriage up into something really solid."

"Oh, Steven, it *is* really solid! We love each other and understand each other, and we're happy!"

"I don't think we do understand each other yet. I don't believe couples do for the first year or so. A marriage has to go on growing. Let's give ours room to grow."

"But Mummy!"

"She's so understanding that she wouldn't be hurt."

"She wouldn't *show* she was hurt. Not to you, anyway. But *I* should know. And the poor darling's so loved having us! Oh no, Steve, we truly couldn't."

"Elizabeth Pryde, will you please come away and live with me, all by ourselves? I'm asking you very seriously."

Elizabeth felt blissfully happy. Sometimes lately she had doubted her importance to Steven, but she need not have worried. "Darling, no, I won't!" she said. "I'd love to, but it wouldn't be fair. Steven, have I been giving too much time to Mummy? I won't any more. I didn't realize"—her voice grew shy, and she ended in a whisper—"how much you needed me, my love."

Steven sat still for a moment with his arm round her. He looked down in exasperation at his wife's amber-coloured head. Then he kissed it and stood up. "There's just time," he said, "for a pipe before we go to bed. I wonder if Godiva will put in an appearance tomorrow? Cigarette, darling?"

"Please." She puffed for a moment and then threw it into the fireplace, where Steven obligingly extinguished it. "All the cigarettes in this house are stale," she said. "I haven't had a decent smoke for days."

"I'll get you some tomorrow."

"Thank you, Steve. Yes, Godiva. Will she turn up, do you suppose? I'm dying to hear what happened."

And sure enough on the Saturday morning, just after Steven had left the house and while Joanna and Elizabeth were still at the breakfast table, Mrs. Holmes bounced merrily in. "Yoo-oo!" she cried. "Where are you, Mrs. Malling? Oh,'ulloh! *And* Mrs. Pryde. Well, that's nice and cosy. Turned colder, hasn't it?" She sat down, beaming, and hitched her bosom into position. "I was ever so sorry I couldn't help you yesterday, dear," she said, "but me old man took me for a outing. Look!" She held out a round arm—very pretty and white-skinned above a roughened hand—on which jingled a charm bracelet.

"Oh, Mrs. Holmes, how pretty!"

"Oh, isn't that sweet!"

"Nice, isn't it?" She fingered the little elephant, the Snow White, the jeep and the other toys with which it was hung. "I *told* Mum not to worry 'er head about my 'ubby. I knew 'e'd come round fast enough when I told 'im me news." She lowered her voice. "I'm expectin' again!" she said proudly. "But don't you worry, Madam; I won't let you down. I can go on workin' till the end and then I daresay Mum will oblige till I'm back."

"*Well*!" said Joanna dazedly. "That's—that's very nice news, Mrs. Holmes!"

"'E's not such a dusty old stick! Just turned nasty for a minute, 'e did, but it soon blew over. Do anything for me, he would." She got up and took her apron off its hook. "Course I wouldn't like to do any *lifting* just now," she said importantly, "but I can always scrub."

"Thank you, Mrs. Holmes; that's very good of you," said Joanna breathlessly, and she left the room, hoping that Libby would follow her. But Libby lingered for a moment, to take a cigarette. "But will you be *able* to work, Mrs. Holmes?" she asked, lighting it. "Won't you feel sick?"

"Well, the sink's 'andy," said Mrs. Holmes placidly.

Elizabeth threw her cigarette impatiently out of the window, and Mrs. Holmes chuckled. "Don't feel like smoking, do you, dear? I can't fancy a cigarette neither. You'll come back to them about the sixth month." She paused in the doorway. "Never mind, dear! I always say there's many a slip!"

Luckily Mrs. Holmes made a neat exit, on this cryptic remark, or Elizabeth would have been rude to her. She stamped indignantly upstairs and into her bedroom, where Joanna found her, a moment later, poring anxiously over a small diary. "Darling!" said Joanna, "isn't that the most sublime answer to the Godiva problem? I'd never have believed it, would you?"

Elizabeth looked up, with an effortful smile. "Yet another little illegit for him to father," she said. "It certainly seems an odd thing to content him."

"Born in wedlock, Libby, and it might just as well be his. In fact as far as that goes they may *all* be his."

"And they really were doing football coupons? Be your age, Mummy!"

But somehow the Holmes subject was beginning to pall, and in a moment the two women separated to do their morning's work. Steven would be back at lunch-time—a prospect that occupied the minds of them both. Elizabeth was not hungry, but she cooked the joint, rather hoping that her lack of appetite would be noticed. She was less efficient than usual this morning and became very tired, but at least she would be free for Steven tomorrow, instead of spending her Sunday morning in the kitchen. At half-past twelve, hot, sticky and with an aching back, she went upstairs to wash, and it was then that the new telephone rang its bell. A moment later Joanna called up the stairs: "Steven won't be back to lunch; he's got to work all afternoon."

"Great *God*!" said Elizabeth, who seldom blasphemed. She appeared at the head of the stairs, comb in hand. "Why on earth didn't he ring up earlier?"

"He just said he was sorry."

"Oh, Mummy, and I've sweated blood over the lunch! I'd have waited till tomorrow if he'd only let me know. What's the good of cooking a great joint and roast potatoes just for you and me? And the plum pie really is perfect! I've done the supper too, so that I'd be free to spend the afternoon with him!"

"Don't let's cut the plum pie. We'll have it tonight."

"Would you mind? Oh, but I've done a trifle for tonight."

"Tomorrow's lunch, then."

"Yes, that would do. We'd better go and carve that wretched joint anyway. Come on, Mummy. *Blast* Steven!"

The afternoon dragged by. Rain fell, and a damp breeze searched out the innermost corners of the house. It would be nice, thought Joanna, to light a fire and have tea before it with hot buttered toast; but of course she couldn't afford either the logs or the butter. She wrote cheques and then sewed, while Elizabeth bent herself round a book, in a position that her mother would have reprimanded a few months ago.

Steven came in for tea. He greeted them curtly, without apologizing to his wife, and proceeded to eat an enormous meal at a rate that would surely injure his digestion. He admitted that he had had no lunch, and Elizabeth forgot her injuries and tried to persuade him to have an egg. Steven showed no gratitude for her care, but only irritation, and at last Elizabeth retired in hurt silence behind the barricade of her book. She had tactfully not mentioned Steven's recent illness, she hadn't scolded him about the lunch, and now look how he was behaving! And this was the man who'd wanted her to live in Wimbledon for his sake.

Joanna could willingly have slapped the two of them. She left the room without a word and escaped by the back door for a walk. She loved them both so much, and they were being so idiotic! How could she possibly help them? If there had been any near end to this intolerable situation she thought that she could have endured it, have played a part every moment of every day and then, when the danger was past, have had a nervous breakdown all by herself. But no living woman, feeling as she felt, could feign detachment and push the others into adult behaviour, and go *on* doing these things for months. She was furiously angry, and her anger refreshed her; it was infinitely less painful than tenderness.

Unfortunately she was incapable of sustained anger with Steven and Libby. She told herself that Steven was behaving like a boor,—but had he not sufficient excuse for boorish behaviour? And Libby was indulging in self-pity—well, could she be blamed? I'm full of it myself, mourned Joanna, but being old (yes, *old)* I can hide my feelings.

What was Steven feeling about her? This was the one question that perpetually troubled her, and now, walking home in the evening, she allowed herself to examine it. Did he feel as she felt, or was she building a mountain from her own emotions alone?

Whenever she went over that scene in the hall when he had opened the telegram she felt certain that Steven loved her, and that his anguish was like her own. She knew it with an almost religious conviction. But she was so habitually unsure of her own attraction that she longed to have this faith confirmed. If she could once hear Steven say that he loved her, she felt that she should need nothing more.

To want so desperately what must ensure Libby's unhappiness appalled her. She kept insisting that Steven's love was the last thing in the world she wanted, and that to blame everything on her own imagination would content her; but she didn't believe a word of it. She dreamt ceaselessly of a full-dress renunciation scene, when she would say wise and noble words that he would always treasure, and Steven would say only that he loved her, he loved her. With this memory to brood upon, she thought that the remainder of her life would be tolerable; without it she would never really know whether she had made a fool of herself.

She came home slowly, fighting a battle. She thought that she would take care that evening not to be alone with Steven, and yet deep within her something calculated how she might be alone with him by accident, and not by her own fault. She would go early to bed and so avoid him. If she came down later in search of a book he might—she must be careful to make no noise or he might hear and join her. That was the one thing she wanted to avoid, she kept repeating.

She was in a turmoil when she came back to the house, but she washed, brushed her hair and helped Libby to carry in the supper as though this were an ordinary evening. Extraordinary how well one could make oneself behave.

After supper she waited until Elizabeth was in the drawing-room and then followed her, bringing an armful of knitting-wool, with which she sat down on her favourite window-sill.

Steven slouched in and stood by the small fire, filling his pipe, and then Elizabeth remembered that she had left the tea-towels out. She went to fetch them, declining Steven's tepid offer of help, and Joanna, caught where she dared not wish to be, bent defensively over her hank of wool. She broke open a skein, and slipping it over her fore-arms, began to wind.

Steven put down his pipe with a little click on the mantelpiece. His footsteps came towards her, and within the circle of her vision appeared his grey trouser legs and a pair of brown sandals of the Indian type. His socks, showing at the toes, displayed Elizabeth's beautiful darning.

Joanna felt a little dizzy, and his voice, after a long silence, hummed oddly in her ears. "Let me hold your wool."

"No, thank you, Steven!" Joanna wound faster, and became entangled. "I like doing it myself," she said breathlessly as she tried to sort it out. "It fidgets me to feel there's someone waiting for me to finish."

"I don't think your way is very successful," said Steven with a hint of laughter in his voice. He bent to pick up her escaping ball of wool. "Don't be obstinate, Joanna. You'd much better let me help."

"No, thank you, Steven!" Joanna's hands shook, and she pulled impatiently at the skein. She could not bear Libby to come back and find Steven domestically holding her wool. "Really," she added on a note of rising hysteria, "I'd rather you didn't."

Elizabeth came in to find her mother, white-faced and with startled dark eyes, gazing up at Steven, while he apparently struggled for her knitting wool. His whole posture, as she saw it from behind, spoke of masculine possessiveness, and Joanna's, as she shrank back against the window, of weak and provocative womanhood.

Elizabeth stood still for a moment, with her heart somersaulting. Then she went over to a chair and sat slowly down with her back to the window. Joanna's voice—an arch voice—came to her hostile ears. "Please, Libby"—laughed the voice—"ask this husband of yours to let me wind my own wool my own way!"

"This husband of yours!" Joanna was aghast at herself. She never talked like that; what on earth would Libby think? She heard her daughter's voice as though from a distance: "Let him help you if he wants to," said the voice disdainfully, and at that Steven left her suddenly, and began to wander vaguely round the room, looking for his pipe.

"On the mantelpiece," said Elizabeth crisply.

"Thank you, darling," said Steven. He sat down beside her, without a glance at Joanna. "What are we going to do tomorrow, Liz?" he asked. "Can you come out with me for the whole day?"

"It's going to rain."

"Oh, damn the rain. I expect the B.B.C.'s wrong, and anyway I don't object to the rain very much, do you?"

"I don't think it's exactly ideal for a picnic." The derisive, high-pitched voice didn't sound like Libby.

Joanna, at whom neither was looking, leant her head against the shutter and pressed her cold hands over her eyes. "Oh, God, help me!" she prayed.

Steven was silent for a moment, and Elizabeth spoke again: "Of course, if we had a car—"

"Yes, wouldn't it be fun? We will have one some day."

"It's surprising how many Majors do have cars."

"Yes, isn't it? They must have private means."

"Oh, Steven, you always say that about everybody. They can't *all* have private means."

"Then they're permanently overdrawn."

"Does it matter?"

"Liz, you know how I feel about that."

"Yes, Steven, it's all very well for you. You go off every day to Tadwych, and you meet hundreds of new people and do interesting things, but I'm stuck here, cooking meals which you don't turn up to eat—"

"I'm sorry about that, and anyway, it was the first—"

"And I never see a soul."

"Liz! There's the whole village!"

"The village! Just because I haven't grumbled, you've thought I *liked* doing all the things they're too damned incompetent to do for themselves!"

"Well, don't you like it?"

Elizabeth's honesty was a nuisance. "In a way. But you don't imagine I could go on for a whole year, do you? It's all so petty compared with what the Mortimers—for instance—are doing."

"Oh, the *Mortimers*!"

"Well? What about them? Don't you like my friends?"

"Of course I like them, but one can have too much of any good thing."

"You were very glad to make use of them when you were ill!"

Steven drew a deep breath and slowly let it escape. He remembered, at last, to light his pipe. Then he said gently: "Liz, sweetheart, I didn't know all this. You ought to have told me you were getting bored. Perhaps I ought to have guessed. Anyway, let's do something nice next week, shall we? Like to go up to a show or something?"

"The trains are awfully awkward after a theatre. Now if we had a car—"

"But we haven't and can't have. We just can *not* afford it, at least until Mother's affairs are settled and I know where we stand."

"You said we could afford to go and live in her house straight away!"

They had both forgotten Joanna's presence. She sat listening in rigid silence.

"That," said Steven slowly, "was rather different. If the trains are awkward we'll go up and stay the night."

"It might be rather fun." Libby's voice sounded softer.

Steven said gently: "Let's make a bargain. If you'll come up with me and go gay for once, I'll make a colossal effort and do something about my moustache."

Joanna, cautiously moving one cramped knee, dropped a pair of knitting-needles on the floor. They clattered like a thousand milk-cans.

"*Oh!*" said Elizabeth. She turned right round and stared at her mother. Then, with a gasp, she said: "I suppose *you've* said you don't like his moustache!"

Steven jerked to his feet. "This is intolerable!" he said, and banged out of the room. The front door crashed behind him.

"Oh!" sobbed Elizabeth. She fumbled her way, weeping, from the room and crept upstairs. Joanna was left alone.

After a moment she stood up, deliberately. The crisis had come now, and she was going to deal with it. She felt quite calm, but her legs, as she crossed the room, might have belonged to someone else. She followed her daughter upstairs.

Elizabeth lay face downwards upon the bed, sobbing and shuddering. She could not have heard her mother come in, but when she felt a hand on her shoulder she jerked it violently away.

"Libby," said Joanna to the wreck of her pretty, well-balanced daughter. "Libby! Stop this nonsense at once and listen to me."

One of Libby's eyes appeared over her arm; it glared incredulously.

"If you go on sobbing like that," said Joanna, as she had said it years ago to her little daughter, "I can't understand a word you say." Elizabeth, who had not attempted to speak, became noticeably quieter. "For goodness sake use some self-control. That's better. Now, then, my darling child, tell me what all the fuss is about."

"He—you—Steven—"

"I know he's cross with you at the moment, but he'll get over it. You did rather nag him about the car, you know."

"It wasn't that!"

"Then in heaven's name what was it?"

Elizabeth sat up slowly and stared at her mother, with mistrustful eyes. "You know quite well what's the matter!"

"I thought it was about a car, but you say not. Was it because he was late for lunch, then? I admit it was exasperating, but aren't you reacting in rather an exaggerated way?"

Elizabeth looked at her with fathomless reproach. "How could you, Mummy? You know it wasn't that."

Joanna sighed. "In that case, you were using the small things as pegs to hang a quarrel on because something more important had hurt you. I don't ask to be told what it was, it's entirely between you and Steven, but if you've got to squabble, I do think you might refrain from doing it in my drawing-room. All newly married couples have their little hells to go through, but as you're unlucky enough to have to share a house you might try to be civilized about it." Libby was gazing at her in bewilderment; there was no wind left in her sails. Joanna allowed her voice to soften. "Darling Libby, the first year of one's marriage is awfully painful, I know. You think that you're absolutely at one with someone, and the next moment they do something you can't understand and you feel utterly at sea, and so terribly disappointed." Libby began to cry again, but quietly, and putting her hand into her mother's. Joanna held her breath for a moment before she went on speaking. "I think I can guess what the trouble was," she said, and the hand in hers twitched. "Don't tell me if I'm right or wrong, but you said something about Aimée's house. Didn't Steven want you to go and live there, and didn't you refuse because of me? No, don't say anything! Sweetheart, it was just like you to be so kind to me, but you were wrong, you know. No wonder you and Steven are getting irritable; your marriage isn't having a chance here. Please, Libby, do change your mind and tell him you'll go."

"Oh, Mummy, I do feel such a beast. I thought—I don't know how I could have thought it! I really was beginning to imagine—"

"If you only thought it, whatever it was, don't tell me about it, darling. Everyone has loathsome thoughts at times."

"But Mummy—" Elizabeth was longing to confess, and Joanna felt that somehow or other she must be prevented from doing so. Once put those suspicions into words and they would never be forgotten. She interrupted in a hurry: "If you're worrying about the things I've done to the house, darling, you really needn't. They'd all have had to be done sooner or later, you know, and in any case I think I'll take in some p.g.'s."

"*You?* Take in p.g.'s?" Elizabeth was dumbfounded.

"Yes, isn't it a good idea?" improvised Joanna. "I need hardly see anything of them, you know, and directly I've saved enough money to have a few repairs done and a bit of redecorating I'll turn them out into the snow."

"They'd pay for having the house whitewashed."

"That, certainly."

Elizabeth was growing interested. "What'd you sting them for?"

"Much more than I did you, anyway! Oh, darling, don't think I haven't loved having you; you *know* it's been heavenly for me. But"—she hesitated—"but, Libby, although we like each other very much, I don't think Steven and I are ever quite at ease together. Probably it's because we both try too hard; you know how it is when you feel you have got to hurry a friendship up instead of letting it grow gradually. It becomes a strain at once."

"I suppose that's true. I do feel ashamed of myself, Mummy. Do you think Steven will understand at all? I don't know how I could have been such an idiot." She began to blush, as she recognized the full enormity of her suspicions. The impulse to confess had passed, and now she wanted to bury for ever her revolting thoughts. Red-faced and humble, she swung her legs off the bed and went over to the dressing-table. "Heavens, what a sight! I hope Steve won't come in yet. I'll just wash my face," she said, as she went to the door. "Don't go, Mummy."

Joanna fell on to the bed and laid her head on Libby's wet pillow. She had just been through the worst hell of her life—an agony which seemed to her now incomparably worse than the death of her husband. Jack had died loving her, and no one had been to blame. But for Libby to be hurt—mutilated—by *her* fault—

She drew an enormous breath and sat up, for Libby was coming back. The poor child was very white now, and crept in looking shamefaced. "I think perhaps I'll go to bed," she said wearily. "I hope Steve won't be long." She sat down at her little davenport, lifted the lid and started to brush her beautiful hair. Joanna watched her through the looking-glass. "Mummy," said Elizabeth, avoiding her eye. "Such a funny thing. I'm six weeks late!"

"Do you mean—"

"Yes," Libby was trying to sound casual. She began to move things about in the davenport. "Isn't it odd? It's never happened before—two or three days at the most!"

"But then, surely, darling—"

"Well, but it's ridiculous, Mummy! I've done *everything* that woman told me—well, practically everything. It can't really be true. I must be run down, I think."

"Six weeks, Libby? That's twice!"

"Yes, that's what's so extraordinary. Do you think—"

"Darling, of course I do. How perfectly lovely!"

Sitting on the bed, she held out her arms, and after a moment Libby came and sat beside her, resting her head on her mother's shoulder.

Joanna sat with her cheek against the shining hair. She had hardly thought of Steven since he slammed his way out of the house, but now, welling up within her and pouring out over her love for Libby, came an intolerable flood of envy. She was old, withered, done, her days of delight over; but she could have blossomed again, she could have made Steven a better wife than Libby ever would, she could have had his child and made him happy.

Libby's voice, a murmur close to her ear, mercifully interrupted her. "I shall feel such an idiot telling Steve. I was so awfully cocksure. I just said, 'Don't worry, leave it all to me', and he believed me! I've been so *inefficient,* Mummy!"

Joanna suddenly began to laugh. "Darling," she said, "it's a good thing to be inefficient now and then! Steven will adore you for it."

In the moment's silence that followed they both heard the front door shut softly. Joanna stood up: "You'll tell him at once, Libby, won't you? And go to sleep happy?"

"I suppose I shall have to." As Joanna left the room, Libby hurried back to the looking-glass. "Thank you, Mummy; you've been an angel." She picked up her powder puff.

"Good-night, my darling," said Joanna. She went to her own room. She was shivering violently and her teeth actually chattered as she lay down on her bed. But in a moment, instead of the thoughts she fearfully expected, there came to her the blest annulment of sleep.

XX

Joanna had the pleasure and pain next day of watching Steven, very quiet and grave, taking care of Elizabeth, who was like a convalescent with her weak smile and her humility. She left them together as much as she could, went to church in the morning and for a sedative walk after tea, and was glad that Libby went early to bed and Steven carried up her supper and his own.

All three of them were tired—too tired to feel at all excited about the baby. But they wouldn't be tired for ever, and soon, Joanna told herself, she would have to watch Libby becoming dedicated and Steven possessive. All men liked to prove their virility by becoming fathers, just as though the world suspected them of impotence. She tried unsuccessfully to find this funny.

Steven went to his mother's funeral, but did not speak to Celia. He wrote to ask when she would be leaving the house, and she replied by inviting him to go and see her. He read out this letter at the breakfast table, and the three of them agreed that there was no need for him to go. No doubt she wanted to stay on; well, let her write her appeal, instead of dragging him away from his work. He asked her to state her business by post. The week dragged by, and once again it was Saturday afternoon.

Steven decided to mow the lawn, and for this purpose he undressed and put on a pair of bathing-trunks which were rather moth-eaten, but not, Elizabeth assured him, where it mattered. She also felt a craving for sunlight, and put on her bathing-dress, thinking, as she fastened the straps, that she would not be able to wear it for long. At present her stomach was as flat and her waist as neat as ever. Perhaps never again, she mourned, shall I enjoy my reflection like this; really it's very noble of women to have babies! I'm horrid, but at least I'm noble too.

Joanna felt hot. She put on an old pair of linen slacks, an aertex shirt and a bent straw hat. Fork in hand, she disappeared across the garden, leaving the young Prydes in possession of the lawn. "Mummy," said Elizabeth, as Steven fixed her deck-chair, "is very retiring these days. I think she suspects that we like being alone!" She beamed up into her husband's face and he kissed her, in a preoccupied way, and went to get the mowing-machine. Dear Steven! she thought. He's so solemn and protective! He thinks I'll break or something. It's rather fun, but when we get into the house I must show him that I'm really quite fit.

Elizabeth shut her eyes. The leaf-shadows flickered on her eyelids and she could hear the mower complaining over the gravel. Now it was on the grass; it settled down to a steady conversational hum and she wriggled in warm comfort against her cushions and fell asleep.

Steven awakened her: "Liz! A car!"

"Oh dear," she said, blinking. He was bending over her, his rather hairy chest heaving and wet with sweat. "Darling, you do look hot. Who is it? Are they in the drive?"

"Yes, blast them! Look."

Through the lilac trees, which were not yet shedding their leaves, she could see a green car, one of those fat cars that she had christened 'Mr. Facing-Both-Ways'. A man slid out of the driver's seat. He wore a green sports shirt with a scarf tucked into the neck, and his grey flannel trousers were so pale as to be almost silver. "Who on earth"—murmured Steven— "can he be? Oh, they must have come to the wrong house. They'll realize in a minute."

"No, Steven. Don't you see it's Derek?"

"Derek who?"

"Celia's Derek, of course. Look."

Derek walked round the car and opened the nearside door. A bulky figure struggled slowly out and stood revealed as Celia, still wearing a smock and wearing it now to considerable purpose. She took his arm, and they walked slowly to the porch, where they rang, no doubt, the bell.

"Oh, my *God*!" said Steven, "why have they come here? I don't want to see them. Where's my shirt?"

"Indoors," said Elizabeth, with dreadful calm. "And so are all my clothes. What shall we do?"

"Can we get round to the back door?"

"They'd be sure to see us."

"They've seen us now. Liz, my girl," and he grinned at her, "we are caught at a considerable disadvantage."

The two visitors advanced. Derek was swaggering and Celia hung back modestly on his arm. Elizabeth and Steven, feeling naked, came to meet them with dignity. "Good afternoon," they said.

Derek answered, "How goes it? Having a bit of sunshine?"

"Come and sit down," said Elizabeth primly.

"I'll get another chair," said Steven.

"No, no. Mother Nature's good enough for me!" Derek helped Celia tenderly into a chair and she handed him a cushion, on which he sat. "As you couldn't come to see us, Major, we thought we'd take a spin into the country and see you. Quiet here, isn't it?" He looked about him.

"If you'll excuse me," said Elizabeth, "I'll go and put on some clothes."

"Don't do that, Mrs. Pryde!" cried Derek. "We like you as you are, don't we, Major? Do give us a treat."

Elizabeth stalked away with a petrified smile on her face. It was mean of her to desert Steven, but she could not stay to be ogled by that man. Loathsome creature! If he had been less obtrusively male she might have ignored him, but she had felt every inch of her skin under his eyes. She hurried upstairs.

When she came down she left the house by the back door and ran to find her mother. "Darling, I've come to warn you. We've got visitors."

Joanna straightened her back. It ached and she rubbed the muscles behind her waist. "Oh, hullo, Libby! Who are they? Mrs. Lane and James? Have we any cake? They said they'd come one day soon."

"It's Celia and Derek, Mummy. Isn't it awful? And poor Steven's got practically nothing on!"

Joanna began to laugh. "Poor, *poor* Steven! Well, you hadn't much on last time I saw you. What on earth have they come for?"

"I can't imagine. It's much too early for tea. I shan't ask them to stay."

"Oughtn't we to show there's no ill-feeling? Particularly as in fact there's quite a lot of it. Oh well, see what happens. Do you want me?"

"It would help if you blew in a little later. Could you bear it?"

"I couldn't bear not to. I must see the famous Celia. Has she washed her hair?"

"It doesn't look like it. And Mummy, she's *enormous* and she's wearing a mauve smock and a black skirt! Mourning, you see."

"And what's Derek wearing?"

"A scarf with fox's masks and horse-shoes and riding-crops all over it. And I bet," said Elizabeth with bottomless contempt, "that he's never even *seen* a horse! I must go back to Steve. Don't be too long."

"I won't."

Elizabeth hurried away to join the group on the lawn. She found Derek holding forth about his car while Steven listened with a blank face. Neither of them was taking any notice of Celia, who looked extremely uncomfortable in her low chair.

Elizabeth said: "Here, Steven, would you like these?" and handed him some shorts and a shirt.

"Thank you very much." He took them and retired, perhaps with needless modesty, behind the trees. Elizabeth supposed that even if you were wearing bathing-trunks you would feel a bit indecent climbing publicly into your shorts.

"Is he very upset?" asked Derek in a hoarse undertone, bending towards her. "About the old girl, I mean."

It was difficult to answer such an impertinent question, but luckily he didn't wait. "We're heartbroken, Celia and me. She was more like a mother to us."

Steven came back and Derek straightened up. "And now," he said, "how'd it be if we talk business, eh?"

"What business?" said Steven.

"About the house."

"There's nothing to discuss. I've told you, Miss—er—" (Steven couldn't remember their surname, if indeed he had ever heard it)—"I've said that we shall need the house ourselves."

"Well, old man, I couldn't care less who wants it. *We* don't. I've got a very nice little flat now, overlooking Hyde Park. I couldn't have left Celia with your poor mother much longer in any case. She needs looking after now, don't you, pet? Do what you like with your house as far as I'm concerned."

"Then to what"—said Steven, very angry and talking like a book—"do we owe the pleasure of this unexpected visit?"

"The furniture, old man. What about the furniture? The total contents of the house is left to Celia, and if you and the little lady," he smiled at Elizabeth, "are going to live there, you might like to make us an offer for it."

Elizabeth was appalled. All those water-colours and embroidered cushions and wobbly little shelves concealed behind folk-weave curtains!

But Steven hesitated. "Well, I suppose it might be convenient, but it would only be to tide us over. We shall want to choose our own furniture. And that being so, any offer we made would be a low one'"

"That's all right, old boy; it's all between friends, and I like to do a good turn when I can. Specially as your dear mother was so good to us. I hope you liked our wreath, by the way. Did you happen to notice it? I think it was the biggest there. Made in the shape of a harp it was. Did you see it?"

"Very kind of you," said Steven stiffly.

"Not at all, Major, not at all. When can you come up and see the stuff? You won't find me unreasonable, I can promise you that."

"What do you think, Liz?"

"I don't know. We'd have to think about it, wouldn't we? Oh, here's Mummy."

Joanna came between the tall, dusty lilacs. Despite her old trousers and loose shirt, her slenderness gave her a certain elegance, and Steven felt for a moment rested as she came forward, trug over one arm, her dark eyes questioning their faces.

"Let me introduce you," said Elizabeth. She struggled for a moment with her memory and triumphed. "Miss—Miss Perkins, Mrs. Malling. And Mr. Perkins."

"How d'you do?" said Joanna, the straw hat bowing slightly. And Derek said: "Pleased to meet you, Mrs. Malling. But it's Mrs. Perkins, not Miss."

"Oh, I'm sorry!" said Elizabeth, blushing. "I didn't know. When—"

"Well, now, Mrs. Pryde, it's a long story," said Derek roguishly, "and I'm not sure I ought to tell you. What do you think, pet; shall I tell them our little secret?"

Celia looked embarrassed. "Oh, no, Derek! Not now!"

"Well, they're sure to know sooner or later." Derek was enjoying himself, and he spoke with pride. "You see, Celia's my wife."

"But"—said Elizabeth stupidly—"you can't marry your sister!"

"That's a good one!" Derek's ugly face had a certain charm when he laughed. "Too true you can't marry your sister, dear lady, but, you see, she *isn't* my sister, and never was!"

He looked proudly from face to face. No one spoke. Joanna and the Prydes were working this out while Celia, embarrassed, lowered her chin on to the curving smock and gazed anxiously through her greasy forelock.

"What exactly do you mean?" said Steven at last.

"We've been married for a long time, old man—about a year," said Derek. "You don't think I'd have had any fun and games with Celia otherwise, do you? She wouldn't have let me, would you, Sweetie? She's not that sort of a girl."

"But why on earth—" said Elizabeth.

"*Well*! You see, we hadn't got anywhere to live. Couldn't get a house for love or money, and to tell the truth," he added confidentially, "I was a bit short of the ready just then. Hadn't a job, hadn't anything. So when Celia heard about this Society for finding homes for unmarried mothers, she said, 'What about it, Derek? Shall we put the clock back a few days and see what the fairies will bring?'"

"A few *months*," said Celia.

"A few months, of course. That's what I said. So Celia got a doctor's certificate about the little stranger and went to see the secretary and, well!, Bob's your uncle!"

Steven was almost stunned. He glanced for help at Joanna, and found her gazing at him with startled eyes. He wondered if he looked queer; he certainly felt it. He felt, for the first time in his life, ready to do murder. He said slowly: "And so you appealed to the charity of a kind and simple old lady by telling a string of lies."

"Charity nothing!" said Derek, shocked. "She wanted a cook, didn't she? She was tickled pink to get such a good one as Celia, and lucky, too, if you ask me. The house was as clean as a whistle!"

"You exploited her," said Steven grimly.

"Oh, come off it, old boy! She *liked* it that way, that was all! Liked to feel Celia needed her."

"She gave—Mrs. Perkins—a far higher wage than any ordinary servant would have had."

"Well, Celia *isn't* an ordinary servant!" Derek was indignant. He went on, in a hurt voice: "If you're going to take this line, I shall be sorry I told you. I thought you'd see the joke."

"*Joke!*"

"Derek," said Celia, "I told you they wouldn't like it. Don't you see, it's the will that's upsetting them?"

"Oh, the will, eh?" Derek was reproachful. "You know, you didn't ought to mind that, really you didn't. Don't be unsporting, Major. Think of the comfort Celia gave the old lady in the last months of her life. And she didn't *know* she was getting anything in the will, did you, ducky?"

"Oh, no, no," said Celia, looking furtive.

"I doubt very much whether the will is valid," said Steven.

Derek laughed. "What's wrong with a will made in favour of 'My dear friend Celia Perkins', eh? No, no, Major; you can't pull *that* one off. Try if you like; I couldn't care less!" He looked about him in search of a friendly face and appealed to Joanna. "Mrs. Malling, you're a woman of the world, I'm sure. Wouldn't you have done the same in my shoes?"

"It was a monstrous thing to do," said Joanna coldly. "Steven, if these people have said all they have to say, they had better be getting back to London."

"Here, I say! Not so much as a cup of tea? Celia, we're not wanted here, and we'll be going somewhere better."

He helped her from her chair, and she stood holding his arm, tight-lipped, moving her eyes from face to face.

"You can keep your furniture," said Steven, "and now get out." He took a step forward and seemed about to hit Derek, who swiftly freed his arm from Celia's clasp and began to smile again, showing the tip of his tongue.

But Steven only walked to the car and opened the door for Celia. He shut her in punctiliously and stood still and silent, waiting for Derek to start.

"Well, cheery-bye, ladies," said Derek, and he grinned and waved to the two women. "I'm taking my wife somewhere where they'll be pleased to see her, now, and give her a good tea and not so many sour looks." He slipped into gear and drove off with a spurt of gravel. He hooted insolently at the gate and rushed off up the road, using every ounce of his excellent acceleration.

"Steven!" twittered Elizabeth. "I thought for a moment you were going to hit him!"

"So did I, but I thought better of it. The chap's a bloody prize-fighter!"

Elizabeth was a little disappointed at this unheroic attitude, but she only said: "I should have been terrified. What a *beast*, what a *pig* he is!"

"Blast him!"

"But the odd thing is," said Joanna as they walked slowly back to their chairs, "that there's a kind of innocence about him."

"*Innocence*? That spiv?"

"Yes, Steven, I really think so. He hadn't any idea he'd done something wrong. He simply doesn't know the difference."

"Oh come, Mamma!"

"He hasn't eaten of the tree. Honestly, I believe a lot of these thugs nowadays haven't. They're callous as a cat is callous, because it's never dawned on them that the other person has feelings. He thought he'd done something clever and funny."

Steven astonished himself by saying: "*Pah!*"

"But *Celia* now—" said Libby.

"Oh, that woman's bad." Joanna looked disgusted. "Nothing innocent about her. She gives me goose-flesh. Let's forget her and have some tea. Steven, will you dispute the will?"

"I shall talk to old Turner, of course, but I shouldn't think there's a hope. It makes me sick. Poor old mother trusting them like that, and all the time they were laughing at her." He looked at Joanna for sympathy, and she looked away.

"He used to keep Celia company when your mother was out," said Elizabeth.

"Oh, don't *talk* about it! I'll knock hell out of the mowing-machine now. Thank God we're alone, the three of us."

He had no sooner spoken than Mrs. Lane's car turned in at the gate.

XXI

ఴ

On the day when the Prydes left her, Joanna, of course, went for a walk. Deliberately she turned along the footpath that she had followed with Steven, and pausing on the hillside where they had watched the storm sweep up the valley, she looked at the neat house which had sheltered them. She had often thought of the dreadful little cripple and wondered whether his daughter still faced the copper jugs to the middle of the shelf. Some day she would go and see him and offer to do something for him. If only he were not so deaf! She leant against a tree and stared at the house. There was a car outside the yew hedge: two cars, very black and shiny. One of them had something bright-coloured on its roof. Joanna screwed up her eyes and wondered what it could be. As she watched, some little black figures came out of the house. They were carrying something. Not—surely it wasn't—"Oh dear!" said Joanna aloud. "So that's what that car is! A hearse!" Her eyes filled with tears as she watched the little figures carry their burden to the flower-laden car. She was not sorry that the old man was dead, but she did regret her own lethargy. He had been unhappy and in pain and she had done nothing about it. Now it was too late. The hearse moved slowly away, followed by the second car, and the house remained, quiet, bland and secretive. Joanna could now see that the blinds were down.

She turned, heavy with her own sorrow, which seemed to embrace all other sorrows, and continued languidly her upward path, passing between sparse trees that were wind-blown and leggy, and round whose roots the leaf mould sent up a delicious smell of decay and of life renewed. Beyond the trees she came into a flat field where mushrooms grew; but she picked none, for who now would greet them with triumphant cries and fry them for supper? Unshared they would give her no pleasure.

She plodded across the field, sat on a gate and lit a cigarette, frowning a little as wisps of hair blew across her face. If she took in p.g.'s they must gather their own mushrooms. They should cater for themselves and have definite hours for using the kitchen. She would herself keep out of it as far as possible, and she would try not to be a cantankerous landlady. She would move some of Libby's furniture into the smallest bedroom, and the p.g.'s, in the Prydes' room, would quickly oust those lingering shadows. There would not be room for her to have both Prydes to stay, and it would seem quite natural for Libby to come down alone when she wanted a few days in the country. As for Steven, who was to come daily by train to Tadwych, there was nothing to bring him out here. If he should make the gesture, later on, of coming to lunch with her, she would invite someone else to meet him. It would all be perfectly simple, if only Mrs. Lane would hurry up and find her some lodgers. She would keep the loathed couple until Steven went abroad, and then, the danger gone, she would at last have her house to herself.

If Steven were to be posted in July, as they all hoped, she must make up her mind to nine months of room-letting. It seemed a long time, but she reminded herself that she could take holidays from her lodgers, while Libby's burden was for nine months inescapable. The baby was to be born in May, and Joanna was ashamed that the prospect gave her no pleasure. Luckily there was still time to flog up some grandmotherly feelings.

She had watched Libby anxiously during these last days and had been sure that the child's self-confidence was damaged. Shame at her own gross suspicions still often engulfed her, and Joanna would see a look of blushing disgust come upon her face. Then she would stop whatever she was doing and hurriedly do something else, and Joanna, who had some hazy ideas about psychology, feared that she was driving her thoughts underground. This, she believed, was a bad thing to do. But how else, for heaven's sake, was poor Libby to live? It was cruel that she must hate herself for what, on that awful evening, her sound instincts had told her.

Celia had moved out of the Wimbledon house, leaving it, to do her justice, in a state of aseptic cleanliness. The admirable Janet Mortimer had produced some friends who were going abroad and didn't want to store their furniture, and they had gladly lent it to the Prydes and had generously refused all payment. Neither Steven nor Elizabeth had any affection for the house with its unhappy associations, but it was so much changed by its new furniture that they hoped to grow fond of it in time.

There had been moments when Elizabeth had put up a show of resistance. Just as their plans were working out she would suddenly begin to worry in case she was treating her mother shabbily. To leave the scene of her own vileness and to have Steven all to herself would be bliss, but—poor, poor Mummy! Fancy having to take in p.g.'s! At these times she would talk about country air for the baby, until Steven or Joanna convinced her that she was worrying herself about nothing.

She had not confessed those depraved thoughts of hers even to Steven. Perhaps some day, when they were at the other side of the world, she might tell him the ludicrous story, and he would be shocked and amused and would tell her—as indeed he often happened to tell her now—that pregnant women couldn't help imagining things. She promised herself that she would often come down and see poor Mummy, who was looking old and haggard and who confessed to sleeping badly. But she didn't think Steven would want to come with her; his week-ends would be too precious.

Joanna could usually divine her daughter's feelings, but today, throwing away her wind-blown cigarette and turning down a lane between high, unkempt hedges, she was wondering if she'd really done the best thing in packing her off to London. The child would be alone so much; might she not remember and brood? In fiction, she mourned, a woman of her age would know all the right answers; with a sure and delicate touch would steer these complex relationships to safety. Never, *never*, would the heroine of a novel have cried out with dreadful archness: "Libby, ask this husband of yours to let me wind my own wool!"

She could not even pride herself on her own tormented reticence. After so many refusals to acknowledge her love, so many ungenerous avoidances of Steven's diffident glance, at the last moment only chance had saved her from spilling all her dammed-up feelings before him. Mrs. Holmes, the Godiva whom she had never taken seriously, had become in the end their preserver.

She was tired to death of her thoughts. Round and round they went, bringing with them a physical pain not unlike indigestion. She had denied herself any reassurance for the long future, when Steven and Libby should be happily united against herself and all the world. She would have no memories to comfort her then. Oh, it was anguish to feel such jealousy of these two whom she loved! How vile of her to want anything for them but perfect happiness! For many nights now she had doped herself with aspirin and muttered recitation, and she began to fear that poetry would itself be poisoned for her soon. Better perhaps to recite the multiplication tables, she reflected with dreary humour.

She stared up resentfully at the hedgerow, where the leaves were beginning to turn. Autumn had never seemed so dismal before. The chestnut leaves were patched with honey colour and nearby hung some leaves that she could not name, darkened to a beautiful opaque brown. How ignorant I am, thought Joanna, even about the country things that have always surrounded me. The next group, however, was ash, its leaves still keeping their midsummer shade of silvery blue-green. Such small details of the changing scene had once delighted her, but she was dead to them today; they awakened no memories, and led her to no favourite line of poetry. "'Season of mists and mellow fruitfulness'," she tried dutifully—but, oh, what was the good?

> "May the rustling harvest hedgerow
> Still the travellers' joy entwine,
> And as happy children gather
> Posies once mine."

But that one linked up with Steven.

Dare she remember 'Autumn', a poem that could at any time affect her to the verge of tears? She murmured it aloud.

"There is a wind where the rose was;
Cold rain where sweet grass was;
    And clouds like sheep
    Stream o'er the steep
Grey skies where the lark was.

Nought gold where your hair was;
Nought warm where your hand was;
    But phantom, forlorn,
    Beneath the thorn,
Your ghost where your face was.

Sad winds where your voice was;
Tears, tears, where my heart was;
    And ever with me,
    Child, ever with me,
Silence where hope was."

Joanna sobbed.

Breakfast this morning had been an agony. Libby had insisted on coming down, and had sat breaking dry toast into smaller and smaller pieces, touching her lips with her tongue and swallowing, until at last she had bolted from the room. Steven and Joanna had sat still, helplessly pitying; they longed to help her and to comfort one another, but there was nothing they could do. After a decent interval Steven followed her, and returned to say that she was back in bed and thought she might manage something to eat in about ten minutes. He then helped himself angrily to a large amount of egg and bacon and ate it much too fast.

Afterwards, while he strapped trunks in the hall, she went up to Libby's room, to find the child looking ghastly. She had managed to dress and was fumbling at her hair. She was almost grey, this morning, and her shoulders drooped. "In a few weeks," Joanna told her, "you'll be looking prettier than you ever have before."

Elizabeth glanced incuriously at her reflection. "Does that mean I look repulsive now?" she asked. "I suppose I do rather. Poor Steven! Mummy, could you help me to sit on that suitcase, when I've finished with this brush and comb?"

"Why not let Steven do it, darling? He said he'd be up in a moment."

"Because," said Libby, and tears came into her eyes, "he'll think I'm so *incompetent*!" She pushed the brush and comb into the case anyhow, and tried to snap the catch. "Oh, damn it!" she said breathlessly, as Joanna came to help her. "I never thought I was wildly clever or artistic or any of those things, but I did think I could be trusted to get things done!"

"You can, darling, more than anyone."

"No, I can't! I don't know how on earth I'm going to manage with this baby; I expect I'll drop it into a hot bath or something. Oh, God! I'm going to be sick again!" She left the room at a stumbling run, and could be heard retching in the lavatory. In a moment she came back, wiping her damp face and smiling. "Better now," she said. "I always thought people made such a fuss about sickness, Mummy! I thought it was rather nonsense, but I was wrong. I've been wrong about so many things lately!"

Joanna, who had seized the moment to repack the brush and comb, leant on the suitcase lid, without exerting pressure. What could she say? If she preached the truth, saying that to know we are wrong is the first step towards being right, she would sound like a quotation from Mrs. Molesworth. She said: "Well, darling, you'd be pretty insufferable if you weren't wrong now and then, wouldn't you? Come and lean on this, but for goodness sake don't heave at it."

The catch snapped quite easily, and Elizabeth said: "Well, anyway, that's one job less for poor old Steve. Gosh! don't you feel marvellous when you've just been sick? It won't last, of course, but just at the moment I feel re-born into a state of grace."

"Dare you chew something, while the going's good?"

"An apple, perhaps?" Libby appeared to be looking inwards. "No, I don't think I'll risk it, thank you, darling. Here comes Steve."

She sat on the bed and smiled, as though inviting him to share with her the oasis in which she lingered. His anxious face relaxed a little, and he touched her shoulder as he went to lift the suitcase. Directly he swung it off the floor it opened, and various things fell out.

"You keep still, Libby," said Joanna, falling on her knees and picking them up.

"I'd better do it."

"Rubbish! I know just where you'd put everything."

She pushed and persuaded the things into place, and Steven watched her morosely without offering to help. Then, in her turn, she sat back to watch him close the case, which he did easily enough. He picked it up cautiously this time, and although it opened at once, nothing fell out.

"H'm," said Steven, "now what?"

He rubbed the palm of his hand along his jaw, making a slight rasping sound that awoke Joanna sharply from her state of semi-consciousness. There he stood, within a yard of her. Her finger-tips imagined the roughness of his chin, which they had never touched and never would touch now.

She said loudly: "It's really too full."

"It's all right," said Elizabeth. "It wants locking, that's all." She opened her handbag, and looked up, frowning. "I gave you the keys, Steve."

"Indeed you did not."

"Don't you remember where you put them?" Elizabeth spoke truculently, but she looked terrified.

"I don't because I've never had them."

"Oh, Steve, I'm *certain* I gave them to you. I'm not a key-loser, now *am* I, Mummy?"

"No, indeed, darling; I do it for us both; but I don't think I've had *your* bunch."

"Rope," said Steven. "Have you a bit of cord, Mamma?"

"I'll look."

"Thank you so much," he said politely, and Joanna drove herself away from him and down the stairs. In a few moments they would be gone. She would not be able to touch or see him. It seemed a pity to waste her chances now.

She was on her knees, trying to remove from a length of cord its satellite muddle of string, when she heard Steven's footfall, and he appeared, rather flushed, in the doorway. He stood there, at a distance, and said formally: "I want to thank you, Mamma, for your great kindness to us both all the time we've been here."

Sitting back on her heels, thin, shabby, worn; with one lock of dark hair falling Hitler-like athwart her brows, she smiled unaffectedly up at him, and said: "Oh, Steven, did you think you needed to say that?"

It was the first time for days that she had looked at him as though she recognized him and spoken naturally without erecting a barrier of formality. In his relief he smiled radiantly, and said: "Liz sent me down to say it!"

They both laughed, quite happy for a moment to be together, and then he came and knelt beside her, not touching her, and took the string from her hands.

Now! commanded her thoughts. Now say it! Quite calmly and quietly say, 'You know that I shall always love you, Steven.' Then he will say it too, and we shall both be strengthened for what lies ahead. It can do no harm now. Say it!

But instead, with an infinite feeling of home-coming, she laid her cheek very softly against his tweed sleeve. He did not feel it at first, and she was waiting for him, calmly, when Mrs. Holmes bounced on a spate of words into the room, and the chance—the lovely chance—was gone. In another moment she was standing up, drained of all strength, and Steven, still on his knees, was frowning up at her. He hadn't known! She had given him nothing, to be his comfort or hers.

She said: "I'll go back to Libby," and then, as Mrs. Holmes darted off, she added shakily: "I know you'll take care of her, Steven; but don't forget to look after yourself, as well."

He wanted to promise her that he would be good to Elizabeth; he wanted to beg her to take care of herself—her tired, sad self whom he might not cherish. But he stayed speechless on his knees and watched her leave the room.

By the time that he had made the suitcase fast, their taxi could be heard in the drive. While the luggage was loaded, the two women sat in the hall. Joanna held Elizabeth's hand and bent to look attentively at the smooth, childish fingers which lay relaxed between her own. Libby's hands had got left behind in time, she thought, for they were still the unfretted hands of a girl at peace. They only became restless when she broke silence to repeat that it could not have been she who had lost the keys. How much, reflected Joanna, those people occasionally suffer who don't usually make mistakes.

"Ready, Liz?" said Steven. He came slowly across the hall, and helped her to her feet.

"Good-bye, Mummy darling," said Libby, as they kissed.

"Good-bye, Mamma," said Steven, taking her hands. His lips did not quite touch her cheek.

They were in. The door slammed. They're really going, thought Joanna incredulously. In another moment I shan't be able to see them any more. If I ran forward now, shouted, screamed, there would still be time to stop them! But she only smiled and waved her hand as the taxi vanished from her sight. There goes my hope, she thought. And for a moment, as she heard the car increase speed on the main road, and settle, in top gear, into a diminishing drone, she thought of Steven not as a person but as her youth, which she had thrown away.

And now, returning from her walk, the thought came again. With Steven I could have had a last flowering, however brief. He was all I had of youth, and now he is gone. It is time for me to grow old. Now, indeed, I must face facts.

She faced them at their worst, all the way down the hill.

XXII

Indeed throughout that winter Joanna continued to face and outface facts and she became, after the torture of the first few weeks, increasingly tranquil. She went doggedly on with her work in the garden and she managed, as she knitted baby clothes, to whip up some feelings of glad expectancy. It was no doubt appropriate that she should now discover a number of white hairs. She showed them, rather mournfully, to her visiting daughter; but Elizabeth, oddly, had been tweaking these from her own head ever since she was sixteen, so she was not very much impressed.

Mrs. Holmes, who had looked for months as though she were about to give birth to triplets, reached in February such awe-inspiring proportions that she was forced to leave her job. Joanna was thankful that she need no longer watch that vast walking egg as it struggled cheerfully about the house, and luckily her young lodgers were leaving too. They had been, she supposed, inoffensive, but she was glad when they went, for their collars were sprinkled with dandruff and when they washed up they put things away on the wrong hooks.

They had been useful at Christmas, when they had begged to have an ancient father to stay, and so ruled out any chance of the Prydes coming down. Elizabeth had expressed disappointment, but afterwards she wrote an ecstatic letter about her first Christmas with Steven, and how they had each filled a stocking to surprise the other, and Steven had made the brandy butter, and they had gone to church and she had surprised herself by crying from happiness when they sang 'While Shepherds Watched'.

Mrs. Lane had promised to find another clean and quiet couple to lodge with Joanna, but in the meantime her big spare room was empty. She thought that a protracted spring cleaning would be her best excuse for never inviting both Prydes to stay. Elizabeth came often, but she had not seen Steven since October. She wondered constantly how he had borne his share—heavier than hers—of their burden. He must have done well for Libby to seem so happy.

At first Joanna had felt sure that she would love Steven for ever. He was always in her mind and usually she ached for him, although there were rare moments of romantic exaltation when she could enjoy the picture of her own renunciation. But she could never glamorize herself for long, and though she tried to write poetry (a thing she hadn't attempted since her marriage), she entirely failed. So her immortality was not to be built in verse. Remembering her discussion with Steven, all those months ago, she wished she could add to her argument. Poets, she now concluded—and indeed all writers—were thumping egoists; they wanted to keep themselves alive for that reason; because their unique feelings were too precious to be lost for ever. I am a thumping egoist too, mourned Joanna, but I have no gift of verse. Really I have no gift of any sort, and I ought to be satisfied with survival as Libby's mother and the baby's ancient ancestor. But I'm not.

She settled, as the winter lagged away, into a state of bearable depression. Except when Elizabeth came down she took little interest in her looks, and the young lodgers clearly thought her a dim old thing. After they'd gone, however, when the snowdrops and crocuses appeared and the larch boughs which she had put in a jug before Christmas—bare except for their delightful cones—astonished her with green tufts and tiny scarlet brushes, she began to wake up. Even now she could not remain dead to the warning of Spring.

On a morning in March, Joanna was on hands and knees, sweeping her bedroom carpet, when she heard the telephone bell. Never a very keen housemaid, she was glad to be interrupted and ran willingly downstairs. She lifted the receiver and was struck at once by a hail of exclamations from Mrs. Lane. Before she had begun to object she was entreated, exhorted, commanded to accept a new lodger.

"A bachelor, my dear, but so nice, a very sensible age and absolutely nowhere to live. Now I know what you're going to say; but do just consider it, please, before you turn him down. He's a solicitor—partner in a firm in Tadwych—and his present digs are folding up under him. He's an absolute darling, and I shall be wildly envious if you have him. You simply must meet. I've given him your address and told him that you're generally in in the mornings. Was that right? Now don't say people will talk, because I don't believe it for a moment. And after all it wouldn't hurt you, would it, if they did? I only wish someone would talk about me!" She sighed loudly, and Joanna drew away her ear which she fancied was tickled.

Her thoughts had leapt the space of fifteen years. What if it should be finicky old Tom coming into her life, after all? That would be a neat trick! But no, when she asked the solicitor's name, it was one that she had never heard. This man was called Barclay-Manson and was aged about fifty. "Such an aristocrat, Joanna!" gushed the voice. "And very intellectural. I'm certain you two would like each other. Please, please, just to satisfy me, don't turn it down without at least meeting him."

Joanna obliged her by demurring. "But I wanted a couple. Who's going to cook for him?"

"Only breakfast and supper, my dear, and he gets those himself. He seems to be most domesticated. *And*"—added Mrs. Lane clinchingly— "James adores him!"

"Oh, well, he can come and see me. But for heaven's sake make it clear that he's got to stick to his own sitting-room. If he starts domesticating himself with *me* in the evenings, out he goes!"

While Mrs. Lane talked on, Joanna wondered how Libby would take this development. No one else would mind her having a male lodger, but Libby did like things to be correct. For such an innocent she had an oddly cynical idea of other people's minds. Then she remembered the baby. Even Libby would admit that a grandmother needed no chaperone. She thanked the still quacking telephone for its kindness and hung up. Funny! she thought as she went upstairs. I had a clear premonition that it was old Tom. He must be sixty-odd by now, and probably long since married. I suppose I'm not the sort of woman whose premonitions mean anything; I never seem to have them at the right moment.

Joanna knelt and took up her brush. Probably this double-barrelled man would be appalling, but she should keep an open mind till she had seen him. (Or as open as her mind *could* be where solicitors were concerned.) She would make it clear that any arrangement they made was temporary, for she longed to have her house to herself.

Sweeping, and inhaling dust, she thought of Elizabeth's latest letter. After all, the darling child hadn't altered very much. "Poor old Godiva," she had written, "still awaiting her Happy Release. (Sorry, I mean Event. Release means death, doesn't it?) I'm sure the doctor ought to hurry it on for her. Won't she be awful with the baby when it's born? I bet it'll have a filthy comforter perpetually stuck in its face. Do you think she'd listen if I told her a thing or two about that, and also about feeding? Those sort of people are *incapable* of working anything out from a book, and I could easily make her out a diet sheet when it's time for mixed feeding." Joanna smiled as she pictured Mrs. Holmes, mother of five healthy children, accepting a lecture from Libby. It would be wonderful to hear the two, each kindly advising the other.

"Julia or Jerome,"—continued Elizabeth—"is going to be no trouble. I'm sure I could feed quads, I have such a fine balcony already. You *must* be good and not worry, like most grandmothers, and snatch it to your heart directly it utters a peep! It's good for their lungs to cry a bit. And incidentally I feel more and more certain that it'll be Julia *and* Jerome, though Steven and Doctor A. only laugh at me! It doesn't seem possible that I can go on swelling for two more months. Steve says I look lovely, bless him, but *he'd* still say so if I looked like the Albert Memorial!!!"

Joanna sat on her heels, brush in hand. Well done, Steven! He had won his fight and she did hope he was enjoying his reward. Critically examining herself, she found that although a part of her wanted Steven to be for ever her disconsolate lover, by far her stronger feeling was the wish for his happiness and Libby's. She did not know in what way he thought of her now, and it startled her to find that she did not greatly mind. For the first time, on this Spring day, she felt what she had been trying for six months to feel.

She thought that their romance had been singularly profitless; it had not even left very tender memories. Words had been lacking to crystallize their love, and without them, as she had feared, little remained. She had expected a torment of doubting whether he had really loved her, and now, to her surprise, she began to doubt not his feelings but her own. Steven was married, and if his married life had not at that time completely satisfied him, it must surely have been at least adequate physically. His love, therefore, was positive. But had not hers for him been the result of propinquity suddenly overwhelming a woman who, though not a virgin, had behaved as one for twenty years? Don't be so disloyal! she silently cried, but the question awaited her reply.

Joanna stood stiffly up and went to her dressing-table. What should I feel, she asked, if he should come into the room now, and without a word take me in his arms? The reflected oval face, with its shadowed eyes and pale, closed lips, was impenetrable. Better admit it, she thought, as she turned away. I should feel embarrassed.

Was Steven really her special sort of person? Was he not just a little bit ordinary? Did her sort of person, in fact, exist at all? Could she really have been so much affected by his hands filling a pipe, his hairy wrists and well-shaped ears? Surely she had not really lain awake, trying to forget that he was with Libby?

Blushing, Joanna went back to her carpet and swept with violence. Very natural, no doubt, she told herself briskly, but also very shaming. Ah well, I daresay lots of women have their last little fling before they settle into old age. I'm glad I've got it over; God knows it was painful while it lasted.

Ah no! Don't let me minimize or resent it. Dear Steven, I shall always be grateful to him, and enriched by what we both felt. It was not his fault that I am too old now to fall properly and lastingly in love. I should like to send him a big box of daffodils this morning, to show that I'm fond of him. I'll do it, too, but of course I shall address the box to Libby.

In sudden lightness of heart, and in defiance of Libby's training, she took the dustpan to the window and emptied it smartly out. And she was horrified to see the cloud of fluff gently descending on to the bare head of a man who stood at the front door. She ducked back with shocked laughter. The head innocently awaiting baptism was bare indeed; a very noble bald forehead, above an eagle nose and legs that managed even from above to look long. Oh dear! gasped Joanna inadequately. It must be Mr. Barclay-Something!

Certainly she felt no hint of a premonition now, for without even waiting to powder her nose she ran downstairs and opened the front door.

Afterword

Two of Diana Tutton's three published novels look at unlikely and taboo relationships – or possible relationships. The odd one out is *Guard Your Daughters*, published in 1953, which follows the eccentric Harvey sisters in their quest for marriage to eligible young men. In her final novel, *The Young Ones*, Tutton writes about a brother and sister who are having a sexual relationship when they believe themselves to be adopted siblings, but who continue after they discover that they are actual biological brother and sister. *Mamma* doesn't approach quite that height of the unthinkable, but a love triangle between a mother, daughter and daughter's husband is not the stuff of traditional romantic fiction.

Sex is certainly not a taboo topic in the novel – in the narrative, in characters' thoughts and in their dialogue. It is present as a concern and as a catalyst in ways that wouldn't have been possible in novels a few decades earlier. The most societally acceptable of these is the idea of Elizabeth (or Libby) losing her virginity to her new husband, Major Steven Pryde. Perhaps the 1950s was the last decade of writing where it could be assumed that the young heroine of a novel would be likely to be a virgin on her wedding night – though far from certain, and almost as far from mattering. Earlier in the century, the revelation of a bride's sexual experience (or otherwise) might be the pivot of the novel – as it was in the previous century in, say, Thomas Hardy's *Tess of the D'Urbervilles*. While neither Elizabeth nor Steven make much of the issue, a less conventional viewpoint is provided in the novel by Elizabeth's friend Janet:

She prided herself on her detachment and understanding, and Steven and Elizabeth were an unfailing source of interest to her. She suspected that their sexual relationship still left much to be desired. Probably Elizabeth was not yet fully awakened; but she would be all right in a year or two, and would probably – when her troubles were over and done with – tell Janet all about them. It was, of course, a thousand pities that Elizabeth should have been so inexperienced. Janet, herself a virgin at twenty-one, intended to change the condition in a year or two, and to marry when she was twenty-five.

Elizabeth and Steven are married by the time of this observation, so Janet considers being 'fully awakened' as something separate and subsequent to losing one's virginity – something which Steven muses on himself:

Perhaps, thought Steven, who had read some of the books appropriate to a bridegroom of his generation, his influence would grow with her growing powers of physical pleasure. At present she seemed disconcertingly placid about the whole thing, so that he felt he must curb his own emotions, which would be, heaven knew, deep and dark enough if he gave them their freedom. Of what passion he was capable he was not sure, but he did feel that their present embraces, while physically they relieved him, were emotionally little more than an introduction.

Steven is 35, Elizabeth 20 and Joanna 41. He is much closer to his mother-in-law's age than his wife's age. This, of course, was not unheard of – but it was unusual. Throughout the 1950s, the average age gap between a husband and wife was about 2.5 years for a first marriage, with the groom being the older. This expanded a little if either or both partners were remarrying, though remained below a gap of three years.

Thus, when the narrative speaks of 'his generation', it is a generation he shares more with Joanna than with Elizabeth. If he was born in the late 1910s, he'd have been too young for the first avalanche of books aimed at educating prospective bridegrooms – like J.P. Gair's *Sexual Knowledge for the Young Man* (1921), which was published simultaneously with a companion volume called *Sexual Knowledge for the Young Woman* – but plenty such guides were still being published. They grew steadily less coy as the century went on, and more willing to acknowledge that women could, like men, have 'powers of physical pleasure'.

As this quotation suggests, *Mamma* might not be unduly prudish about sex, nor is it particularly overt. There is a certain coyness to terms like 'powers of physical pleasure' and 'fully awakened', for instance. Perhaps the least sexually progressive aspect about the novel (or at least the characters in it) is the response to the hints that Steven's mother might be in a lesbian relationship with Celia. Steven reacts with disgust, and neither Joanna nor Elizabeth are willing to broach the issue openly or particularly empathetically.

Gay sex between men wouldn't be legalised in the UK until 1967. While lesbianism was never officially illegal in the UK, writing about it explicitly would technically contravene the Obscene Publications Act 1857. This Act was in the process of being altered when *Mamma* was published, and the definition of 'obscene' was becoming less stringent, but a new Act wouldn't be in place until three years later. Having said that, other novels appeared in the 1950s that were far more open about lesbian relationships – such as Patricia Highsmith's *The Price of Salt*, filmed in 2015 as *Carol*. Certainly, *Mamma* was not considered scandalous when it was published – for instance, a contemporary review described it as 'an amiable amble'.

While it might not put Elizabeth or Janet beyond the pale to have had sex before marriage, the novel also shows what happens to those (particularly those from a lower social class) for whom sex has led to its natural consequences. The airy philosophies of people like Janet are a little at odds with the experiences of women who have to deal with society's actual reactions. Steven's mother is concerned for unmarried mothers, and 'belonged to a society which found work for these unfortunates in homes where their babies would be welcomed'. The euphemistic word 'unfortunates' shows that enlightenment is far from universal, even if Joanna thinks the society 'an excellent idea [...] she wondered whether it might solve her servant problem'.

Joanna is perhaps more open-minded than some, but sufficiently bound within her class to refer to the 'servant problem' – that is, the difficulty of procuring servants, particularly those who had taken on war work in either of the two World Wars, and were reluctant to return to household service. The phrase was first used in the First World War and became prevalent in the interwar period – though the expectation that one would have servants had certainly decreased significantly by the 1950s. By 1951 there were about 800,000 people employed as domestic servants, compared to 1.4 million only two decades earlier. Increasingly, domestic staff were choosing not to 'live in', and households the size of the Malling/Pryde home were exactly the ones that might have to become self-sufficient on the domestic service front. As the novel opens, Elizabeth is 'in the final stages of a course in Domestic Science', but there is still a societal chasm between the relative expertise of an 'unfortunate mother' and a wife with an accredited course.

If discussion of the 'servant problem' persisted in some forms in Britain of the 1950s, it wasn't the only popular 1920s viewpoint that had a legacy in the era *Mamma* was published. While Freudian psychoanalysis never regained the cultural dominance it enjoyed in the early twentieth century, it influences the sort of opinion Elizabeth puts forward about celibacy. While some are damned for having sex, others are damned for not:

"I don't see," said Elizabeth, smiling, "how anyone at all young *can* live without sex and not get warped."

Steven's feelings changed abruptly. Of all the tactless remarks! But Joanna answered peacefully: "Quite a lot do."

"Well, they all get a bit peculiar."

"I don't think that's altogether true."

"Janet says it comes out in all sorts of funny little ways."

"Well, good Lord, we've all heard *that* one," said Steven impatiently. "But it's by no means universal."

"Even if it's not visible," calmly continued Elizabeth, "it's still there. In fact if you can't see it it's probably worse."

"Darling," said Joanna, looking, as Steven gratefully noticed, not hurt, but amused, "we've all heard that, too."

"Often," added Steven.

"Oh, all right!" said Elizabeth, not at all offended. "But all the same, Janet says—"

"A course in so-called psychology," said Steven nastily, "doesn't guarantee a profound knowledge of human nature."

There is little suggestion, in the narrative, that Joanna's widowed celibacy is causing her to become 'peculiar', and Elizabeth certainly doesn't suspect the turn of events that leads to her mother and her husband being attracted to one another. As it turns out, what initially connects Joanna and Steven on a deeper level is not sexual attraction, but a meeting of minds when it comes to poetry.

As the three enjoy a crossword, they have to enter a five-letter poet with the central letter 'n'. After some debate, they land upon John Donne, a metaphysical poet of the early seventeenth century, who turned away from poetry and towards sermons when he was ordained (and later Dean of St Paul's). Stephen can quote from the opening of one of Donne's *Elegies*, and they move on to 'The Flea', an erotic poem that wasn't published until after Donne's death. The theme, as is explained, is 'He tries to persuade his lady to go to bed with him, and says she may just as well, as the same flea has already bitten them both'.

ৰু ৰু ৰু

Tellingly, it isn't entirely clear in the conversation whether it is Joanna or Steven who is giving this summary.

Joanna and Steven turn from 'Ecstasy' by Donne to 'Ode to a Nightingale' by John Keats, and to 'Fare Well' by Walter de la Mare (who died the year *Mamma* was published), each time without giving the title of the poem and expecting the other to identify it without prompting. This is the context for the conversation where Elizabeth suggests that celibacy makes one peculiar – even while her mother and husband are discovering a deeper intimacy in a shared set of literary reference points, which shut Elizabeth out.

> It had been a delightful surprise to find him alive to poetry, and clearly he cared for it more than he was willing to admit. It occurred to her that she had never before met a man who was interested in it; she had, of course, known very few men well.
>
> Certainly Jack had tried, but either you could be excited by poetry or you couldn't; Libby, like her father, never would be, although she was educated to the pitch of recognizing quotations, and knowing, with uncompromising certainty, which poets were 'great' and which were 'considerably over-rated'.

While Joanna and Elizabeth can share references to Louisa M. Alcott's *Little Women*, talking about Mrs March, Meg and Laurie without needing to explain the allusions to each other or (initially, at least) to the reader, Elizabeth's own recollections of poetry are a little less elevated than Steven's or Joanna's. Imagining the hypothetical sound of frogs or crickets at a future idyll with her husband, she thinks of 'some lines from Edward Lear':

> The little beasties' twittering cry
> Rose on the fragrant air

The lines are from Lear's 'The Cumberbund', subtitled 'an Indian poem' and first published in the *Times* of Bombay in 1874. In it, Lear uses Urdu words out of context, treating them as 'nonsense' words (in a manner that would be unlikely to be published today). This was clearly rather lost on Elizabeth, who remembers 'beasties' rather than the original 'Bheesties', a variant of the Urdu 'bhisti' meaning an Indian servant who supplies water. Perhaps the error was Tutton's, though it seems more likely that she wanted to highlight Elizabeth's rather lukewarm relationship with literature.

It's another Walter de la Mare poem, 'Autumn', that Joanna recites to herself towards the end of the novel – reflecting that there is 'silence where hope was' and being driven to sobbing. But the final lines of *Mamma* make the reader question whether that hope is really over. As she goes to greet 'Mr Barclay-Something', we are told that she has 'no hint of premonition' – asking the question, naturally, of what she is failing to prophesy. Diana Tutton might turn to the unconventional and the taboo in her themes, but it appears that *Mamma* might end just as the most conventional sort of love story is beginning.

Simon Thomas

Series consultant **Simon Thomas** created the middlebrow blog Stuck in a Book in 2007. He is also the co-host of the popular podcast Tea or Books? Simon has a PhD from Oxford University in Interwar Literature.